John Dawson Ross

Scottish Poets in America

With biographical and critical notices

John Dawson Ross

Scottish Poets in America
With biographical and critical notices

ISBN/EAN: 9783337028961

Printed in Europe, USA, Canada, Australia, Japan

Cover: Foto ©Raphael Reischuk / pixelio.de

More available books at **www.hansebooks.com**

SCOTTISH POETS

IN AMERICA

WITH

BIOGRAPHICAL AND CRITICAL NOTICES,

BY

JOHN D. ROSS,

Editor of "Celebrated Songs of Scotland."

NEW YORK:

PAGAN & ROSS, PUBLISHERS,

352 PEARL STREET.

1889

PRESS OF
WILLIAM PAGAN, JR.,
352 Pearl Street.
NEW YORK.

TO

THE HON. CHIEF JUSTICE, DAVID MCAD

OF NEW YORK CITY,

A lover of Literature, and the author of various works,·

THESE BRIEF SKETCHES OF SCOTTISH POETS IN AMERICA

are respectfully and with permission

Dedicated.

It is an ungenerous silence which leaves all the fair words of hones
earned praise to the writer of obituary notices and the marble-worker.

Oliver Wendell Holme

POETS REPRESENTED IN THIS WORK.

Thomas C. Latto.

There's the clerk wha can tak a bit kiss 'hint the door,
And gladden us a' wi' his sang and his lore,
The honors o' sang, o' guid auld Scottish sang,
To him and to his may they ever belang.

John Crawford.

SCOTTISH POETS IN AMERICA.

THOMAS C. LATTO.

I left him in a green old age
And looking like the oak, worn but still steady,
Amidst the elements, while younger trees
Fell fast around him.

I RECENTLY paid a visit to Mr. Thomas C. Latto, the distinguished author of many of the most humorous Scottish lyrics of the present century. The shades of evening were silently wrapping the snow-clad world in darkness as I entered the threshold of his comfortable home and, with a feeling more of veneration than gladness, grasped the hand which he invitingly extended to welcome me. My visit was necessarily of brief duration, but it shall live in my memory and be cherished as one of those rare events only met with at long intervals in the journey of life. It was the first time that I had stood in the presence of the author of many of the most familiar songs of my boyhood; songs which had charmed and delighted me with their exuberant humor, and which now intertwine themselves and nestle among the happiest recollections of my early years. Nor was this the most important feature to me, in connection with my visit to the talented song-writer and poet. Here was one who had mingled with many of the illustrious men whose very names I had revered from infancy, and whose works had been a beacon of enjoyment and delight to me for so many long years! Men who had made themselves famous by the treasures they had added to, and by which they had enriched, the general literature of Scotland, and then laying aside their pen, had passed from the world and joined one another in "the land of the leal." It was therefore with more than ordinary interest that I listened to the conversation of Mr. Latto, and as he proceeded and recollections of by-gone days and events became awakened in his mind, I could notice that his eyes brightened and his face seemed to glow with a singular pleasure. He certainly had a wonderful store of reminis-

cences and anecdotes of men and books, which he related in a style
peculiarly his own. These included James Hogg, the author of "The
Queen's Wake;" Professor William Edmonstoune Aytoun, author of
"Lays of the Scottish Cavaliers" (to whom Mr. Latto acted as private
secretary for four years); Allan Cunningham, the editor of Burns's
works; Professor John Wilson ("Christopher North"), of Noctes
Ambrosianæ fame; James Ballantine, author of "Castles in the Air;"
Macaulay, Talford, Mrs. Hemans, Mrs. S. H. Whitman, "the bright-
est woman of New England" and the well-known defender of Edgar
A. Poe, David Macbeth Moir ("Delta"), author of "Mansie Waugh;"
Henry Scott Riddell, author of "Scotland Yet," besides Charles Gray,
David Vedder, Robert Gilfillan, Hew Ainslie, Alexander Smart, Robert
Nichol, and many others equally famous, all of whom he had known
and with whom he had associated or corresponded. Truly, such of
his reminiscences as he imparted to me were of an interesting and
profitable nature, and if he could only be induced to publish a collection of them in book form the literary world would be greatly enriched
thereby. He was, in early life, a prominent contributor to Whistle
Binkie, the Ladies' Own Journal, Blackie's Book of Scottish Song, the
Glasgow Citizen, Blackwood's Magazine, and many other standard
works and publications, and his recollection of his contemporaries at
this date would undoubtedly prove not only interesting but valuable
reading. His own reputation as a poet had already been established,
and his poem on Sir Walter Scott, which appeared in Blackwood's
Magazine about this time, drew from the editor of that publication the
acknowledgment that "Of all the poetical tributes which had been laid
on the tomb of the great magician, that of Latto was the most graceful
and the most original."

Mr. Latto is now well advanced in years. He was born at Kings-
barns, Fifeshire, on the first of December, 1818, and received the best
part of his education at St. Andrew's University. He was noted
among his schoolmates as being of a very reserved and retiring disposition, and strange to say these traits are characteristic of him even
to this day. While his name and his writings are well known throughout the United States and Canada very few Scotsmen even in this city
are aware of the fact that their gifted countryman has resided for a
number of years in a pleasantly situated cottage in the suburbs of
Brooklyn. After engaging in one or two mercantile pursuits, both in
Edinburgh and Glasgow, Mr. Latto decided to take up his residence

in this country. He arrived here in 1851, and since then has supported himself and his family to a great extent by his untiring literary labors. In the midst of these labors, however, the muse has been his constant and fascinating companion, and he has continued to contribute to the press both of Great Britain and America many sterling gems of poetry and song on a variety of subjects. His most popular songs are his humorous ones, and of these, "Sly Widow Skinner," "When we Were at the Schule" and "The Kiss Ahint the Door," are probably the most widely known. They have been sung in nearly every part of the world, certainly in every part where Scotsmen have found a resting place. The following is a copy of "The Kiss Ahint the Door," with an additional stanza (the fourth) which Mr. Latto has added to the song so as to render it more complete:

> There's meikle bliss in ae fond kiss,
> Whyles mair than in a score;
> But wae betak' the stowin smack
> I took ahint the door.

O laddie, whisht! for sic a fricht
 I ne'er was in afore;
Fu' brawly did my mither hear
 The kiss ahint the door.
The wa's are thick—ye needna fear;
 But, gin they jeer and mock,
I'll swear it was a startit cork,
 Or wyte the rusty lock.
  There's meikle bliss, etc.

We stappit ben, while Maggie's face
 Was like a lowin' coal;
An' as for me, I could ha'e creept
 Into a mouse's hole.
The mither look't—saff's how she look't—
 Thae mithers are a bore,
An' gleg as ony cat to hear
 A kiss ahint the door.
  There's meikle bliss, etc.

The douce gudeman, tho' he was there,
 As weel micht be in Rome,
For by the fire he fuffed his pipe,
 An' never fasht his thoom;

But, titterin' in a corner, stood
  The gawky sisters four—
A winter's nicht for me they micht
  Ha'e stood ahint the door.
      There's meikle bliss, etc.

Wee Rab, that sneck-the-woodie imp,
  Could scarcely hide his glee,
As owre his sclate he hotched an' shook,
  Thrang at his "Rule o' Three."
That lang-drawn whistle that he wheept
  Was herald o' mischance;
He kent the music was begun
  An' wha was gaun to dance.
      There's meikle bliss, etc.

"How daur ye tak' sic freedoms here?"
  The bauld gudewife began;
Wi' that a foursome yell gat up—
  I to my heels and ran.
A besom whiskit by my lug,
  And dishclouts half a score;
Catch me again, tho' fidgin' fain,
  At kissin' 'hint the door.
      There's meikle bliss, etc.

"The Kiss" was made the subject of a painting by an eminent Scottish artist, and exhibited in the Royal Academy at Edinburgh some few years ago.

"When we were at the Schule" originally appeared in "Blackie's Book of Scottish Song," without the author's name being attached to it, but in the index of authors it is properly credited to him. Some twenty years ago an article appeared in the *New York Weekly Dispatch*, claiming that the song was written by a John Paterson, whose widow was then living in Grand Street. It seems that this party had been in the habit of singing it for many years as one of his own productions; but the matter having been brought to the notice of Mr. Latto, he had no difficulty in proving that Paterson was laboring under a hallucination. We append a copy of this celebrated song, of which it was said by the Rev. George Gilfillan "Every line is a memory. In the whole compass of Scottish lyrical poetry there is nothing more graphic or delightful."

WHEN WE WERE AT THE SCHULE.

The laddies plague me for a sang,
　I e'en maun play the fule;
I'll sing them ane aboot the days
　When we were at the schule.
Though noo the frosty pow is seen,
　Whaur ance wav'd gowden hair,
An' mony a blythesome heart is cauld,
　Sin' first we sported there.

　　　　When we were at the schule, my **frien'**,
　　　　　When we were at the schule;
　　　　An' O, sae merry pranks we play'd,
　　　　　When we were at the schule.

Yet muckle Jock is to the fore,
　That used our lugs to pu',
An' Rob, the pest, an' Sugar Pouch,
　An' canny Davie Dow.
O do ye mind the maister's hat,
　Sae auld, sae bare an' brown,
We carried to the burnie's side
　An' sent it soomin' down?

　　　　When we were at the schule, etc.

We thocht how clever a' was plann'd,
　When, whatna voice was that?
A head is raised aboon the hedge,
　" I'll thank ye for my hat!"
O weel I mind our hingin' **lugs,**
　Our het an' tinglin' paws,
O weel I mind his awfu' look,
　'An' weel I mind the taws!

　　　　When we were at the schule, etc.

O do ye mind at countin' time,
　How watchfu' he has lain,
To catch **us** steal frae ithers' slates
　An' jot it on our ain?
An how we fear'd at writin' hour,
　His glunches an' his glooms,
How mony times a day he said,
　Our fingers a' were thooms?

　　　　When we were at the schule, etc.

I'll ne'er forget the day ye stood,
  ('Twas manfu' like,) yoursel',
An' took the pawmies an' the shame,
  To save wee Johnnie Bell;
The maister fand it out belyve,
  He took ye on his knee,
An' as he gaz'd into your face,
  The tear was in his e'e.

          When we were at the schule, etc.

But mind ye lad, yon afternoon,
  How fleet ye skipp'd awa',
For ye had crack't auld Jenny's pane,
  When playin' at the ba'.
Nae pennies had we; Jenny grat;
  It cut us to the core;
Ye took ye're mither's hen at nicht
  An' left it at her door.

          When we were at the schule, etc.

An' sic a steer his granny made,
  When talepyet Jamie Rae
We dookit roarin' at the pump,
  Syne row'd him down the brae.
But how the very maister leuch,
  When leein saddler Wat
Cam' in an' threep't that cripple Tam
  Had chas'd an' kill'd his cat.

          When we were at the schule, etc.

Ah, laddies, ye may wink awa',
  Truth maunna aye be tauld;
I fear the schules o' modern days
  Are just sic like's the auld.
An' are na we but laddies yet,
  Wha' get the name o' men?
How sweet at ane's fireside to live
  Thae happy days again;

              When we were at the schule, my frien',
                When we were at the schule,
              An' fling the snawba's ower again
                We flang when at the schule.

Mr. Latto's pathetic compositions are of the very highest order. They contain the genuine ring of the true poet, and in each instance are clothed in great beauty and tenderness. Here is one which was published in Blackie's Book of Scottish Song as far back as 1845. For sweetness and simplicity it is equal to anything of its kind ever published, and if we mistake not it is one of the author's special favorites :

THE BONNIE BLIND LASSIE THAT SITS I' THE SUN.

O hark to the strain that sae sweetly is ringin',
    And echoing clearly o'er lake and o'er lea,
Like some fairy bird in the wilderness singin',
    It thrills to my heart, yet nae minstrel I see,
Round yonder rock, knittin', a dear child is sittin',
    Sae toilin' her pitifu' pittance is won,
Hersel' tho' we see nae, 'tis mitherless Jeanie—
    The bonnie blind lassie that sits i' the sun.

Five years syne come autumn she cam' wi' her mither,
    A sodger's puir widow, sair wasted an' gane:
As brown fell the leaves, sae **wi'** them did she wither
    And left the sweet child on the wide world her lane.
She left Jeanie weepin', in His holy keepin'
    Wha shelters the lamb frae the cauld wintry win',
We had little siller, yet a' were gude till **her,**
    The bonnie blind lassie that sits **i' the sun.**

An' blythe now an' cheerfu' frae mornin' to e'enin'
    She sits thro' the simmer, an' gladdens ilk ear,
Baith auld and young daut her, sae gentle and winnin',
    To a' the folks round, the wee lassie is dear.
Braw leddies caress her, wi' bounties would press her,
    The modest bit darlin' their notice would shun,
For though she has naething, proud-hearted this wee thing,
    The bonnie blind lassie that sits i' the **sun.**

The late **Dr.** John Brown, author of " Rab and His Friends," **once** said, "Among the song-birds of Scotland, Latto has a true note of his own," and a writer in the *Caledonian Mercury* concluded a criticism of his poems by saying: " Here are not only the germs of true poetry, but the bud, the blossom and the very flower of song," opinions which **every** true lover of the lyrical muse must heartily endorse. The following song, written a few months ago, will prove that Mr. Latto has lost none of his poetical fervor even at this date. The title is the familiar proverb—

"WE NEVER MISS THE WATER TILL THE WELL RINS DRY."

Be lookin' out for fell auld age in sunny days o' youth;
Keep rain draps that ye dinna need ere comes the autumn drouth;
Let aye some pennies ye can spare be cannily laid by;
" We never miss the water till the well rins dry."

The wee bit stockin' fittie, that has its private neuk,
Comes just as handy in the end as weel-lined pocket beuk;
Tak' tent an' no be wasterfu', the winter's drawing nigh;
" We never miss the water till the well rins dry."

But be na mean an' greedy, I canna thole the coof,
Wha sees the beggar at his door an' doubles up his loof;
O dinna let him gang his wa's wi' mutter'd bitter cry:
" We never miss the water till the well rins dry."

There's plenty gude within this warld fu' quietly to be done,
Wark needfu' to be hurried through an' mair to be begun;
But charity maun hae the means nor pity lack supply;
" We never miss the water till the well rins dry."

There's just ae water I wad hint that ne'er shortcoming knows;
The mair ye quaff o't, aye the mair your pitcher overflows—
The water o' the WELL O' LIFE; come, drink your fill an' try;
Its brim is gurgling ever bright; its fount is never dry.

Few poets have written so many noble and meritorious sonnets as
Mr. Latto has done, and scarcely a day passes without his adding one
or more of these to his already large collection. We quote three of
his latest inspirations in this respect:

ALLAN RAMSAY.

Not all the poets dree'd a wretched lot;
    Among them there is one that I can name,
    Whose happiness was equal to his fame—
Just " Honest Allan," the illustrious Scot.
Genial old man! his chiefest glory is,
    Before declining in the vale of years
    He stood without a rival 'mong his peers;
" One Half of Round Eternity " was his;
    " Lochaber " and the " Lass o' Patie's Mill,"
The " Gentle Shepherd " and his " Peggy " sweet
Can yet all Scottish hearts with rapture fill.
Still do our milkmaids his blythe strains repeat;
    Good cause had he for his complacent smiles—
    His country's choice as Laureate of the Isles.

ROBERT FERGUSSON.

Poor ill-starr'd Robert! I have grieved for thee,
  Kind, joyous, fired with genius' generous glow,
  And, save the pendulum too fast would go—
Embodiment of mirth's wild witchery;
From Ramsay's lays oft snatching inspiration,
  Indeed, improving upon honest Allan,
  He kythed into the daintiest "rhyming callan',"
Helping e'en Burns to his immortal station.
The "Daft Days" will receive the meed of praise,
  Until the "Holy Fair" with age grows dim;
The "Farmer's Ingle" shed its cheery blaze,
  While Robin's "Cottars" chant their evening hymn;
High Priest of Nature! nobler was the tone
Caught up by thee from lowly Fergusson.

ROBERT BURNS.

Dying at thirty-eight, two feverish years
  He snatched, in which to pour those deathless lays
  That 'tis in vain to emulate or praise,
So surely have they distanced all compeers;
It is a marvel, did we but reflect
  How many cultured failures struck the lyre,
  Till at one swoop his mountain-muse of fire
Hailed him as God's anointed—sole elect.
And now where is the man, save he alone,
  With immortality's bright singing robe;
Whose songs are sung to earth's remotest zone—
  Whose birthday is a joy throughout the globe?
A simple ploughman from the braes of Ayr
Enjoys a triumph that no king can share.

Recently Mr. Latto has taken a special liking to making translations from the Danish, Swedish and Icelandic poets, and such of
these translations as he has given to the press have been very favorably commented upon. As one writer remarks, "They are marked
by the same vigor of execution, felicitous grace of diction and genial
human sympathy that early won for him the place he holds among
modern Scottish poets." It is only a few years since he mastered the
Scandinavian languages, and on this account is entitled to more than
the usual amount of credit for his labors in this direction. Here is
one of his latest translations:

THE NATIVITY.

(From the Danish of Oehlenschlager.)

Each spring, when mists float o'er the plain,
The infant Jesus is born again;
Angels in river, in grove and in air,
Look for the Saviour; he is there.
Nature, as silent the blossoms ope,
Bedecks herself in the green of hope.

Before the innocent shepherds' sight,
Who look to the sky in the Syrian night,
God's angels take thro' the fields their way;
They hover and glide in the moon's pale ray,
Singing, " To-day is born the child
Of Spring—of Mary, the meek and mild.

The drink he quaffs is of purest dew;
That tender smile to the godhead flew;
To heaven he stretches his childish hands
And the earth is wreathed as with rosy bands;
His prattle the zephyr, his cradle the straw,
His eyes the bluest earth ever saw.

To Bethlehem ! ye herds of the green hillside,
That your souls may be soften'd and sanctified;
Awhile from your cares and toils withdraw
To look on the child in the lowly straw,
That so his holy smile this day
May raise your hearts from earth away."

Up swept the seraphs like meteor flame,
But the shepherds held onward to Bethlehem,
And lo ! what a marvelous change is wrought,
On hearts with troublous doubtings fraught,
For they turn again from the pasture sod,
Kneel down to the child and believe in God.

And The STAR darts light from the azure dome,
To point to the King of the Orient's home;
Bright rays of glory stream from the choir,
And the shepherds sink humbly, then back retire
Blessing the Saviour's holy face
That smiles in his mother's fond embrace.

And still there rise from the grim black mould
REDEEMERS in purple, and velvet and gold,
Half of the meadowland, half of the air,
Babes of the wilderness, fragile and fair,
Their chalices charged with a rapture intense—
The fragrance of myrrh and of frankincense.

Mr. Latto is a man with a large and Christian heart, a benevolent nature, a sound judgment and a taste for literature and all that is good and beautiful. Added to these qualities he is greatly esteemed by those who know him personally as a genial companion, a cultured scholar, and a friend to whom they can point with pride. He possesses one of the finest private libraries in Brooklyn, a library that is filled with rare and curious literary treasures, and over the door of which might be truly inscribed, "A Paradise for Book-worms." May he live for many years in the full enjoyment of the gifts which nature has bestowed on him, and the well-deserved reputation which his works have gained for him.

EVAN MacCOLL.

Age sits with decent grace upon his visage
And worthily becomes his silver locks;
He wears the marks of many years well spent,
Of virtue, truth well tried and wise experience.

Evan MacColl, a poet who, for more than half a century, has charmed the lovers of Gaelic poetry throughout the world, has now reached the venerable age of eighty years. He was born on September 21, 1808, at Kenmore, Lochfyne-side, Argyleshire, and was the youngest but one of a family of six sons and two daughters. His father was a man of many excellent qualities and of considerable learning, but he was especially noted among his neighbors for his rich store of Celtic song. His mother, a descendant from the Camerons of Cowall, was well versed in the legendary and fairy lore pertaining to the Highlands. She was a charitable and kindly-disposed woman, and she infused a moral and religious influence into the hearts and thoughts of her children which has never departed. The MacColl family, although thrifty and industrious, was by no means a rich one, and Evan began at an early age and continued for many years afterward to lend assistance in the labors connected with farming and fishing. At odd times he attended school.

These, however, must have been happy and memorable years to our author, as amidst their toils and hardships many of his most celebrated Gaelic lyrics were composed. Mr. John Mackenzie, in his "Beauties of Gaelic Poetry and lives of the Gaelic Bards," informs us that "at a very early age he displayed an irresistible thirst for legendary lore and Gaelic poetry, but, from the seclusion of his native glen, and other disadvantageous circumstances, he had but scanty means for fanning the latent flame that lay dormant in his breast. He, however, greedily devoured every volume he could procure and when the labors of the day were over would often resort to some favorite haunt where, in the enjoyment of that solitude which his father's fireside denied him, he might be found taking advantage of the very moonlight to pore over

the minstrelsy of his native country until lassitude or the hour of repose compelled him to return home." By the time he had reached his
twenty-third year his wonderful Gaelic productions had made his name
famous throughout Scotland and in many parts of England.

In 1831 his father, with the unmarried members of the family, emigrated to Canada. Evan, however, could not be induced to accompany
them. In 1836 he published his first volume, under the title of "The
Mountain Minstrel." It contained poems and songs, both in Gaelic
and English, and was warmly received by the public and the press.
In 1838 appeared his "Clarsach nam Beann" and a second edition of
his first work, which was followed by a third edition in 1849. In 1839
he was appointed to a clerkship in the customs at Liverpool. Ten
years later he obtained a six months' leave of absence to enable him
to visit his friends in Canada and recuperate his health, and while
there was induced to exchange his position at Liverpool for a more
remunerative one in the provincial customs of Upper Canada. He
settled in Kingston in 1850 and remained at his post until he was
superannuated in 1886. His muse has been exceedingly fruitful during his long residence in Canada, and we are not surprised that many
of his productions have been inspired by the recollection of the scenes
and incidents connected with his boyhood's home. Here is one of
his best known lyrical pieces on this subject:

THE HILLS OF THE HEATHER.

Give the swains of Italia 'mong myrtles to rove,
Give the proud, sullen Spaniard his bright orange grove,
Give gold-sanded streams to the sons of Chili,
But, O, give the hills of the heather to me !
Then, drink we a health to the old Highland Bens,
Whose heads cleave the welkin, whose feet press the glens;
What Scot worth the name would not toast them with glee ?
The red heather hills of the Highlands for me !

The hills whose wild echoes delight to prolong
The soul-stirring pibroch, the streams' gushing song,
Storm-vexed and mist-mantled though often they be,
Still dear are the hills of heather to me.
Then, drink we a health to the old Highland Bens,
That fondly look down on the clan-peopled glens;
What Scot worth the name would not toast them with glee ?
The red heather hills of the Highlands for me !

Your carses may boast of their own fertile farms,
Yet give me the glens shielding well in their arms
Blue lakes grandly glassing crag, cliff, tower and tree—
The red heather hills of the Highlands for me!
Then drink we a health to the old Highlands Bens,
Their deer-haunted corries and hazel-wood dens;
What Scot worth the name would not toast them **with glee**?
The red heather hills of the Highlands for me!

'Tis there 'neath the tartan beat hearts the most leal—
Hearts warm as the sunshine, yet firm as the steel;
There only this heart can feel happy or free;
The red heather hills of the Highlands for me!
Then, drink we a health to the old Highland Bens;
Glad leaving to England her flats and her fens;
What Scot worth the name would not toast them **with glee**?
The red heather hills of the Highlands for me!

Numerous other notable quotations might be made from our author's
works, touching the **scenes** of **his** boyhood, or showing the genuine
warmth of his love for **the** fatherland. They are grand and impres-
sive at all times, and seldom fail **to awaken** pleasant memories in the
mind of the reader. How grand **and** realistic for instance is his **de-**
scription of the river Beauly as it surges **from the** Highlands down to
the Lowlands:

'Tis grand thy crystal flood to **view**
     Benvaichard's borders leaving,
Nor less to see the Strath below
     Thy fuller flow receiving;
          But grander far
          To see thee where
     Its narrowing bounds thou'rt cleaving
Through rocky ridges opening **wide**
In very terror of thy tide.

Now through the Druim's dark gorges deep
     Methinks I see thee going,
Half hid 'mid woods that love to keep
     Fond watch upon thy flowing;
          From rock to rock,
          With flash and shock,
     And fury ever growing—
A giant fettered, it is true,
Yet bound all barriers to subdue.

The patriotism with which MacColl is imbued, however, is something altogether apart from his love for Scotland. The land wherein reposes the dust of his ancestors is the most sacred portion of the globe to him, and he stands ever ready, both with pen and voice, to uphold its dignity and honor. A good illustration of this spirit may be found in the reply which he sent one morning to a certain professor who had, in a public speech delivered the previous evening, ventured the assertion that "Scotchmen must admit their country to have been once conquered: '

Scotland, a conquered land ! Learned sage,
Pray tell us how, and in what age ?
Not so read *I* historic page.

Thou canst not deem a mere invasion—
A brief disputed occupation—
To be the conquest of a nation ?

Think'st thou the homage of a knave
Binding on those he would enslave ?
Let Baliol answer from his grave !

Scotland a conquered land ! Ho, ho !
Proud Edward found it was not so
When dying—vainly still her foe.

No pandering, then, to Saxon pride !
Pretensions by our sires defied
Shall we not also cast aside ?

Forget'st **thou Carun's crimsoned stream ?**
Is Bannockburn **a myth or dream ?**
And Wallace a **mere minstrel theme ?**

Thou speak'st of Cromwell ? **Be it so;**
Cromwell was never Scotland's foe—
How then her conqueror, prithee, show ?

Her friend and freedom's, north he came;
Her noblest sons backed well his aim,
And scotched misrule in Cromwell's name.

Hold up thy head, then, Scotia ! When
Thy sons forget that they are men
Thou may'st **be** conquered—not till then !

MacColl's language is poetic in every sense of the word. His poetry is a realm of fascinating, intellectual beauties, always bright, and pure, and original. Few, indeed, are the poems which he has written that

are not studded with rare and striking metaphors, thus showing with
what a luxuriant, poetic imagination he is endowed. We listen in
wonderment while his muse joins in the joyous carol of the lark, or
hovers over the roaring cataract, the mighty woods, the shady glens,
and the heather-clad hills of his native land. We watch him as he
traces with his magic pen the scenes and incidents of his early life, and
they become familiar and endeared to us. He conjures up the legends
and romances which cling like the ivy to the battlements and crumb-
ling walls of the once famous castles and strongholds of the Highlands,
and the grandeur and glory—the victories and defeats—the superstitions and crimes of a by-gone age become vividly portrayed and re-
called to our minds. He casts his spell, like Burns, over many of the
commonest objects of every-day life, and they assume a new beauty
and importance. He pictures to us the various beauties of nature,
shows us the brighter side of life, sings to us of mirth, love, patriotism,
duty, humanity and piety, and as we wander among his poetical productions we are made to realize that we are for the time being com-
muning with the innermost thoughts of one who is a true poet. The
following is a translation by the late Lachlan MacLean (Glasgow) of
one of his most renowned poems:

THE CHILD OF PROMISE.

Thy life was like a morning cloud,
  Of rosy hue at break of day;
The envious sun appears, and soon
  The rival glory melts away.

Thy life was like May's sunny beams
  By shadows brushed o'er field and flower;
Or like the bow of heaven that sheds
  Its glory in a fleeting shower.

Thy life was like new-fallen snow,
  Gracing some sea-beach lately bared;
The tide returns with heedless flow—
  The sky-born guest hath disappeared.

Thy life was like some tuneful harp
  Abruptly stopped when sweetest strung;
Or like "the tale of other years"
  To expectation half unsung.

Thy life was like a passing gleam
　Of moonlight on the troubled main,
Or like some blissful dream which he
　Who dreams, may never dream again.

O child of promise bright ! although
　'Twere wrong to grudge to heaven its own,
Our tears, withal, will often flow
　To think thy sun so soon gone down.

Our author reveals to us his intimacy with nature through many of his finest poems. Embodied in his " May Morning in Glen-Shira," for instance, we have the following delightful description of the month of May:

O May ! thou'rt an enchantress rare—
Thy presence maketh all things fair;
Thou wavest but thy wand, and joy is everywhere.

Thou comest and the clouds are not—
Rude Boreas has his wrath forgot,
The gossamer again is in the air afloat.

The foaming torrent from the hill—
Thou changest to a gentle rill
A thread of liquid pearl, that faintly murmurs still.

Thine is the blossom-laden tree,
The meads that white with lambkins be,
Thine, too, the nether world that in each lake we see.

Cheer'd by thy smile, the herd-boy gay
Oft sings the rock-repeated lay,
And wonders who can be the mocker in his way.

Thou givest fragance to the breeze,
A gleaming glory to the seas,
Nor less thy grace is seen in yonder emerald leas.

Many valuable testimonials of esteem and respect have been tendered to Mr. MacColl during his lifetime, one in particular taking the form of a very fine portrait of himself, presented by his townsmen. The noblest one, however, and the one which will outlast all the others, is a poem by his friend, Mr. Duncan MacGregor Crerar, a gentleman known among his countrymen as the Breadalbane Bard, on account of

the many beautiful poems which he has written on the classical and
historical scenes of his native Perthshire. The poem was first published in the Celtic Magazine, Inverness, Scotland, and has since been
characterized as "a tribute to the genius of the poet which reflects
equal lustre on the subject and the singer." We quote it here as we
feel confident that it will always be mentioned in connection with
MacColl's poems:

TO EVAN MacCOLL.

My greeting to thee, Bard revered,
  Sweet minstrel of Loch Fyne!
Heaven bless, and shield, and prosper aye,
  Mo charaid! thee and thine.
May time deal ever tenderly,
  MacColl, with thine and thee!
Long may thy tuneful Highland harp
  Throb sweetest minstrelsy.

The sterling virtues of the Gael,
  Their deeds of bravery,
Their guileless hearts so warm and true,
  Who can portray like thee?
And sweetly dost thou sing the charms,
  The gracefulness divine,
Of Highland maids, in speech endeared—
  Thy mother tongue and mine.

"Iona" "Staffa," and "Loch Awe,"
  "Loch Lomond" and "Loch Fyne,"
The "Brander Pass" and "Urquhart's Glen,"
  Thou grandly doth outline.
Thy "Child of Promise," beauteous gem,
  A plaintive, soothing psalm;
Thy "Falling Snow" brings to the heart
  A sweet, a holy calm.

Thine own "Glenshira," by thy Muse,
  Is now a classic land:
Its scenes of grandeur have been limned
  With skill by Royal hand.
O bless her, princess of our race!
  That rose without a thorn,
So dearly cherished in our hearts,
  The loved Louise of Lorne.

Thine odes, thy sonnets, and thy songs
　　All rich in melodie,
Shall with delight be read and sung
　　While Awe flows to the sea.
O Bard beloved ! in boyhood's morn
　　I sang thy mountain lays;
With joy perused thy poesie
　　'Mong famed Breadalbane's braes.

I dreamed not then the rich delight
　　My future had in store—
Thy noble friendship, treasured dear,
　　Within affection's core.
The happy *ceilidhs* to thy home,
　　The charming converse there;
Thy Highland hospitality,
　　How cordial, and how rare !

Though fair Canadia, now thy home,
　　Be full of charms to thee;
Thy heart oft yearns to see Argyll,
　　And thine own " Rowan Tree."
My wishes warm to thee I waft,
　　Charmed songster of Loch Fyne;
And oh, may heaven's blessings rest,
　　My friend on thee and thine !

We cannot conclude our sketch of this eminent poet in a more
appropriate manner than by repeating **the words** of **his** friend and
biographer, Mr. Charles Sangster.

"Mr. MacColl," he writes in 1873, "is considerably past the middle
of life, but **bids fair** to weather the storm of existence **for** many years
to come. In private life he is, both by precept and example, all that
could be desired. He has an intense love for all that is really good
and beautiful, and a true and manly scorn **for** all that is false, time-
serving and hypocritical; there is no narrow-mindedness, no bigotry
in his soul. **Kind** and generous to a fault, **he is** more than esteemed,
and that deservedly, by all **who** properly know him. **In the** domestic
circle, all the warmth in the **man's** heart—the full glow of genuine
feeling and affection—is **ever** uppermost. He is a thoroughly earnest
man, in whose daily walk and conversation, as well as in his actions,
Longfellow's ' Psalm of Life ' is acted out in verity. In his friendships, **he is** sincere; **in** his dislikes, equally **so.** He is thoroughly

Scottish in his leanings, his national love burns with intensity. In poetry he is not merely zealous, but enthusiastic, and he carries his natural force of character **in all** he says and does. Consequently he is not simply a wooer, but a worshiper of the muse. Long may he live, the 'Bard of Lochfyne,' to **prostrate** his entire heart and soul in the Temple of the Nine."

An English edition **of** MacColl's poetical works was published by Messrs. Hunter, Rose **& Co.**, Toronto, in 1883. Attached **to** this **volume is** an excellent biographical essay by the editor of **the Celtic** Magazine, Alexander Mackenzie, F. S. A. To the latter we beg to acknowledge our indebtedness for much of the information herein **stated** in connection with the life of our author. A new edition of his poems with a number of additional pieces has just been published, and to this we would kindly refer such of our readers as may desire to become better **acquainted** with the **writings of** the gifted *Eoghan MacColla.*

DUNCAN MacGREGOR CRERAR.

Whoe'er amidst the sons
Of reason, valor, liberty and virtue
Displays distinguished merit, is a noble
Of nature's own creating.

SCOTLAND is proud, and justly so, of the many eminent men of letters which she has given to the world. Since the year 1375, when John Barbour produced his great historical poem, "The Bruce," down to the present time, her history is replete and sparkles with the illustrious names of her many talented sons who have won both honor and renown through their literary abilities. Nor has it been in one particular branch that these gifted individuals have labored so earnestly, and thus gained for Scotland a pre-eminence in literature second to no other nation. All branches have been represented and enriched by the magical touch of their pens, from the quaint and primitive looking almanac of by-gone days to the large and wonderful encyclopedias of modern times. But it is certainly through their contributions to the poetical literature of their country that the greatest number of Scotsmen have acquired an enviable and well merited reputation, and as the names of the various Scottish poets and their works are familiar to all of our readers, we shall not occupy unnecessary space by quoting or referring to them at any length here. The traditions and history, the scenery and associations of Scotland, are all favorable to the cultivation of the muse, and as is well known many of the finest gems of poetry and song in our language have emanated from the Bards of that country. Many of these Bards from time to time have strayed from their native hills and glens and settled down in the new world. Among others Mr. Duncan MacGregor Crerar, the honorable Secretary of the Burns Society of this city, is worthy of special attention. Mr. Crerar is a poet of acknowledged ability and of wide reputation. In Scottish circles he is always referred to as "The Breadalbane Bard." His style is marked by earnestness of moral purpose and a purity of diction which sometimes rises into religious fervor, and often takes **the form of** embalming in verse the virtues and talents **of** his fellow men **whose** characteristics have **won** his esteem, or who by moral or intellectual superiority have gained his friendship.   In the latter quality **the** numerous sonnets which **he has** produced of an elegiac or complimentary nature, **each** of **them a** gem in itself, might furnish **a** volume, **and we feel** assured that **the** publication of these **melodious** embodiments **of** thought would **place** Mr. Crerar as an **acknowledged** superior to any living poet in **America** in this department **of literature.**   Although Mr. Crerar has been many years **in America,** and is thoroughly cosmopolitan in his habits **of** thought **and modes of expression,** his muse ever looks back lovingly to the fatherland.   **The home of his youth** has become sanctified by separation, **and the** majestic scenery of his native Perthshire rises before his imagination in all the vividness of its reality.   The purple glory of the heather-clad hills, the flash of **loch and** stream, the warble of the wild birds, the bloom of dewy flowers, seem to pass in a ceaseless panorama before him.   The associations **of** youth have thus furnished the theme **of some of his sweetest lyrics, as for instance in his**

CALEDONIA'S BLUE BELLS.

Hail, bonnie Blue Bells! ye come hither to me
With a brother's warm love from far o'er the sea;
Fair flowerets! ye grew on a calm, sacred spot—
The ruins alas! of my kind father's cot,
     Caledonia's **Blue Bells,** O bonnie Blue Bells!

What memories dear of that cot ye recall,
Though now there remains neither rooftree nor wall!
Alack a-day! lintel and threshold are gone,
While cold 'neath the weeds lies the hallowed hearthstone!
     Caledonia's Blue Bells, O bonnie Blue Bells!

'Twas a straw-roofed **cottage, but love abode there,**
And peace and contentment aye breathed in its air;
With songs from the mother, and legends from sire,
How blithe were we all round the cheerie peat fire!
     Caledonia's Blue Bells, **O bonnie** Blue Bells!

Our sire long asleep, his fond mem'ry endeared;
The mother still spared us, beloved and revered;
Sweet Blue Bells with charmed recollections entwined
Of scenes in my childhood forever enshrined.
     Caledonia's Blue Bells, O bonnie Blue Bells!

Mr. John Laird Wilson, the well-known New York critic, speaking of the above lyric, said: " The accompanying song speaks for itself, It needs no praise of ours. Coming warm from the heart, it finds its way to the heart. Breathing piety, patriotism, filial and brotherly love, it touches all the best chords of our common humanity. It has in it the warmth of Highland blood, the flavor of Breadalbane heather, the freshness of the mountain breeze. We congratulate Mr. Crerar on this fresh revelation of true poetic genius; and we advise him to throw aside his excess of modesty, and to trust the public with a fuller and more adequate manifestation of his powers. ' Caledonia's Blue Bells ' will win for its author many friends; but we, who know what is in store for us, impatiently await better things."

Among Mr. Crerar's other poems in connection with the associations of his youth we would mention " My Bonnie Rowan Tree" and "The Eirlic Well." The subjects of these poems are very simple, but the poems are clothed in such beautiful and touching language that we linger over them with feelings of love and respectful admiration. His two beautiful poems addressed to the Marquis and Marchioness of Breadalbane are also worthy of special notice. We take sincere pleas- ure in re-printing those two pieces here, as the first is a well-deserved compliment to a nobleman who is one of the most progressive and liberal-minded Scotsmen of the day, and the other is a just tribute of respect to the many sterling qualities and accomplishments of a talented and kind-hearted lady:

TO THE MOST HONOURABLE THE MARQUIS OF BREADALBANE.

Beloved Breadalbane ! greetings waft I thee,
    On this thy dear, thine honoured natal day;
    That Heaven long spare thee, earnestly I pray
Full many, many glad returns to see.
Thy rule is wise o'er vast domains and wide,
    Rife in good actions for thy people's weal;
    Each duty shared by helpmate kind and leal
Whose work and walk are ever at thy side.
Rule wisely on, for noble is the race
    O'er whom your governance holds loving sway;
Yours their deep gratitude for acts of grace,
    Their warmest blessings crown you every day!
How rich, how sweet, and joyous the reward,
Your people's love and their sincere regard!

TO ALMA, MARCHIONESS OF BREADALBANE.

Lady beloved! My warmest thanks to thee
 For thy most gracious gift—thine image dear—
I waft across the wide Atlantic sea,
 With gladdened heart and gratitude sincere.
Here beauteously and faithfully portrayed
 Thy graceful form and lovely classic face;
O noble lady, thou art winsome, fair,
 And genial, kind, and full of heaven-born grace

Nor do I thank thee less for friendly words
 And warm regard for thine so far away;
No distance can undo the cords of love
That bind us to the home of childhood's day.
Sweet as the fragrance of fresh heather bloom,
 The praises reach us of thine acts benign;
Thy charming courtesy and kindness rare
 We in our hearts will treasure and enshrine.

O wife devoted of Breadalbane's Lord !
 True Freedom's cause a friend has found in thee;
'Twas thine own hand that bravely raised the flag
 Which led our Perthshire on to victorie.
Heaven bless you both with peace, and spare you long
 To kindly rule your every strath and glen;
No land is richer in romance and song;
 No men are braver than Breadalbane men !

Mr. Crerar has been particularly fortunate in securing the friendship of nearly all of the distinguished literary Scotsmen who have visited America during the last twenty years. George MacDonald, William Black, the Earl of Rosebery, Alexander Strahan, Marchioness of Breadalbane, Prof. James Geikie, Prof. John Stuart Blackie, and many others are among his hosts of admirers and correspondents. Mrs. William Black, among many other tokens of kindly remembrance, sent him, on one occasion, a spray of white heather, which immediately called forth the following lines:

A SPRAY OF WHITE HEATHER.

I lovingly greet thee, sweet spray of white heather,
  With a heartfelt emotion I would not conceal!
Thou com'st from a friend true in shade and bright weather,
  Who in kindness is warm as in friendship she's leal.

  Good fortune and luck **aye** attend me together,
    Is the wish thou dost bring from the donor to **me,**
  Charmed emblem of both! bonnie spray of white heather,
    From the land of my fathers far over the **sea.**

Fair token, thou'rt chaste as the heart of the sender,
  Bringing fond recollections of life's early day—
Of kin, friends, and country, and ties the most tender,
  Ere from **kin, friends,** and country I wandered away.

  Good fortune and luck aye attend me together,
    Is the wish thou dost bring from the donor to me,
  Charmed emblem of both! bonnie spray of white heather,
    From the land of my fathers far over the sea.

I never may see, pretty spray of white heather,
  Caledonia's loved glens and her mountains so grand;
I may ne'er again with the dear ones forgather,
  But my blessings on them and my dear native land!

  Good fortune and luck aye attend me together,
    Is the wish thou dost bring from the donor to me,
  Charmed emblem of both! bonnie spray of white heather,
    From **the** land of my fathers far over the sea.

Thou gift of a friend! I will treasure thee dearly,
  Till my journey shall end in that long peaceful rest,
When some loving hand mine had oft pressed sincerely
  May with tenderness place thee, sweet spray, on **my breast.**

  Good fortune and luck aye attend me together,
    Is the wish thou dost bring from the donor to me,
  Charmed emblem of both! bonnie spray of white heather,
    From the land of my fathers far over the sea.

Although Mr. Crerar excels in pieces of an elegiac nature, he has written many short pieces full of a joyous hopefulness looking on **the** brighter side of life and a sweet assurance of a glad hereafter. Of these his " To-morrow " is probably the best:

TO-MORROW.

Away with grief; dull care, away;
   Away with canker, pain and sorrow;
Where black clouds scowl and frown to-day,
   The sun will brightly shine to-morrow.
The weary heart, when sore depressed,
   Too oft, alas! will trouble borrow,
But joy will banish what distressed,
   And eyes that wept will smile to-morrow.

Why should we grieve though friends forsake—
   If one is left that's true and thorough
In adverse hours, who will partake
   And share our woe or weal to-morrow?
No peaceful place of rest is this,
   Here no immunity from sorrow,
But an enduring home and bliss
   Await above when comes the morrow!

It would give us **sincere pleasure** to present **a few** of Mr. Crerar's sonnets to our readers, but **we will confine ourselves to** the one already given and the two following. They are entitled "To Robert Gordon, Esq.," and "To William Black, Poet and Novelist." Mr. Gordon was **long and** well known as one of the leading bankers in our community. **He** returned to his native shores **a few** years ago, hence the lines:

TO ROBERT GORDON, ESQ.

Farewell, dear friend, since farewell it must be;
   Our hearts **are heavy,** and our **tears are** flowing,
   For sorrowfully grieve we at thy going,
As true affection's grasp we give to thee.
We grudge thee not to our loved fatherland,
   Whither our warmest wishes with thee **go:**
   Thy record pure; thou leav'st behind no foe.
Undimmed thine honour, and unstained thy hand!
We'll miss from circle charmed and curling fray
   Thy cheerie voice and ever genial face;
Thy name will cherished be when far away,
   Thou worthy son of Kenmure's noble race.
Forget us not: remember auld lang syne.
Heaven's blessing rest, leal friend, on thee and thine!

TO WILLIAM BLACK, **POET AND** NOVELIST.

'Tis thine to wield a chaste and charmèd pen
   That thrills and gladdens hearts in every clime,
   With story modern or of olden time,
Congenial comrade, faithfullest of men!
Thy leaves are redolent of heather breeze;
   With deft skill thou pourtray'st each beauteous scene,
   Glen, strath, and loch, and setting sun serene,
In inland shire or lonely Hebrides.
The people thou creat'st bear Nature's mould.
   Endowed with dignity and grace are they;
   Life's march they cheer with some sweet Scottish lay,
Or psalm, or ballad of the years of old.
Write ever on, loved friend, for at thy gate
Admiring millions do thy lines await!

Probably the finest of all Mr. **Crerar's** productions is his poem on Robert **Burns.** This poem was composed for and read at one of the annual dinners of the Burns Society of this city. It was afterward published in book-form by Marcus Ward & Co., and received quite an ovation from the press and public. As one writer remarks :—" It has the true ring of poetry, and within a comparatively small space it hits off the salient features of Burns' character and commemorates the principal subject of his works." We quote two verses as a specimen of the whole:

"He touched our country's ancient harp
   With truest patriotic fire;
Forth thrilling came soul-stirring strains,
   Man's nobler actions to inspire.
The cottar's fireside, 'neath his spell,
   Becomes at once a hallowed shrine;
His hymn to Mary swells the heart,
   And fills the eye his Auld Lang Syne."

    *   *   *   *

"Not to his native land alone
   His genius and his fame belong,
In other climes is treasured dear
   His matchless legacy of song.
His melodies have echoing gone
   To continents and isles afar;
They cheer and gladden hearts alike
   'Neath Southern Cross and Polar Star."

Prof. John Stuart Blackie, in one of his letters to Mr. Crerar, says: "I am now among 'Yarrow's Braes and Ettricks Shaws' tasting a little rural quiet and pastoral rest. I have read your Songs with peculiar pleasure. 'Caledonia's Blue Bells', 'A Spray of White Heather', and 'Tomorrow' being my special favorites. It is delightful to see with what pious joy the Highlanders cherish the heroic traditions, and the sweet memories of their country when far across the sea. Next to the Bible, popular song is the great moral force that makes rich the blood of the world; and a man that keeps a singing bird in his heart, holds a claim even more potent on occasions to disarm the Devil than a text of Scripture." Among the other well-known poems by Mr Crerar, we would specially refer to the following: "Mementos of My Father's Grave," "A Christmas Greeting to Mr. and Mrs. James Brand," "My Hero True Frae Bennachie," "A Guid New Year," addressed to Mr. Thomas Davidson Brown, "To Mr. William Drysdale, of Montreal," "The Victory Won," "In Memoriam : Jane Jardine Marsh," "Gone Before," and the three exquisite pieces—"A Full Blown Flower," "A Bridal Greeting," and "The Orange Wreath for Heaven's Crown," which are now bound together and issued (privately) as an "In Memoriam Souvenir" of the late Mrs. Fuller, daughter of Mr. and Mrs. Walter Watson. Before closing our selections and extracts from the contributions of Mr. Crerar to the poetical literature of our time, we desire to present to our readers a poem composed on the occasion of the death of Mr. David Kennedy, the Scottish vocalist. He died at Stratford, Ontario, on the thirteenth of October, 1886.

SUNG INTO HEAVEN !

Sung into heaven ! meet end to thy long day;
Rare songster ! who sang Scottish song and lay
In earth's four quarters, and on every sea,
Hearts ever gladdening with thy minstrelsie.
Thine was a magic power to soothe or thrill,
The eye with joy or sorrow's tears to fill,
To kindle love, rouse patriotism's fire,
When to impassioned strains attuned thy lyre.
How sweetly blended with thy melodie,
The charmed notes of thy gifted family,
A group, alas, we never more shall see!
Proud of the name and fame thy genius won,
Our native Perthshire, mourns her minstrel son;

Foss, fanned by breezes from Loch Tummel's shore—
Thy brave sires' cradle-land in days of yore—
Broad Scotland, and all lands that thou **did'st see,**
Join now in one grand coronach to thee.
To her who was thy helpmate leal through **life,**
Thy faithful, loving, **and** belovéd **wife,**
And to thy comely, sweet-voiced children dear,
All with one heart waft sympathy sincere.
Sung into heaven ! by thine own filial band;
Thy blessing, parting kiss, and grasp of hand;
Sung into heaven ! in a sweet, holy calm,
Thine own voice **melting in the** farewell psalm!

Duncan **MacGregor Crerar** was born **at** Amulree, Glenquaich, Perthshire, **December 4,** 1837. He received a good education, and was destined by his parents for the ministry. These **intentions,** however, were abandoned on the death of **his father.** In **1857 he went** to Canada, where he engaged for **a number of years in mercantile** pursuits. He also served for some time **in** the active militia **on the** frontier, and in recognition of his valuable services, **the** Canadian Government, when under the direction of his warm friend, **the** Honorable Alexander MacKenzie, gazetted him Honorary Lieutenant **of** the company with which he served. **For** many years he has been engaged on **a** large poem which **is now** completed, and about to **be** published. One of his friends **says : " This** poem will **have** immense attraction for lovers of the beautiful **in** nature, but particularly those who are familiar with the matchless **scenery,** the family histories and the legendary lore of Perthshire." **In conclusion we would** state that Mr. Crerar is one of the most genial of men, kind, sympathetic and generous in all his actions. In his own quiet, unobtrusive way, and unknown to the world, he has rendered assistance to many when they found the clouds **of** adversity hovering over them: and there are few men similarly circumstanced who can boast **of** so large and so sincere a following of friends.

JAMES KENNEDY.

To whom the lyre and laurels have been given,
With all the trophies of triumphant song—
He won them well, and may he wear them long!

MR. KENNEDY was born at Carsegownie, Forfarshire, in the year 1848. According to a memoir of him which appears in "Modern Scottish Poets," he "is of Celtic origin, being descended through his father from the Kennedys of Lochaber, and through his mother—from whom he inherits his literary taste and poetic temperament—from the Mackintoshes of Glenshee. We also learn from the same source that after the suppression of the rebellion, 1745-6, "A branch of the Kennedys settled in Forfarshire and sought employment in the extensive quarries of that county. Their descendants chiefly followed the same occupation, and the poet's father rose to be a moderately successful contractor. Dying, when barely past the meridian of life, his widow was left burdened with the task of rearing a family of ten children, of whom James was the seventh, and some of whom were in infancy." Mr. Kennedy studied at the village school for a few years and at the age of twelve began the battle of life on his own account as a farmer's boy. A few years later he removed to Dundee, where he entered upon an apprenticeship as a machinist. At this time he was an enthusiastic athlete and was credited with being a Hercules for his size. The casket of medals now in his possession bears witness to the many wonderful feats both of skill and of strength which he performed. Apart from the celebrity which he acquired as an athlete, however, he became interested in the agitation then in progress for the bettering of the agricultural classes in Scotland, and was soon known as one of the most active promoters of the cause. It also seems to have been about this time that he discovered his ability at verse-making. He had written a few pieces of a lyrical nature, and these had been accorded a prominent place in the columns of one of the local journals. This had encouraged and stimulated him to make greater efforts,

and he decided to begin a diligent course of **study in** the different branches **of** English education. He also devoted **whatever time he** could spare in carefully reading the works of Ramsay, Fergusson, Burns, Scott, and the other master poets of Scotland, and as a result his mind gradually conformed to their style of composition. As time wore on he became a regular and popular poetical contributor to a number of newspapers and magazines, and when he had reached his twentieth birthday his fame as a poet of more than ordinary ability had **been** firmly established in many parts of Scotland. He began to contemplate a visit to America, however. He believed that there was a larger and a more remunerative field here for the better class of mechanics than there was in **any part** of Great Britain, and he resolved to put his belief to **a** practical test, for a time at least. Acting on a sudden impulse he appeared before his friends one morning and bade them good bye, and ere the shades of that evening had fallen, he was being wafted from the land of his forefathers to the shores of the new world. We can easily imagine that it was not without the deepest emotion that he gazed, for what might be the last time, on the stern outlines **of** his native land as they slowly receded from his sight. To him the fatherland was the one fair spot on earth, and his love for it was akin to that for his Bible. It was the land of which he so proudly sings :

> Where the rowans hang like lustres
>   Red within the shady dells;
> And the sweet blaeberry clusters
>   Blue among the heather-bells;
>
> Where the laverock and the lintie
>   Sing their lilts o' pure delight;
> And the robin whistles canty
>   To the warbling yellow-yite;
>
> Where the deeds o' martial glory
>   Hallow like hill and dale;
> Where the wild, romantic story
>   Casts its charm o'er ilka vale.
>
> Where sweet poesy pipes her numbers
>   Till the minstrel's airy dream
> Haunts the wild where echo slumbers,
>   Sings in ilka crystal stream;
>
> Where true manhood dwells serenely,
>   Moulded in heroic grace,
> And fair virtue, meek but queenly,
>   Beams in woman's angel face.

He landed in New York early in 1869, and for the next three years travelled extensively throughout the States, and worked in many of the principal locomotive shops in the country. Returning to New York in the Summer of 1872 he settled down here, and a few months afterward published his first great poem, a metrical romance, which was favorably received by the American people, and of which a large edition was rapidly sold. He also resumed his studies, and we learn from the work already mentioned that "by attending the New York Evening High School, and while still following the calling of a machinist, he made the most laudable efforts to remedy the deficiencies of his early education. In a few years he graduated in the regular literary course. In 1875 he was awarded the first prize for English composition. In 1876 he was commended both for excellence in oratory and for rapid progress in the study of the Latin language. His periodical contributions to the press, both of Scotland and America, demonstrated his growing culture. His language was rapidly becoming more vigorous and pure, and his thought more elevated." At this time Mr. Kennedy was united in marriage by the late Rev. Henry Ward Beecher, to Miss Isabella Lowe, an estimable young lady from his native hills, and one who has since proved herself a true helpmate to him in every sense of the word. The first great grief that overshadowed their lives was in the death of their first born, an affectionate and robust little boy who passed to the unseen world about his third year. On this sad occasion Mr. Kennedy produced one of his finest and most touching little poems. We can all appreciate the heavy sorrow, while many of us no doubt, at some period of our lives, could have re-echoed the wish expressed in the verses entitled

WEE CHARLIE.

"I shall go to him, but he shall not return to me."—II. Samuel, 12th c. 23d v.

> O gin my heart could hae its wiss
>   Within this weary warld o'care,
> I'd ask nae glow o' balmy bliss
>   To dwell around me evermair.
> For joy were mine beyond compare,
>   And O how happy would I be,
> If heaven would grant my earnest prayer,
>   An' bring wee Charlie back to me.

He cam' like sunshine when the buds
  Burst into blossoms sweet an' gay,
He dwelt like sunshine when the cluds
  Are vanish'd frae the eye o' day.
He pass'd as daylicht fades away
  An' darkness spreads owre land and sea,
Nae wonder though in grief I pray,
  O bring wee Charlie back to me.

When pleasure brings her hollow joys,
  Or mirth awakes at friendship's ca',
Or art her varied power employs
  To make dull time look blythe an' braw.
How feckless seem they ane an' a'
  When sad remembrance dims my e'e;
O tak' thae idle joys awa
  An' bring wee Charlie back to me.

But vain's the cry, he maunna cross
  Frae where he dwells in bliss unseen
Nor need I mourn my waefu' loss,
  Nor muse on joys that micht hae been.
When cauld death comes to close my een
  Awa beyond life's troublous sea,
In everlasting joy serene,
  They'll bring wee Charlie back to me.

It has truly been said that "Mr. Kennedy's lyre is not an instrument of one string. He passes with apparent ease from touching pathos to broad humor, and sings with scarcely greater fervor of Caledonia than of the Union's 'bright flag's starry fold' with its 'blended crimson, blue and gold.'" In the realm of descriptive poetry he is unrivalled by any of his contemporaries. He portrays natural scenery in the most delightful and graphic of language, and many of his passages become linked to our memory by their simple beauty and truthful delineations of nature. In some instances they almost seem like a mirror reflecting back with wonderful reality the scenes amid which we passed our boyhood's days. Noran Water, for instance, is an excellent descriptive poem. It is too long for quotation here, but an idea of its many beautiful passages may be gathered from the following extract :

O Noran ! how I see thee dance
  By heath-clad hills, alone, unseen,
Save where the lonely eagle's glance
  Surveys thee from his crag serene.

Forever joyous thou dost seem,
  Still sportive as a child at play,
Who, lost in pleasure's careless dream,
  Makes merry music all the day.

By fairy nooks I see thee flow,
  Nor pausing in thy artless song
Till where the fir trees spreading low
  Obscure thy stream their arms among.
There, sweet amid the shady gloom,
  Thou hear'st the blackbird chant his lay,
Thou see'st the pale primroses bloom,
  And silent ling'rest on thy **way;**

Then forth thy waters dazzling come
  Where sweet-brier scents the balmy breeze,
And where the wild bees softly hum
  Faint echo of thy harmonies.
Green spiky gorse thy banks adorn,
  Gold tassell'd broom thy fringe-work **weave,**
While feather'd choirs from dewy morn
  Make melody till dewy eve.

        *   *   *   *   *

Then on by pleasant farms **that breathe**
  Of calm contentment's happy clime,
Or laughing where the ivy's wreath
  Clings round the ruins of olden time
And on where stately mansions rise,
  Or lowly gleams the cottage hearth;
Unchanged thy smile still meets the **skies,**
  Unchanged still rings thy **song of mirth.**

Mr. Kennedy is possessed of a large and manly heart, **and** he looks
with undisguised enjoyment upon the humorous side of human nature.
What **he** terms his character sketches are full of genuine wit, and
provoke bursts of laughter **whenever they** are read. They are all the
more enjoyable by having a **pleasing and** wholesome moral attached
to each. In addition **to these he** has written many short pieces of a
humorous and **satirical** nature. In this respect those of **our readers**
who are familiar with the peculiarities and expressiveness **of the**
Scottish dialect will greatly appreciate the following :

ST. ANDREW AND THE HAGGIS.

Ae time Saunt Andrew—honest carl,
When on his travels though the warl,
He fand himsel' in great distress
In Macedonia's wilderness,
Grim hunger gnawed his wame within,
The cauld sleet soaked him to the skin;
An' buffeted wi' winds unruly
He lookit like a tattie dooly;
An' trauchled ae way or anither
Tint cowl and bauchles a'thegither,
An' skelp'd on barefit though the gloom
In patient, perfect martyrdom.

A' shivering like a droukit mouse,
He halted at the half-way house,
An' spreading out his open palms
Fu' meekly beggit for an alms.
The landlord steer'd na frae the bit,
But e'ed the Saunt frae head to fit,
An' said :—"You idle, gangrel crew,
Coarse crumbs should sair the like o' you
I set ye doun this bill o' fare:
The shakin's o' the meal-pock there,
Some harigalds, an' sic' like trash.
That puir fowk use for makin' hash.
Tak' them, an' mixed wi' creeshie dreep,
Boil in the stammack o' a sheep;
An' gin your greedy gab be nice,
There's ingans an' a shak' o' spice:—
Fa' to,—mak' guid use o' your time,
An' ken the rift o' stappit wame."

The Saunt in silence—shivering, cauld,
Made up the mess as he was tauld;
An' bent him canny owre the pot,
An' render'd thanks for a' he got;
An' ate his meal wi' cheerfu' grace,
An' never thraw'd his honest face !

An' aye sin' syne, on Andrew's nicht
We see this extraordinar' sicht,—
How social Scots owre a' the warl'
Will leave the fu' cog an' the barrel,
An' smack their lips, an' rive like mad,

At sic a dish as Andrew had.
An' 'gainst the pangs o' flesh and bluid
They'll roose it up an' ca' it guid,
Though feeling in their hearts' ain gloom
Some **pangs** o' Andrew's martyrdom !

Among Mr. Kennedy's smaller poems his **"Address to the** Mosquitoes," **"Auld** Scotia in the Field," " Bonnie Noranside " and "Angus Rankin's Elegy " are specially **worthy of notice,** while his verses entitled the " The Songs of Scotland " surpass everything hitherto written **in verse** in connection with that subject. Of his larger poems, " The Southern Cavalier " is decidedly **the best.** It is a remarkable **piece of** poetical fact and fiction blended together, and through which **there** rings, says the *Fifeshire Journal* " an honest echo of the passion and beauty of Tennyson's ' Maud.'" Mr. Kennedy numbers among his personal friends **many of the most** prominent scholars and authors of the day. Among the latter is Mr. Robert Buchanan, the eminent poet **and novelist.** They have a very sincere regard for each other's merits, **and during Mr.** Buchanan's sojourn in this country, some three years **ago, the two poets spent many** happy and profitable hours in each **other's company. A few days** after Mr. Buchanan sailed for home, Mr. Kennedy indulged his muse in the following lament, which, by **the way,** was widely quoted by the British press:

LAMENT

On the occasion of the departure of Robert Buchanan,
the British poet, from America.

My muse fu' dowie faulds her wing,
An' nought but sabs an' sighs she'll bring:
An' sad-eyed sorrow bids me sing,
                    Her tears to draw,
How, like a pilgrim journeying,
                    Our bard's awa !

O Rab was bright an' warm an' free,
Like sunlight on a simmer sea !
He aye was fu' o' mirth an' glee
                    An' wit an' a';
An' graced wi' gifts of poesy—
                    But Rab's awa !

O blithe it was I trow to trace
The sweet saul in his manly face,
His blue een sparkling kindly grace
        On ane an' a';
Rab dearly lo'ed the human race—
        But Rab's awa !

The puir newspaper chields may mourn,
If Rab should never mair return;
His words cam like a bick'rin burn
        An' filled them a':
He did them mony a friendly turn—
        But Rab's awa !

Play-actor billies round him **hung,**
An' listen'd to his silv'ry tongue,
That sweet as ony clair'net rung
        In house or ha':
He was the pride o' auld an' young—
        But Rab's awa !

The lang-haired literary louns
That live real puir in muckle touns,
Will miss him for the royal boons
        He shower'd on a,'—
Gold dollar bits as big's half crowns,—
        But Rab's awa !

O when he **met** wi' men o' spirit,
Real clever chields o' modest merit,
Owre oysters an' a glass o' claret,—
        O then—hurrah !
The very earth they did inherit,—
        But Rab's awa !

That day he gaed on board the ship,
He gied my hand a kindly grip,
An' while a tremor shook his lip,
        Said—"Tell them a'
They'll never frae my memory slip
        When I'm awa."

Quo' I wi' heart as saft as jeel,
"Braw be your chance in fortune's wheel,
May seas slip past your sliding keel
        Wi' canny jaw,
An' may the bodies use ye weel
        When far awa."

Sin syne I muse on fortune's quirk:
She shines, then leaves me in the mirk;
I canna sleep nor wreat nor wirk,
            Nor ought ava,—
I'm doited as a daunder'd stirk
            Sin Rab's awa.

But whiles round friendship's wreathéd urn,
Hope's vestal fires fu' brightly burn;
An' though the vanish'd joys I mourn
            That blossomed braw,
Wha kens but Rab may yet return?—
            Though Rab's awa!

In addition to his poetical works, Mr. Kennedy is the author of a serial story, entitled "Willie Watson," and he has written numerous articles on various subjects. He re-visited Scotland in 1883, and was warmly welcomed by many eminent persons who had become acquainted with him through his works. His latest volume of poetry, entitled "Poems on Scottish and American Subjects," has passed through two extensive editions, and we understand that he is now engaged in the preparation of a new and larger edition of his poetical writings. He is employed by the Elevated Railroad Companies and has charge of a section of their works. A welcome guest at every Scottish social gathering, he is also a capital extemporary speech-maker on these and other occasions. He is a resident of this city, and, surrounded by the members of his family, enjoys the comforts and pleasures of a happy home. Life did not run smoothly with him at the beginning, but he met its vicissitudes with courage and good will, and to use the language of another poet, "Out of it all has come the plain fact that he can now sit under his own vine and fig-tree with no one to make him afraid."

Since the foregoing sketch was written, Mr. Chas. T. Dillingham, New York, has published "The Deeside Lass, and Other Poems," by Mr. Kennedy. Of this work, W. D. Latto, Editor of *The Peoples' Journal*, says : "I have read 'The Deeside Lass' with much interest and admiration. The composition is good. The best bit in the poem is the interview between the 'Dominie and the Minister.' The description of their toddy drinking and their 'cracks' is first-rate;" and J. Logie Robertson, author of "Horace in Hamespun," writes: "I have read 'The Deeside Lass' with pleasure, chiefly because of the freshness of the style. The descriptive parts of the poem are very good. The best bits of characterization are Lady Meg and Black Tam. Lady Meg's piety is refreshing. Tam is a splendid character."

PROF. JAMES C. MOFFAT.

—The warrior's name,
Tho' pealed and chim'd on all the tongues of fame,
Sounds less harmonious to the grateful mind
Than his, who fashions and improves mankind.

AT Glencree, in the South of Scotland, on the thirtieth day of May, 1811, there was born of poor but honest and industrious parents a child, who in course of time grew up, and at an early age began the battle of life as a shepherd's boy. Tending his flocks day by day among the hills and glens, far from his home and his friends, he was thus led into a closer companionship with nature in all her wonderful beauties than he would otherwise have been, and soon he began to discover that there were

" Books in the running brooks,
Sermons in stones,
And good in everything."

Gradually his mind expanded, and imperceptibly a desire for knowledge and an earnest wish to become something better and nobler than what he was naturally took possession of his heart. Up to his sixteenth year he had received little, or, at all events, a very imperfect education, but at this age he apprenticed himself to a printer, not with a view of learning that trade, but simply as a means of obtaining access to books. His duties here occupied his attention for ten hours each day, yet so willing a scholar was he that during his spare hours in the course of a few years he had mastered Latin, Greek, Hebrew, a little of Persian and several other European languages. Such in brief was the boyhood of James C. Moffat, the now venerable and greatly respected Professor of Church History in the Theological Seminary at Princeton. In 1833 he emigrated to America, and shortly after his arrival in New York, through the advice and assistance of a few friends, entered the junior class at Princeton College and graduated in 1835. He was then offered and accepted a position as private tutor to two young gentlemen who were about to study at Yale College, and one of whom afterwards ranked among the most eminent Greek scholars in Europe. We now quote from the Princeton Review : "At the end of about two years Mr. Moffat returned to Princeton as Greek tutor, in which capacity he continued till September, 1839, when he accepted the appointment to the Professorship of Greek and Latin in Lafayette College, then under the presidency of Dr. Junkin. In the Spring of 1841 he removed with Dr. Junkin to Miami University, O., where he had been called to the department of Latin, and subsequently Modern History was added to his work.

"In the Spring of 1851 he was licensed to preach the Gospel, and from September of next year he taught Greek and Hebrew in a theological school which had a short existence in Cincinnati. Having been elected to the Professorship of Latin and History at Princeton, he returned to that place in the Spring of 1853. Upon the resignation of Dr. Carnahan and the election of Dr. McLean to the presidency, several changes were made in the faculty and Dr. Moffat was transferred to the Chair of Greek, which he held for a period of seven years, retaining still the lectureship of history until a professor was appointed to that department. In 1861 he was elected by the General Assembly to the Chair of Church History in the Theological Seminary at Princeton." With Church History he retained Greek Literary History until 1877. Having thus as briefly as possible outlined the career of Professor Moffat, let us now turn our attention to him as a poet. After a careful perusal of his poetical works, we unhesitatingly pronounce his right to take a high rank not only among Scottish-American poets but among the poets of America. The principal features of his poetry are a graceful and melodious versification, a purity of language, the originality and perfect justness of his reflections, and a contemplative seriousness that reminds us of the meditative pathos of Wordsworth. His muse has no eye for frivolity ; to her "Life is real, life is earnest," and we have not seen even among his earlier and shorter pieces any absence of that stately dignity which is such a characteristic of the work of his mature years. Of his many published volumes the first of a poetical kind published in this country and entitled "A Rhyme of the North Countrie," (Cincinnati, 1847), the prelude to the principal poem in the work gives us a key at once to the mainspring of his poetic feelings—the love of the fatherland, which he thus apostrophises :

> Wild land of poesy, when free
> From daily cares to youth and thee
> My thoughts return, what visions lie
> Like evening clouds before my eye !
> The winding stream, the mountain glen
> And sunny lawn appear again ;
> While every spot its legend brings
> Of love and past beloved things.

The prelude introduces to us the story of the heir of a Scottish house whose worldly circumstances have been reduced, but who wins the love of a high-born lady, and in a heroic endeavor to win fortune and fame, undertakes the command of an expedition to the Polar regions.   Years pass and no news of the hero until a wandering sailor tells the story of the finding of a lost ship and a frozen crew in the northern seas.   The descriptive passages in the work are particularly fine, the versification elegant and melodious.   Take, for instance, the hero's last look at the home of his beloved:

> The moon is on the eastern height
>   His silver on the seas,
> But fairer to the poet's sight
> The glimmering of that humble light
>   Among the ancient trees ;
> For it has shone on one possessed
>   Of human life's most envied boon
> And prized more dearly to his breast
>   Than all the rest beneath the moon ;
> And at this lovely place and hour
> When nothing but that ancient tower
> .   Upon the wooded steeps above
> Can thought of human life impart,
> Its gentle rays come on his heart
>   Like messengers of love.

The description of the Polar regions, the attitudes of the frozen crew, with the accompanying weird natural phenomena, are admirable examples of invention and graphic description to which no brief selection could give an adequate illustration.   We pass, however, to notice his happy faculty of writing short poems, chiefly of a moral or didactic kind.   They embrace a variety of subjects, but the most striking are those which contain a survey of the beautiful in nature ; a subject with which he ever links a broad human sympathy.   As an illustration of this let us quote a little poem which he composed during a visit to Europe immediately after the Franco-German war ;

TO THE RHINE AT COLOGNE.

We've met, old Rhine, among the hills,
    And thou wast young and playful then,
Disporting with the wanton rills
    And rushing wild from glen to glen.

I've met thee in a **fuller stream,**
    Where still the haughty Alps arose,
Flowing in majesty supreme,
    And gathering tribute from their snows.

When brooks with loud complaining din,
    Harassed and tortured in the race,
Through rocks and gorge, o'er ledge and lin,
    Sought refuge in thy strong embrace.

And here, in thy maturer age,
    In tranquil force and grandeur spread,
Conferring traffic's heritage
    Upon the lands thy floods have made,

Diffusing far on every hand,
    Thy gifts and energies benign,
I bow before thy wide command,
    And hail thee monarch, mighty Rhine.

So may the people, through whose coasts
    Thy far-assembled waters wind,
Their strong but long-divided hosts,
    Of honest worth and fertile mind,

Endowed with learning's richest dower,
    Harmoniously at length combine
Into one vast benignant power,
    As thou art here, imperial Rhine.

Many of the professor's short poems are of a religious kind, and as such display an abiding faith in God's goodness to men. "A Cry in Battle" may be taken as a specimen of this:

A CRY IN BATTLE.

There is a war which I must wage,
    A victory I must win ;
A fiend has cast the mortal gage,
    And dares me from within.

His hate is vigilant and keen,
　His forces manifold ;
His strategy is broad, unseen,
　His charge sustained and bold.

Insidious craft have I to meet,
　Whose arts deceive the eye ;
To fight is to provoke defeat,
　Yet I must win or die.

Great Son of God, whose piercing glance
　Through all designs can see,
My hope for victory in defence
　I rest alone on thee.

Again, many of his short poems take a lyrical form, and of these his
" Tamers of the Ground " is probably the most widely known.

TAMERS OF THE GROUND.

There is conquest of force in taming the horse
　Till he brooks to be driven and bound,
But prouder by far the victories are
　Of the men who tame the ground—
Who tame the ground and its wilful powers,
　And determine **the work** it must do,
Till it leaves its own, and executes ours,
　With obedience docile and true.

For they are true workers together with God,
　In maturing the earth to his plan,
And in teaching her dull and unmeaning sod
　To glow with the thinking of man—
Who compel her rude life to surrender the wold,
　The marsh and the jungle to yield
To him who can out of her deserts unfold
　The wealth of the fruit-bearing field.

Delights there may be on the restless sea,
　Though treacherous, barren and bare ;
But the grateful land ever blesses the hand
　That tends it with wisdom and care.
Then health to the heroes, who tame the ground,
　And hold it in bountiful thrall,
For they lap the earth with their conquests around
　Enriching, benignant to all.

The greatest, however, of the learned professor's poems is "Alwyn:
A Romance of Study," published by Messrs. Anson D. F. Randolph
& Co., of this city, in 1875. It is a lengthy work of seven cantos,
written in the Spenserian stanza, and deals chiefly in an analysis of
the mind of a student passing through the various studies of the
acquired knowledge of the ages. This subject, simple as it may
appear, opens a wonderful panorama of facts and fancies, which pass
transfigured before the intellectual eye, and illustrate not only the
vast scholarship of the author but his intimate knowledge of natural
phenomena. The endless array of pictures that pass before us are
drawn from every conceivable source, from the lovely grandeur of far-
spreading seas, from the wild sublimity of mountains, from the shrouded stillness of the white North, from the dazzling brilliancy of tropical
forests, from the heart of man and from all animate nature. The effect
of each new experience of observation is finely pointed out in the
growing intellectual power of the hero of the poem, and the incentive
to study and a true conception of the power of knowledge with the
highest reverence and faith in revealed religion, may be gathered as
the general effect of the whole work. Indeed the religious sentiment
is ever held, and justly so, as the highest attribute of man. The effect
of forests in this sentiment is grandly expressed in the first canto:

> And much he sought the forest dense and old,
>   A strange unhuman charm resided there ;
> And in the sombre twilight, damp and cold,
>   Which bade the venturous foot of man forbear,
>   He found attractions such as dangers wear.
> An awful thought that the Almighty God,
>   Such as he reigned ere man was made, and ere
> Christ was revealed, still had his dread abode,
> In these old shades, to him was like a wizard's rod.

> Majestic trees, earth's ancient garniture,
>   Primeval forests, which so fondly cling
> To the wild places, which your life secure
>   From the destroying enemy, ye bring
>   Conceptious of creation's early spring,
> Ere man's vicegerency had yet begun,
>   And when in herb and stream and living thing,
> In heat and cold and cloud and golden sun
> God solitary reigned and all his will was done.

Not only does this intimacy with nature form one of the chiefest beauties of the work, but through this quality we are led to a higher appreciation of such men of eminence, whose works are touched upon in this masterly poem. Even when we cannot follow the learned professor into his perfect knowledge of the work of the Greek and Roman poets and philosophers we feel a closer intimacy with them after seeing the kaleidoscopic reflex of their works such as is here presented on every hand. Take Cicero for instance :

> "Most fertile genius of the Roman name,
> Whose glowing tones of eloquence bestow
> But half thy green inheritance of fame ;
> Pure statesman hero, toiling to reclaim
> A sinking country and a vicious age,
> Who lived a life scarce faction dared to blame,
> And nobly died to stem the tyrant's rage—
> Hail freedom's martyr, hail benign eclectic sage !"

If space permitted, we would be pleased to analyze this poem to its close, but we can only add that as a whole it is one of most remarkable ever published in America. In finish of versification it certainly has no superior. It gives added sanction and stability to the power of knowledge and to the faith and practice of true religion as constituting the highest law of the moral universe.

Besides his poetical works, Prof. Moffat is the author of a Life of Dr. Chalmers, published in Cincinnati, 1853; Introduction to the Study of Æesthetics, 1856; Comparative History of Religions, 2 vols., 1871-3; Song and Scenery, or a Summer Ramble in Scotland, 1874; Church History in Brief, 1885; and he has contributed about seventy historical articles to the Princeton Review and other periodicals. In conclusion, we cannot close our brief comments on the poet-professor without alluding to the exalted estimate in which he is held as a man. His pure and noble life carries with it the royal reward of a heart still sweet and young. The shepherd's boy with the keen eye and the bright smile is still there; the journeymen printer, with the quick hand and the kind word for a fellow workman, is still there. Add to this the talented scholarly professor, the profound theologian; and through this combination of manly and noble qualities, the light of poesy shines as sunshine among the forest leaves, blessing and beautifying the whole.

HEW AINSLIE.

His life was gentle; and the elements
So mixed in him, that nature might stand up
And say to all the world '*this was* a man.'

HEW AINSLIE is entitled to a prominent place among Scottish-
American poets. Early imbued with a taste for the ballad and song
literature of his country, he contributed much to it that was both
valuable and beautiful, and his name shall descend to posterity
enshrined among the galaxy of sweet singers who have made the land
of the mountain and the flood famous among nations as a land of
poetry and song. Hew Ainslie was born at Bargeny Mains, in the
parish of Dailly, Ayrshire, on the fifth of April, 1792. His father at the
time held a responsible position on the estate of Sir Hew Dalrymple,
and, being in possession of sufficient means, resolved upon giving his
son a better education than that usually accorded to boys in Scotland
at that date. A private tutor was accordingly procured, who prepared
him in the elementary branches of study at home, after which he was
sent to the parish school at Ballantrae, and later on to the Ayr Academy. He remained at the latter place until he reached his fourteenth
year, when failing health compelled him to discontinue his studies and
return home. Gen. James Grant Wilson, in his excellent work, "The
Poets and Poetry of Scotland," tells us that "Sir Hew was at this time
engaged in an extensive plan for the improvement of his estate, under
the direction of the celebrated landscape gardener, White, and a
number of young men from the South. Young Ainslie joined this
company, as he says, 'to harden my constitution and check my over-
growth. Among my planting companions I found a number of
intelligent young men, who had got up in a large granary a private
theatre, where they occasionally performed for the amusement of the
neighborhood the 'Gentle Shepherd,' 'Douglas,' etc., and in due time
I was, to my great joy, found tall enough, lassie-looking enough, and
flippant enough to take the part of the pert 'Jenny;' and the first

relish **I got for** anything like sentimental song was from **learning** and **singing the** songs in that pastoral—auld ballads that **my mother sung—** **and she** sung many and sang them well—having been **all** the poetry I **cared for.** For three years, which was **up** to the time we removed **to** Roslin, I remained in this employment, acquiring a tough, sound constitution, and at the same time some knowledge of nursery and floral culture." Shortly after this **however he was** sent to Glasgow, where he entered upon the study of law, but **this** proving too uncongenial an occupation for one possessing his temperament, he **soon** resigned his position and returned to his home. Another situation was procured for him in the Register House, Edinburgh, and here he performed his duties faithfully for a number of years. He also acted for some time as the amanuensis of the celebrated Professor Dugald Stewart. At the age of twenty he married, and ten years later, finding that his salary was inadequate for the maintenance of his family, he resolved to emigrate **to America.** He certainly expected **that** he would better his **condition** by coming to this country, and **yet it** was with a **very** sorrowful heart that he bade farewell to his native land.

THE LAST LOOK OF HOME.

Our sail has ta'en the blast,
　　Our pennant's to the sea,
And the waters widen fast
　　'Twixt the fatherland and me.

Then, Scotland, fare thee well—
　　There's a sorrow in that word
This aching heart could tell,
　　But words never shall record.

The heart should make us veil
　　From the heart's elected few—
Our sorrows when we ail—
　　Would we have them suffer too?

No, the parting hour is past;
　　Let its memory be brief;
When we monument our joys
　　We should sepulchre our grief.

Now yon misty mountains fail,
　　As the breezes give us speed—
On, my spirit, with our sail,
　　There's a brighter land ahead.

> There are wailings on the wind,
>   There are murmurs on the sea,
> But the fates ne'er proved unkind
>   Till they parted home and me.

He arrived here on the twenty-second of July 1822, and shortly afterwards purchased a small farm at Hoosick, Rensselaer County, N. Y. This proved an unwise speculation for him however, and after struggling with it for nearly three years, he was glad to retire from it. Then Robert Owen's settlement at New Harmony, Ind., was tried and pronounced a failure. A few years later he removed to Cincinnati, where he entered into partnership with Messrs. Price & Wood, brewers, and henceforth his lot may be said to have fallen in pleasant places. Success followed nearly all his future movements, and, being prosperous, he was happy and contented. But amidst this prosperity his thoughts would ever turn to scenes of bygone days, and he would find time to sing of

THE LADS AN' THE LAND FAR AWA'.

When I think on the lads an' the land I ha'e left,
An' how love has been lifted, an' friendship been reft;
How the hinnie o' hope has been jumbled wi' ga',
Then I sigh for the lads an' the land far awa'.

When I think on the days o' delight we ha'e seen,
When the flame o' the spirit would spark in the een ;
Then I say, as in sorrow I think o' ye a',
Where will I find hearts like the hearts far awa ?

When I think on the nights we ha'e spent hand in hand,
Wi' mirth for our sowther, and friendship our band,
This world gets dark, but ilk night has a daw' !
And I yet may rejoice in the land far awa' !

In 1864 Mr. Ainslie resolved to pay a visit to Scotland. With what eagerness and joy he crossed the Atlantic for this purpose, may be judged by the following lines, entitled "A Hameward Sang." His love for Scotland must indeed have been stamped very deeply on his heart when, on nearing it after an absence of over forty years, his imagination gave him the impression that the trees seemed to look upon him with fond recognition, while even the very brutes had a social look about them and seemed to welcome him back to his early home.

A HAMEWARD SANG.

Each whirl o' the wheel,
  Each step brings me nearer
The hame o' my youth—
  Every object grows dearer,
The hills and the huts,
  The trees on that green,
Losh ! they glour in my face
  Like some kindly auld frien'.

E'en the brutes they look social,
  As gif they would crack ;
And the sang o' the bird
  Seems to welcome me back.
Oh, dear to our hearts
  Is the hand that first fed us,
An' dear is the land
  An' the cottage that bred us.

An' dear are the comrades
  Wi' whom we once sported;
But dearer the maiden
  Whose love we first courted.
Joy's image may perish,
  E'en grief die away ;
But the scenes o' our youth
  Are recorded for aye.

He remained for some years in Scotland and on the continent, enjoying the friendship of many of the most eminent men of letters of the time. Returning to America he took up his abode permanently with his eldest son George, at Louisville, Ky. Mr. Ainslie was a poet in the truest sense of the word. His love for Scotland no doubt stimulated his muse to sing forth her praises in songs which will ever retain a place in the hearts of his countrymen, but apart from this he has left us numerous ballads and lyrical pieces which we would not willingly let die. Many of these are of a very pathetic nature, and, in addition to their being very beautiful, they contain excellent sentiments expressed in the simplest of words. Take for instance his

DOWIE IN THE HINT O' HAIRST.

It's dowie in the hint o' hairst,
  At the wa'-gang o' the swallow,
When the wind grows cauld, and the burns grow bauld,
  And the wuds are hingin' yellow ;

But oh, it's dowier far to see
The wa'-gang o' her the heart gangs wi',
The dead-set o' a shinin' e'e—
That darkens the weary warld on thee.

There was mickle love atween us twa—
  Oh, twa could ne'er be fonder ;
And the thing on yird was never made,
  That could ha'e gart us sunder.
But the way o' Heaven's aboon a' ken,
And we maun bear what it likes to sen'—
It's comfort, though, to weary men,
That the warst o' this warld's waes maun en'.

There's mony things that come and gae,
  Just kent, and just forgotten ;
And the flowers that busk a bonnie brae,
  Gin anither year lie rotten.
But the last look o' that lovely e'e,
And the dying grip she ga'e to me,
They're settled like eternitie—
Oh, Mary ! that I were wi' thee.

"Perhaps," says Mr. Thomas C. Latto, "the finest of Hew Ainslie's songs is the 'Bourocks o' Bargeny,' which I transcribe from the manuscript of the good old Bard, now lying on my desk. He copied it for me at my request October 16, 1868, and felt much gratified when I expressed my opinion that, though the theme had been attempted several times, notably by Robert Chambers in 'Young Randal' and by Robert Nicoll in 'Bonny Bessie Lee,' it had never been handled with greater delicacy and success than in his own simple lines. The Bourocks (*i. e.* Cotter houses) o' Bargeny is indeed a gem.

'I left ye, Jeanie, bloomin' fair
  'Mang the bourocks o' Bargeny,
I've found ye on the banks o' Ayr,
  But sair ye're alter'd, Jeanie.
I left ye like the wanton lamb
  That plays 'mang Hadyed's heather ;
I've found ye noo a sober dame—
  A wife and eke a mither.

I left ye 'mang the leaves sae green
  In rustic weed befittin';
I've found ye buskit like a queen
  In painted chaumer sittin'.
Ye're fairer, statelier, I can see ;
  Ye're wiser nae dou't Jeanie,
But oh ! I rather met wi' thee
  'Mang the bourocks o' Bargeny !'"

In 1822 Mr. Ainslie published his first **work, viz.** : "A pilgrimage **to the Land of Burns."** Several large editions **of this** work **have** been issued and sold. In 1855 he published **"Scottish Songs, Ballads and** Poems," **and this** also received a cordial welcome from the public and **press.** Three different editions **of his** collected writings **have since** been publshed **and** disposed of. **Many of** his earlier poems are to **be** found in the publications **of the Messrs.** Chambers, of Edinburgh, and in "Whistle Binkie," "Gems of Scottish Song," etc. Mr. Ainslie died at Louisville, Ky., at the venerable age of eighty-six. From **an** obituary notice which appeared a few days after his death written by Mr. Latto, we clip the following :—"A truer Scotchman than **Hew** Ainslie never trod the heather. In person tall, stately and agile **even in advanced years, his** face was the index of his character—frank, open, **honest, genial and** manly. He looked the personification of Wallace **wight or Bruce the** bold, and in a personal encounter **he** would have been a match for half a dozen ordinary men. His head was beautifully **set** on his square shoulders and **his** broad, **lofty brow** betokened a rare and transcendent genius. At one of the meetings of the Burns Club, Brooklyn, E. D., it was stated that Ainslie, before he left Scotland for the first time, had had the honor of kissing Burns' 'bonny Jean' by the banks of the Nith, on the spot where he had composed one of his deathless lyrics. Full of years and of honors, it must be consoling to his family in their bereavement to know that his long life closed so peacefully, but never can his place be filled in the hearts of those who, like the writer, knew and loved **him."**

HON. WILLIAM CANT STUROC.

The general voice
Sounds him for courtesy, behavior, language,
And every fair demeanor, an example ;
Titles of honor add not to his worth,
Who is himself an honor to his title.

WILLIAM CANT STUROC was born in the old town of Arbroath in the
year 1822. He was the twelfth child of a family of thirteen, and as his
parents' circumstances in life were not of the best, it became neces·
sary to put him to work at a comparatively early age. His education
therefore while not altogether neglected, can truly be said to have been
of a limited description. During the short time however that he
remained at school it is interesting to note that he was credited with
being " a persistent, dogged, unconquerable boy, with a sharp, inquisi-
tive turn of mind, bold and self-reliant, and a leader among his schoolmates." He learned the trade of a wheel-wright with his father, but so
determined was he during those early years of his life to better his education and to push himself forward in the world, that before he had
reached the age of twenty he had read through and studied as carefully
as possible nearly all of the English classics. To-day he can pause
and look back with complacent satisfaction on the heroic and laudable struggles of his youth, and he may feel proud of the fact that apart
from the honors which his merits have won for him in various fields,
he now stands prominently before the world as one of the finest specimens of the self-made men of the present century. In 1846 he resolved
to emigrate to Canada. He arrived in Montreal in May of that year,
and while supporting himself during the succeeding four years by his
trade, eagerly embraced every opportunity that presented itself whereby
he could add to the knowledge which he had already acquired. He
became a frequent contributor to Canadian newspapers and magazines,
and many of his articles written at this date show that he possessed

considerable literary ability, **besides a** sound discriminating **judgment.**

Life in Canada however soon failed to please him. In 1850 **he crossed over to** the **United** States and took up his abode in Sunapee, **N. H.**

Here he became acquainted with the late Hon. Edmund Burke, **and** by him **was induced** to commence the study **of law.** Zealously applying himself to his new task he **was** rewarded in 1855 by being admitted to practice as an attorney **in the courts of** New Hampshire. Since that time he has made Sunapee his home, and while attaining the highest degree of eminence in his profession, has also acquired an honorable reputation **as** an orator, a poet and one of the ablest statesmen in **New** Hampshire. By his gentle demeanor, his genial disposition and his numerous acts of Christian kindness he has gained the **respect and** the love of all classes. His home and surroundings are thus **described** in a recent issue of the Granite Monthly :—"Along the banks of Sugar River, on the shore of the lake, and crowning surrounding hillsides cluster fifty or sixty dwelling-houses, interspersed among which rise the spires of three church edifices, the roofs of a hotel, post-office, five stores, school-house, and the town hall. Some of the residences are elegant and commodious and compare favorably with the same class of structures in larger villages. The oldest and one of the best-looking dwelling-houses is the one owned by the Hon. William Cant Sturoc, in the heart of the village. We found that gentleman at home in his library, a man fifty-seven years of age, looking what he is, the educated, hospitable, ardent Scotchman. The blood of Bruce and Wallace is in his veins, **the** fire of Burns and Scott in his brain. Next to his adopted country he **loves** Scotland, and he has often breathed that affection in exquisite verse. It is a pleasure **to hear** him read Burns and other Scotch poets. As a lawyer and politician, he has no little distinction. He was the democratic candidate for State **Senator in** district number ten in 1876. His proudest title, however, **is that of the** 'Bard of Sunapee.' " The following is his well-known descriptive **poem** entitled

LAKE SUNAPEE.

Once more, my muse ! from rest of many a year,
  Come forth again and sing, as oft of yore ;
Now lead my steps to where the crags appear
  In silent grandeur, by the rugged shore,
That skirts the margin of thy waters free,
Lake of my mountain home, loved Sunapee !

Meet invocation! to the pregnant scene,
  Where long ere yet the white man's foot did roam,
Strode wild and free the daring Algonquin ;
  And where, perchance the stately Metacom
Inspired his braves, with that poetic strain
Which cheer'd the Wampanoags, but cheer'd in vain.

Clear mountain mirror ! who can tell but thou
  Hast borne the red man, in his light canoe
As fleetly on thy bosom as e'en now
  Thou bear'st the pale face o'er thy waters blue ;
And who can tell but nature's children then
Were rich and happy as the mass of men?

Sweet Granite "Katrine" of this mountain land !
  Oh jewel set amid a scene so fair !
Kearsage, Ascutney, rise on either hand,
  While Grantham watches with a lover's care,
And our dark "Ben" to Croydon sends in glee,
A greeting o'er thy silvery breast, Lake Sunapee !

How grand, upon a moonlit eve, to glide
  Upon thy waters, twixt the mountains high
And gaze within thy azure crystal tide,
  On trembling shadows of the earth and sky ;
While all is silent, save when trusty oar
Awakes an echo from thy slumbering shore.

Oh, lovely lake, I would commune with thee !
  For in thy presence naught of ill is found ;
That cares which wed the weary world to me,
  May cease to harass with their carking round.
And I a while 'midst Nature's grandeur stand,
On mount of rapture 'twixt the sea and land.

For where shall mortals holier ground espy,
  From which to look where hope doth point and gaze,
Than from the spot that speaks a Diety,
  In hoary accents of primeval praise ?
And where shall man a purer altar find,
From which to worship the Almighty Mind ?

Thy past is curtained by as deep a veil
  As shrouds the secrets which we may not reach ;
And then, 'twere wisdom, when our quest doth fail,
  To read the lessons which thou *now* dost teach ;
And in thy face, on which we look to-day,
See hopes to cheer us on our onward way.

Roll on, sweet lake ! and if perchance thy form
  Laves less of earth than floods of Western fame ;
Yet still we love thee, in the calm or storm,
  And call thee *ours* by many a kindly name.
No patriot heart but loves the scenes that come,
O'er memory's sea to breathe a tale of "Home."

And when the winter in its frozen thrall
  Binds up thy locks in braids of icy wreath,
Forget we not thy cherish'd name to call,
  In fitting shadow of the sleep of death !
But morn shall dawn upon our sleep, and we,
As thou in spring-time wake, sweet "Sunapee !"

Mr. Sturoc has been an ardent and successful wooer of the muses since his earliest years. He has given to the world many excellent poems and lyrical pieces, which have been awarded the highest praise from the press and literary men in general, but his extreme modesty and unwillingness to exhibit his talents in this respect before the public, has in a great measure retarded his popularity as a poet, both in America and in Great Britain. "The little fugitive crumbs," he says, "which I have cast carelessly upon the waters have been received on both sides of the Atlantic with more favor than they really deserve, yet, though 'owre the seas an' far awa', I always take a warm and hearty interest in all that concerns Scotland." There is however, a notable difference between his early poems and those of a more matured period of his life. Take for instance one of his pieces which appeared in the *Glasgow Citizen* in 1845. It begins,

My Katie is a winsome flower,
  As ever bloomed in cot or ha',
An' heaven forbid its dewy leaves,
  Should ere untimely fade or fa,' etc.

There is hardly a line in this production that is in any way worthy to stand beside the beautiful lines which he gave to the world later on under the title of " Mary " and which we herewith append. An American paper noticing this poem at the time of its first publication very justly remarked that " It stamped its author, not only as a ripe scholar, but as possessing rare poetic gifts."

MARY.

I saw a vision in my boyish days,
　So bright, so pure, that in my raptur'd dreaming,
Its tints of emerald and its golden rays
　Had more of heavenly than of earthly seeming ;
The roseate valley and the sun-light mountain
　Alike, enchanted as by wand of fairy,
Breathed out as from a high and holy fountain,
　On flower and breeze, the lovely name of Mary

That youthful vision, time has not effaced,
　But year by year the cherish'd dream grew deeper,
And memory's hand, at midnight hour oft traced,
　Once more, the faithful vision of the sleeper ;
No chance or change could ever chase away
　This idol thought, that o'er my life would tarry,
And lead me, in the darkest hours, to say—
　"My better angel is my hoped-for Mary."

The name was fix'd—a fact of fate's recording—
　And swayed by magic all this single heart ;
The strange decree disdained a novel wording,
　And would not from my happy future part ;
As bright 'twas writ, as is the milky way—
　The bow of promise is a sky unstarry—
That sheds its light and shone with purest ray
　Through cloud and tempest round the name of Mary.

Burns hymn'd his "Mary" when her soul had pass'd
　Away from earth, and all its sin and sorrow ;
But mine has been the spirit that hath cast
　A gleam of sunshine on each blessed morrow ;
And crown'd at last, this trusting heart hath been,
　With fruits of faith, that nought on earth could vary,
For I have lived until my eyes have seen
　The vision real, in the form of Mary.

A special feature of Mr. Sturoc's poetry is the simplicity of language
used by him. He places his thoughts before us in a clear and concise
style, and his words, beautiful and appropriate in each instance, seem
to flow as naturally from him as do the streams and rills down the sides
of the mountains and the glens of his native land. Take the following
"song" as a specimen of this :

I ken'na gin the lanesome birds,
  When winter's snaws fa' dreary, O.
Forget their canty summer hames
  In woods and glens sae cheery, O.

But weel I ken this heart o' mine,
  Tho' fortune gars me wander O,
Beats leal to ilka youthfu' scene
  An' distance makes me fonder, O.

For in my dreams, by day or nicht,
  Tho' wealth and beauty bind me O,
I'm wafted far owre sea an' land,
  To friends I left behind me O,

An' there I see ilk weel-kent face,
  An' hear sweet voices many O.
But dearest still the smile and word
  O' charming, winsome Jenny O

In nearly all of our author's poetry we find an underlying reference and unquestionable love for the land of his boyhood.

This is more to be wondered at when we take into consideration the fact that it is now more than forty years since he left Scotland. Time however has in no way changed her to him; and her history, traditions, scenery and people are ever before his mind. In some cases his enthusiasm for the fatherland becomes uncontrollable, and his muse bursts forth into patriotic strains as noble and as grand as those which emanated from Henry Scott Riddell and others. The following poem, for instance, written not very long since, will always be accorded a prominent place in Scottish minstrelsy :

MY NATIVE SCOTTISH HILLS.

Though cold and bleak my native land,
  Though wint'ry are its looks,
The mountains towering, dim and grand,
  Though "ice-bound" are its brooks ;
Yet still my heart with fondest pride,
  And deepest passions thrills,
As, gazing round me, far and wide,
  I miss my native hills !

The spreading prairies of the West
  May yield their richest store ;
And other tongues may call them blest,
  And chant their praises o'er ;

But I shall sing, in humble song,
  Of mountains, lochs and rills—
The scenes my childhood dwelt among—
  My native Scottish hills.

Oh native land ! Oh cherished home,
  I've sailed across the sea,
And, though my wandering steps may roam,
  My heart still turns to thee !
My thoughts and dreams are sweet and bright
  With dew which loves distills ;
While every gleam of golden light
  Falls on the Scottish hills.

And, when my mortal race is run,
  And earth's vain dreams are o'er,
And, far beyond the setting sun,
  I see the other shore—
Oh, may my resting place be found
  Secure from all life's ills,
Some cheerful spot of hallow'd ground
  Among the Scottish hills.

A sincere religious sentiment, well worthy of note, also pervades
many of Mr. Sturoc's musings. However much his public career may
have brought him in contact with the world there is no misdoubting
the Christianity of the heart that can sing

So what we have of gifts and graces given,
  Are only lent us for life's little day ;
Nor shall we do the high behest of heaven
  If gifts are hidden, or be cast away ;
And whom the hand of destiny hath sealed,
  As seer and singer for his fellows all,
'Tis his to scatter o'er earth's fertile field
  The seeds that drop at inspiration's call

          *   *   *   *

Then let me sing ! O worldlings, let me sing !
  Mayhap my warblings with their notes of cheer
Will heal some heart that cherishes a sting
  Or wake the hopeless from their sleep of fear !
And thus I give what first to me is given ;
  My heart still grasping at the good and true,
And trust the rest to high and holy heaven,
  Which measures doing by the power to do.

The Manchester Daily Mirror and American, in an article describing our author says: " He has many of the elements of the genuine orator. He is one of the best debaters in the legislature—better than a majority in Congress whose names appear daily in the papers during the sessions of that body. He is deliberate in utterance, makes himself heard by all the house, and speaks with earnestness and to the point. In July, 1867, he received from Dartmouth College the honorary degree of Master of Arts. He holds a commission as Justice of the Peace and as Notary Public from the Governor of N. H. His democracy is of the Jeffersonian type and his faith in constitutional liberty as firm as the granite hills." Mr. Sturoc keeps up a regular correspondence with his many literary friends, both in this country and Scotland, and frequently receives a rhyming epistle from some of his poetical contemporaries. The following brief but complimentary one is by Mr. Duncan MacGregor Crerar, and is addressed

"TO WILLIAM CANT STUROC, ON RECEIVING HIS PORTRAIT"

My wishes warm I waft to thee,
Belovéd bard of Sunapee !
I prize, and will as years roll on,
Perhaps, dear friend, when thou art gone,
This welcome gift, this portrait true
Of thee, ta'en at three score and two ;
Those kindly eyes and locks of gray
Will call up many a byegone day
Made glad by letters charmed from thee,
Belovéd bard of Sunapee !
Heaven grant thee strength and spare thee long
To sing thy tunesome woodland song,
Till dell and dingle, lake and corrie,
Join in the strain and sound thy glory !

Mr. Sturoc, while getting on in years, is still hale and hearty. His intellect is as clear to-day as it has been in years gone by, and we trust as he gradually lays aside the cares of public life that he will continue to charm us with more of that genuine poetry which he has already produced, and which he is still capable of producing.

WILLIAM LYLE.

The fame that a man wins himself, is best;
That he may call his own. Honors put on him
Make him no more a man than his clothes do,
Which are as soon ta'en off.

WILLIAM LYLE, whom the *Dundee Weekly News* extols as being "one of the sweetest toned of living poets resident in America," was born at Edinburgh in the year 1822. His father having died at a comparatively early age, the entire responsibility and care of the boy devolved upon his mother, a noble Scottish woman who, with limited means and a sincere faith in God's goodness, earnestly strove to perform the duty allotted to her.

Our author received the rudiments of his education at the Lancasterian school of his native city, and at the age of twelve removed with his mother to Glasgow, where a few years afterward he became apprenticed to a potter. He was always a bright. observing boy, and being possessed of good common sense he soon became conscious of the fact that his education was very deficient in many respects. He therefore began to apply himself diligently to study and to the reading of standard books. In addition to this he enrolled himself as a scholar in one of the evening schools, and soon had the satisfaction of knowing that he was making rapid progress in the cultivation of his intellectual faculties. He also made rapid progress in learning the various branches of the trade at which he was occupied, and as soon as his apprenticeship was finished he readily obtained a position as journeyman at a salary which enabled him to better himself in many ways. In 1850 he became united in marriage to Miss Jessie Wylie, third daughter of Mr. Robert Wylie. of Kincardine on the Forth. She was an intelligent and fascinating young lady, and her loving nature and sweet companionship stimulated him to brave, and eventually overcome, many of the obstacles which beset his pathway in life at the time. She was the first to inspire his muse, and he has acknowledged

her worth and his love for her in **many of his finest pieces**. Under
the title of "Queen Janet," he sings:

Beside a wee burn there stan's a wee cot,
  An' a bonny wee lassie in it ;
Gin the gowd were mine that gilds a king's lot,
  I wad pairt wi' it a' this minute
If there I micht bide for aye by the side
  O' the bonny wee lassie in it.

Red roses speel roon' its auld-fashioned door,
  Less sweet than the roses within it ;
Outside the birdies mak' sic an uproar—
  Inside is the song o' the linnet.
The birds in the glen are jealous, I ken,
  O' the bonniest lassie in it.

Richt past it the burnie rins tae the sea—
  Losh me ! hoo my love wad ootrin it,
Gin I thocht her heart was waitin' for me,
  Wi' her twa witchin' een abune it,
The song I wad sing wad make the wuds ring
  An' fairies wad help me tae spin it.

Saft blaw the win's o' winter's cauld day
  Aroon' that wee cot an' wha's in it ;
An' when its my ain, as sometime it may
  (For I'll play my best cards tae win it).
I'll sit mysel' doon an' think I've a crown
  In the true love of my Queen Janet !

In 1862 Mr. Lyle was offered and accepted a position in England,
and while there published a number of meritorious poems which commanded a great deal of attention. One in particular, of **considerable**
length, was entitled "The Grave of Three Hundred," **and had refer-**
ence to the great Barnsley Mine disaster. This poem was published
in book form and had a very extensive sale. It was dedicated by permission to the late Lord Lytton, and copies were presented to and
accepted by her majesty Queen Victoria. Some years later our author
decided to emigrate to America. On his arrival here, he took up his
residence in Rochester, N. Y., where he has since remained, and where
he has long held a position of trust and responsibility. Like all other
Scottish poets in America, while upholding the dignity and grandeur
of his adopted **country**, he is intensely enthusiastic on the subject of

his native land.   **His whole** soul is completely wrapped up in his **ad-**miration for her, and he never seems to tire of singing her praises. Take the following **as a specimen of** his muse in this particular:

THE LAND OF THE HEATHER

Come sing me the songs of old Scotland,
  If ye would be merry awhile,
And strike **the** wild harp of her minstrels,
  If ye would my sorry beguile.
O chant the wild lays of her heroes,
  Whose blood **has** baptized every **vale,**
And sing me the songs of her martyrs,
  That oft **lent a joy to the gale.**

      Hurrah for the land of the heather!
        The dear little land of the North,
          Where true hearts and brave ones together,
            Tell mankind what freedom is worth.

The earth is enriched with her lessons,
  And time is embalming her name :
Disgrace never tarnished her tartans,
  Or mantled a brow with its shame.
Bright gold may not burst from her valleys,
  Nor silver be washed from her streams,
But there is a gold in her glory—
  Her valor all silver outgleams.

      Three cheers for the land of the heather !
        The dear little land of the North,
          Where true hearts and brave ones together
            Tell mankind what freedom is worth,

Through all the archives of the nations,
  'Tis writ how her fame has been bought,
Still wearing the chaplet of honor
  Wherever her claymore has fought.
O, **hearts from** the birthplace of **freedom**
  Forget not the soil ye have **trod,**
Through time and through distance **remember**
  The noble old land and her God.

      Hurrah **for** the land of the heather!
        The dear little land of the North,
          Where true hearts and brave ones together
            Tell mankind what freedom is worth.

The above is but one probably out of a hundred poems which we might mention, written by Mr. Lyle, each of which sparkles with references of the warmest nature to Scotland. Even a sprig of heather sent to him by a friend, calls forth the following affectionate sentiments:

Bonnie wee sprig o' the dear purple heather,
　Fresh frae the auld lan' my heart lo'es sae weel ;
Twa cronies hae met when we've come thegither ;
　Auld love revived wi' a kiss I maun seal.

Ye come like a warlock, wi' queer thochts surroonded
　Ye bring tae my heart lang syne simmer days,
Ere life's angry storms my young dreams confoonded,
　When freedom an' I ran wild on the braes !

Ye speak **o'** the ploys by the rock and the river ;
　Ye tell me o' frien's lang deid an' awa ;
Ye mind me o' music noo silent for ever ;—
　I wadna be true if tears didna **fa'.**

Puir withered stranger, lang miles frae yer mither,
　Ye needna be fleyed though far frae yer hame ;
Fortune is kind—ye ha'e met wi' a brither,
　Wha never looks cauld on ane o' yer name.

Bide near my heart, braw **son o' the** mountain,
　For his sake wha sent ye, an' for yer ain ;
The bluid o' a Scot maun be cauld at the fountain
　When he can look on sic a gift wi' disdain.

Yes, bide near my heart, an' aften ye'll cheer me,
　When fortune's hard thumps frae the warl' I **dree** ;
In fancy I'll dream that I hae a frien' near me,
　Though your hame an' mine is ower the wide **sea.**

Bonnie blue sprig, ye'll be dawtied an' nourished,
　An' no ae strip frae yer plume shall be torn ;
Ye'll keep the wish warm that I hae long cherished,
　Tae see the auld lan' whaur we twa were born.

They say sometimes the spirit will linger
　Near the lo'ed places when life is nae mair ;—
If sae, can ye blame the heart o' the singer,
　That breathes sic wish in its sang an' its prayer?

Mr. Lyle is a voluminous writer of poetry besides being the author of a number of tales and sketches. During the twelve years which the New York *Scotsman* was in existence scarcely a week elapsed without a new poem being contributed by him to its pages. He has already composed material enough to fill six large volumes and he still continues to write with unabated vigor and zeal. He is thus well and favorably known to the Scottish residents both in this country and Canada, and he has hosts of admirers on the other side of the Atlantic as all of his principal poems have been extensively copied by the Scottish press. His themes are numerous, and his poems, considering the very large number of them, display considerable power and originality of thought. Humor and pleasing sarcasm also form a special characteristic of many of his compositions. A good illustration of these latter qualities may be found in the poem entitled:

A CRACK WI' BOBBY INGERSOLL.

Noo, Rab, my lad, I want tae say
A word or twa in frien'ly way
    Tae ye, my chiel.
Ilk ither week ye mak' a din
About the clergy and their sin—
A' praying folks through thick and thin
    Ye thump them weel.

Ye've got a notion in yer pow
That there can be nae after lowe—
    That there's nae hell.
Ye mak' some folks believe it's sae,
An' crack yer jokes tae them—for pay ;
But whaur ye get yer logic frae
    I cannna tell.

Noo, if there be nae hell tae dreid,
Whatever mak's ye fash yer heid,
    An' guid time spen'?
Beside there's ae thing puzzles me,
Tae after life ye'll no agree .
Hae ye been ower the lake tae see—
    Hoo dae ye ken?

It's this way, Rab, as sure as death—
We are na gaun tae pin our faith
    Tae your coat tail.
Ye may hae notions in yer brain—
Juist keep them there—they're a' yer ain ;
Aye, when ye try sic tae explain,
    Yer sure tae fail.

When braggin' o' yer duty dune,
Yer suppin' wi' a muckle spune,
    For mair than you
Hae loved their brithers juist as weel,
Wha ne'er denied there was a deil,
And wi' their bluid this truth did **seal—**
    The Bible's true.

Rab, heids are heids, ye ken yersel',
An' heids as guid as yours can tell
    Juist what they think :
Maybe the worthies we could name
Tae sense had quite as soond a claim
As ye hae; and for honest fame
    Were nae sma' drink.

Sae haud ye, man, an' dinna squeeze,
Yer conscience for twa-three bawbees
    Gie us **a** rest !
Gin ye think Jonah gulped the whale,
Sae let it be—baith heid and tail ;
But losh ! man, Rab, let ilk ane sail
    As he thinks best.

Our author has been connected **for** a number of years with the Scottish Society of Rochester. He takes a deep interest in everything pertaining to the welfare of this patriotic organization, and no member is better known **or more** highly respected **than** he is. It has been customary with him **for** many **years past to present** the society with an original and **always** able and pleasing **poetical** address, on **the** occasion of its **annual observance** of the birthday **of** Robert Burns, and he has **thus** worthily borne the title of Poet Laureate of the society, an **honor** which his brother members conferred upon him many years since in recognition of his talents. These addresses are of considerable length, and if they were collected together and pub. lished in book form they would make a very interesting and unique little volume. We cannot conclude our brief sketch of Mr. Lyle and his works without referring in the highest terms to his English compositions. They are certainly equal to his poems in the Scottish dialect, **and prove** that he possesses true poetic genius. The following **poem** in this respect will speak for itself:

THE MURDER AT HOLYROOD.

Night's ebon curtain fell once more
  On quaint Edina, Lothian's pride;
Again the pointed gables wore
  The mystic robes of eventide,
And stood up gaunt and grim and hoar,
  Like spectral giants, side by side.

The narrow streets were still and lone,
  No taper with its fitful glare
From odd projecting casement shone,
  Or struggled with the murky air,
While now and then the night guard's tone
  In query curt cried, " Wha gangs there ?"

Dark, silent city, little dream
  Your honest burghers while they sleep
That horrid murder's daggers gleam
  In ruthless hands, and curses deep
Will mar the peace of happy themes
  When morn shall rise on eyes that weep.

At Holyrood—sweet royal name—
  In stately room, of fashion old,
Lit by lambient spirit flame,
  Sat Scotland's Queen, and, roundly told,
All of the friends her lot could claim,
  Alas, how few were in the fold.

A plaintive air from skillful hand,
  Remembered her of happy days
In sunny France, the summer land,
  Ere sorrow fell upon her ways,
While beauteous lips in concert planned
  To meet the minstrel's witching lays.

To some hearts come when skies are glad,
  And Nature smiles her sweetest smile,
A premonition, softly sad,
  Like shadow from some unseen isle,
Thus oft our thoughts in gloom are clad,
  With sunshine overhead the while.

A presence seemed to fill that room
  No one could name and none could see,
A creeping terror, and a gloom
  Lip feared to mention.   Minstrelsy,
However sweet, had sound of doom,
  And nameless sorrow soon to be.

Hush, hark, a ring of rattling mail
  Steals on the startled ear and then
The crash of timber, cheeks grow pale
  And hearts beat high—it comes again!
Eft soon that sound has told its tale—
  The room is filled with armoured men.

Sprang the fair Sovereign from her seat:
  " What means this outrage ? how my lords,
Have ye no shame ? or is it meet
  To face your Queen with flashing swords ?
Douglas! on guard, these traitors greet!
  Death with this treason well accords."

Swift the stern Ruthven crossed his blade
  With youthful Douglas, whose slim steel,
Unused to war's more trenchent trade,
  Snapped at the hilt, ere he could feel
The gash the sullen earl had made.
  Or note his doublet's bloody seal.

" 'Tis not with striplings we would war,"
  Cried Murray, as he viewed the fight.
" This popinjay and his guitar
  Must no more blast the nation's sight.
Madame, stand back, for by my star,
  And God's own Son, he dies to-night."

Then hauberks flashed, on floor and stair
  Gleamed naked swords behind whose blades
Each bosom was a tiger's lair,
  Where vengeance lurked in stygian shades.
" Hound," the fierce Ruthven howled, "prepare;
  Scotland is tired of masquerades."

Then flashed the Stuart's pallid face,
  She bounded dogs and prey between.
So meekest hearts to grandeur brace
  When danger shows and wrong is seen.
Stamping her foot with royal grace,
  She stood there every inch a queen.

" Caitiffs and curs, this boy shall feel
  Through our own heart your traitor blows.
Unhand me, Darnley! thus you seal
  Your marriage vow, thus treason grows.
Guards, without there.   This last appeal
  Is from your Queen, whose friends **are foes**."

"*Lords of the Covenant*, is hate
  A tenant of the church you own?
We've heard you all of mercy prate.
  Is this its outcome? this its tone?
Mother of God, look on our fate—
  For thou art more than crown or throne."

Few words were said, few were to say,
  'Twas chance and thrust with lightning speed;
Poor Rizzio fell, his doublet grey
  Dabbled in blood. Oh, hellish deed;
Man becomes demon when his sway
  Is held in common with his creed.

Drag the dead minstrel from the place
  He loved so well, by his Queen's side.
Cold dews of death o'erspread his face;
  Winds tell his mother of her pride—
Tell her his name bore no disgrace,
  But men were cruel, and he died.

The sun arose o'er Arthur's throne
  In liquid floods of golden brown.
Poor hunted Mary sat alone,
  And viewed the dead with mournful frown.
She knew it not, but she had gone
  One step nearer the martyr's crown.

Thus every time the sun shall rise,
  Its rays will fall on varied scenes;
Some hearts give song and some give sighs,
  While some are kings and some are queens,
Some from hovels send weary cries,
  Nor recks the sun what all this means.

Mr. Lyle is at present arranging for the publication of a new volume
of poems which his friends have at length induced him to place before
the public. It will be entitled "The Martyr Queen and Other Poems,"
from which "The Murder at Holyrood" is an extract, and we feel
assured that the little volume will receive a hearty welcome from all
true lovers of Scottish poetry. Its publication will undoubtedly add
to the fame of its author, although this is hardly necessary, as he
has already earned a reputation for himself of which he may justly
feel proud.

WILLIAM WILSON.

A truer, nobler, trustier heart,
More loving or more loyal, never beat
Within a human breast.

" Having summered and wintered it for many long years with your dear father, I ought to know something of the base and bent of his genius, though, as he hated all shams and pretensions, a very slight acquaintance with him showed that independence and personal manhood, 'as wha daur meddle wi' me,' were two of his strong features; while humor, deep feeling and tenderness were prominent in all he said or wrote. * * I loved him as a man, a poet and a brother, and I had many proofs that my feelings were reciprocated." So wrote Hew Ainslie of William Wilson in a letter addressed to General James Grant Wilson, the esteemed editor of " The Poets and Poetry of Scotland " and of the " Cyclopædia of American Biography." William Wilson was born at Crieff on the twenty-fifth of December, 1801. He was educated with great care, and early began to take an interest in poetical matters; indeed, many of his own verses, written before he had reached his tenth year, prove that even at this tender age he was possessed of superior poetical talents. He is said to have inherited these gifts from his mother, a patriotic Scottish lady who ever delighted in singing the old Jacobite songs and ballads, which she did with much sweetness and pathos. At the age of twenty-two Mr. Wilson removed to Dundee, where he edited for some time the *Literary Olio*, and to which he contributed largely, both in poetry and prose. He afterwards went to Edinburgh and entered into business on his own account as a commission agent. While there he is credited with having contributed no less than thirty-two valuable poems in less than three years to the Edinburgh *Literary Journal*, a well-known publication then under the editorship of Henry Glassford Bell, late Sheriff of Lanarkshire.

Through his connection with this periodical he was brought into contact with nearly all of the prominent literary men of the time, and
among others with Robert Chambers, then a young man just beginning
his wonderful literary career, with whom he formed a warm friendship
which was only terminated by death. He was also a great favorite
with Mrs. Grant, of Laggan, who claimed the privilege of naming his
eldest son, by his second marriage with a member of an old Border
family, after her husband, the Rev. James Grant. This lady the
young poet first saw while on a visit to his friend the "Ettrick Shep-
ard," who delighted in his spirited singing of old Scottish songs and
ballads.

In 1833 Mr. Wilson emigrated to America and took up his residence
in Poughkeepsie, N. Y. Here he established a book-selling and publishing business, which he conducted with great success for nearly
thirty years. For a portion of this period he had for a partner a
brother of Bishops Alonzo and Horatio Potter, and for a few years
before his death, his son, General Wilson. But during all these years
he continued to pour forth his heart in song, and many of his finest
pieces were composed at brief intervals amid the cares and anxieties
of this busy portion of his life. Many of these compositions were
given to the world anonymously, and in this manner did not at once
attain the popularity which they afterward achieved. They are now
classed with the more illustrious of Scottish poems, however, and Mr.
Wilson has long since been accorded a prominent place among the
bards of his country. He was indeed a true Scottish poet, simplicity,
tenderness, pathos or humor being characteristic of all his writings.
Apart from his poems, however, his lyrical compositions have made
him a universal favorite with his countrymen everywhere. Few Scotsmen, even in America, for instance, are unacquainted with his

AULD JOHNNY GRAHAM.

Dear aunty, what think ye o' auld Johnny Graham?
   The carle sae pawkie and slee!
He wants a bit wifie to tend his bein hame,
   And the bodie has ettled at me.

Wi' bonnet sae vaunty, an' owerlay sae clean,
   An' ribbon that waved boon his bree,
He cam' doun the cleugh at the gloamin' yestreen,
   An' rappit, an soon speert for me.

I bade him come ben whare my minnie sae thrang
  Was birlin' her wheel eidentlie,
An', foul fa' the carle, he was na' that lang
  Ere he tauld out his errand to me.

" Hech, Tibby, lass ! a' yon braid acres o' land,
  Wi' ripe craps that wave bonnilie,
An', meikle mair gear shall be at yer command,
  Gin ye will look kindly on me.

" Yon herd o' fat owsen that rout i' the glen,
  Sax naigies that nibble the lea ;
The kye i' the sheugh, and the sheep i' the pen,
  I'se gie a', dear Tibby, to thee.

" An', lassie, I've goupins o' gowd in a stockin',
  An' pearlin's wad dazzle yer e'e ;
A mettl'd, but canny young yaud for the yokin'
  When ye wad gae jauntin' wi' me.

" I'll hap ye and fend ye, and busk ye and tend ye,
  And mak' ye the licht o' my e'e ;
I'll comfort and cheer ye, and daut ye and dear ye,
  As couthy as couthy can be.

I've lo'ed ye, dear lassie, since first, a bit bairn,
  Ye ran up the knowe to meet me ;
An' deckit my bonnet wi' blue-bells an' fern,
  Wi' meikle glad laughin' an' glee.

" An' noo woman grown, an' mensefu' an' fair,
  An' gracefu' as gracefu' can be—
Will ye tak' an auld carle wha ne'er had a care
  For woman, dear Tibby, but thee ?"

Sae, aunty, ye see I'm a' in a swither,
  What answer the bodie to gie—
But aften I wish he wad tak' my auld mither,
  And let puir young Tibby abee.

Another of Mr. Wilson's lyrical compositions which has won for
itself a well-merited popularity is the one entitled " Jean Linn." This
was not only a favorite with the author but was also admired and
highly spoken of by Dr. Robert Chambers, N. P. Willis, Hew Ainslie
and other prominent authorities.

JEAN LINN.

Oh, haud na' yer noddle **sae hie ma doo!**
Oh, haud na' yer noddle sae hie!
The days that hae been may be yet again seen,
Sae look na' sae lightly on me, ma doo !
Sae look na' sae lightly on me !

Oh, geck na' at hame hodden gray, **Jean Linn,**
Oh, geck na' at hame hodden gray !
Yer gutcher and mine wad thocht themsels fine
In cleidin' sae bein, bonnie May, bonnie May—
In cleidin' sae bein bonnie May.

Ye mind when we won in whinglee, Jean Linn,
Ye mind when we won in whinglen,
Your daddy, douce carle, was cotter to mine
An' our herd was yer bonnie sel', then Jean Linn,
An' our herd was yer bonnie sel', **then.**

Oh, then ye were a' thing to me, **Jean Linn !**
Oh, then ye were a' thing to me !
An' the moments scour'd by like birds through the sky,
When tentin' the owsen wi' thee, Jean Linn,
When tentin' the owsen wi' thee.

I twined ye a bower by the burn, Jean **Linn,**
I twined ye a bower by the burn,
But dreamt na' that hour, as we sat in that bower,
That fortune wad tak' sic a turn, Jean Linn,
That fortune wad tak' sic a turn.

Ye busk noo in satins **fu'** braw, **Jean Linn,**
Ye busk noo in satins fu' braw!
Yer daddy's a laird, mine's i' the kirkyard,
An' I'm yer puir ploughman, Jock Law, Jean **Linn,**
An' **I'm yer puir** ploughman Jock Law.

While **Mr.** Wilson wrote largely in his mother tongue, he has **also** given us many valuable gems of English poetry. Of these his "Richard Cœur De Lion " **is** the best. This is the piece which Mr. William Cullen Bryant claimed to be "more spirited than any of the ballads of Aytoun."

RICHARD CŒUR DE LION.

Brightly, **brightly** the moonbeam shines,
  On the **castle** turret-wall;
Darkly, darkly, **the** spirit pines
  Deep, deep in its dungeon's thrall.
He hears the screech-owl whoop reply
  To the warden's drowsy strain,
And thinks of home, and heaves **a sigh**,
  For his own bleak hills again.

Sweetly, sweetly the spring **flowers spread**,
  When first he was fettered there ;
Slowly, slowly the sere leaves fade,
  Yet breathes he that dungeon's **air**.
All lowly lies his banner bright,
  That formost in battle streamed,
And dim the sword that in the fight
  Like midnight meteor gleamed.

But place **his** foot upon the plain,
  That banner o'er his head,
His good lance in his hand again,
  With Paynim slaughter red,
The craven hearts that round him now,
  With coward triumph stand,
Would quail before that dauntless brow,
  And the death-flash of **that** hand.

Among Mr. Wilson's other short pieces his " Sweet Lammas Moon,"
" A Welcome to Christopher North," " Jeanie Graham," "Sabbath
Morning in the Woods," and " Britania " are worthy of special notice.
The following extract in connection with our author **is** taken **from the**
" Autobiography **and** Memoirs of Robert and William Chambers:"—
"Among the persons to whom my brother applied for materials **for**
the work ('Popular Rhymes of Scotland') was William **Wilson, a**
young man of about his own age who had similar poetical **and** archæ-
logical tastes, **and** for a time edited a literary periodical in Dundee.
Between the **two** there sprung **up an** extraordinary friendship which
was not weakened by Wilson some years later emigrating to America.
The letters which passed between them bring into view a number of
particulars concerning my brother's literary aims and efforts. Writing
in January, 1824, to Wilson, whom he always addresses as 'Dear
Willie,' he **refers** gratifyingly to the 'Traditions,' and the manner

which the book had brought him into notice. "This little work is taking astonishingly, and I am getting a great deal of credit by it. It has also been the means of introducing me to many of the most respectable leading men of the town, and has attracted to me the attention of not a few of the most eminent literary characters. What would you think, for instance, of the venerable author of the 'Man of Feeling' calling on me in his carriage to contribute his remarks in MS. on my work! The value of the above two great advantages is incalculable to a young tradesman and author like me. It saves me twenty years of mere laborious plodding by the common walk, and gives me at twenty-two all the respectability which I could have expected at forty.'" Mr. Wilson died at Poughkeepsie on the twenty-fifth of August, 1860. The last of his work were the following verses, written in a feeble and faltering hand a few days before his death:

WANING LIFE AND WEARY.

Waning life and weary,
  Fainting heart and limb,
Darkening road and dreary,
  Flashing eyes grow dim ;
All betokening nightfall near,
  Day is done and rest is dear.

    Slowly stealing shadows
      Westward lengthening still
    O'er the dark brown meadows,
      O'er the sunlit hill.

Gleams of golden glory
  From the opening sky,
Gild those temples hoary—
  Kiss that closing eye :
Now drops the curtain on all wrong—
  Throes of sorrow, grief and song.

    But saw ye not the dying
      Ere life passed away,
    Faintly smiled while eying
      Yonder setting day :

And, his pale hand signing
  Man's redemption sign—
Cried, with forehead shining,
  Father, I am thine !
And so to rest he quietly hath passed,
  And sleeps in Christ, the Comforter, at last.

A few years after Mr. Wilson's death a portion of his poems were published in a small volume, with a memoir by Mr. Benson J. Lossing. A second and enlarged edition appeared in 1875, and this has since been followed by a third edition. Many of his poems made their first appearance in Blackwood's Magazine or Chambers' Journal, and selections from his writings appeared in Whistle Binkie, The Modern Scottish Minstrel, Blackie's Book of Scottish Song, The Cabinet, and in Longfellow's "Poems and Places." In concluding the brief memoir attached to his father's poems in "The Poets and Poetry of Scotland," General Wilson says:—"The idea of this work originated with William Wilson, but urgent demands upon his time, together with failing health, interfered with its execution. The task devolved upon his son, who has as an act of filial duty, no less than a labor of love, endeavored to complete his father's unfulfilled literary project." Granting that the completion of this work was "an act of filial duty and a labor of love," it is still due to General Wilson to say that he has given us one of the best and most valuable books on the subject of Scottish poets and poetry which has so far been published.

ANDREW McLEAN.

Tho' modest, on his unembarrassed brow
Nature hath written:—Gentleman.

Mr. Andrew McLean, the eminent Brooklyn journalist, is also a
poet of sterling merit. He is a native of Renton, in Dumbartonshire,
where he was born in 1848. After studying for a few years at the
village school of Alexandria he became apprenticed to a carpenter,
and remained at this trade until he was nearly fourteen years of age.
It cannot be said, however, that he took much interest in this occupation; certainly it did not in any manner harmonize with his tastes; and
we may judge from the following verses that it afforded him considerable relief when Saturday night approached and the work of the week
was nearly over. Then his thoughts left the bench and the workshop,
and he rejoiced that :

> The wearisome week is over,
>   With its burden of fret and toil ;
> To-morrow I'll smell the clover
>   And tread the daisied soil,
> And chant a tune as I lightly go
> More merry than any the greenwoods know
>
> Where the streamlets glint and shimmer,
>   Through shadows of maple gloss,
> And strolling sunbeams glimmer
>   On fern and rambling moss,
> An hour I'll spend and drink the balm
> That the brooklets brew in the woodland's calm.

He began to have a desire for some kind of occupation where
energy, determination and ambition were requisite qualities to success,
and where the services of one possessing these would command
recognition and advancement. We are not surprised therefore to find

him at this time eagerly gazing **beyond the** Atlantic **to the shores of** the new world and resolving to strike out for himself and begin life anew under the flag of the great republic. He had hardly reached his fifteenth year when he left his home and proceeded to Glasgow. Here **he** gladly entered into an engagement with the captain of an American vessel to perform certain duties, for which he was to be allowed a free passage across to New York. The recollection many years afterward of this eventful period of his life inspired his muse, and in spirit he became a boy again with a farewell song on his lips to his native land:

Deep crimson heather bloom,
Rich yellow blushing broom,
Sweet, fragrant Scotch bluebell,
        Farewell ! farewell !

Song-hearted, throbbing lark,
Gray cushat crooning dark,
Shy, plaintive "bonnet blue,"
        Adieu! adieu !

Broad-bosomed, silver lake,
Leven's rippling, sunny wake,
Grim, grizzly mountains high,
        Good-bye ! good-bye !

Scenes that I loved and roved among :
Rocks that echoed my earliest song ;
Birds I knew in the nesting days ;
Flowers I plucked by the woodland ways ;
Lake of silver and sunny stream—
Beauteous all as a sinless dream ;
I say farewell, good-bye, adieu,
But life shall end ere I part from you ;
Ye are present wheresoever I be,
Thy life is mine; I am part of thee.

Arriving here during the excitement of the war, McLean entered the navy and served with distinction and honor until its close. On his return he took up his residence with some friends in Brooklyn, and after spending some time as a student in a commercial college, **he** decided to adopt journalism as a profession. He obtained a position on a daily as a reporter, and it did not take long for the management of the paper to discover that they had made **a** valuable acquisition to their staff. He proved himself an original and terse writer on all subjects. After serving in one or two other positions he became assistant editor of the *Brooklyn Daily Eagle*. On the death of Mr. Kinsella he became editor-in-chief; but in 1886 he severed his connection with the Eagle and started what is now not only the recognized organ of the Democratic party in Brooklyn, but a first-class evening newspaper generally, namely, the *Brooklyn Citizen*. Mr McLean is certainly a hard and conscientious worker in the newspaper field, and the public has not been slow to recognize his talents in this respect. "The true Scottish 'grit' of McLean is proved by his antecedents," writes one of his literary friends. "He is an eloquent and effective public speaker, and the skill and ability he has displayed in conducting an influential daily are generally conceded. Engaged as he is, he has but few leisure hours to devote to poetry; and yet such is the energy of the man that he has actually written much—no small portion of which bears the stamp of poetical genius." The following is one of his best known poems:

THE JEWELS OF BLARNEY.

'Tis told us pleasantly, by the simple peasantry
　　Whose hearts ne'er wander tho' their words may stray,
How an earl's daughters into Blarney's waters
　　Cast all their jewels on a hapless day ,
There to be pendant till some late descendant,
　　Finding from war and bigotry release, .
Shall bid the fairies on whom the care is,
　　Bring them to deck his coronet in peace.

There's another story, presaging glory,
　　And something better, which the peasants tell :
For witching reasons, in happy seasons,
　　When the earth is under the new moon's spell,
Come flocks all white, from the breast of night,
　　Calmly to graze near the pearly strand ;
So that favored eyes may at least surmise
　　That a spotless future awaits the land.

These old traditions and superstitions
　　Yield a moral that fits our time and place—
They've a counterpart in each human heart
　　That throbs with the heat of an ancient race ;
The Bigot's word and Oppression's sword
　　Made a lake far deeper than Blarney knows,
And in its water Good Will's fair daughters
　　Once buried jewels more rare than those.

Clancarty's earl ne'er owned a pearl
  To compare with the gem of brotherhood ;
Nor in any mine doth a diamond shine
  Like the soul that longs for another's good.
No glittering schist, or soft amethyst
  Can rival the beams of a friendly eye ;
The emerald fades and the topaz shades
  In the flashing light of a purpose high.

On a new made plain I observe again
  The Blarney flocks with their spotless dress,
And a shepherd near, from the fairy sphere,
  Maketh signs which my heart is swift to guess :
Our Age is the heir to the jewels fair
  That Good Will buried in evil days,
And we shall see in our own land free
  The diadem on his forehead blaze.

Let us sing old songs and bury old wrongs,
  And draw from the past, not gloom but cheer ;
The angry moods of our fathers' feuds
  Should be given no place in our gatherings here :
Let our children boast when our healths they toast
  At the festal boards of the years to come,
That their fathers' choice was for friendship's voice,
  And in favor of striking rancor dumb.

Mr. McLean is a poet of excellent fancy and power. His compositions, as a rule, evince a true sympathy with nature, and there is a tenderness and melody, besides a quaint simplicity, displayed in all of them. Many of them also contain pleasing and thoughtful ideas, expressed in the choicest of language. Take for instance his poem entitled :

THE FOUNTAIN OF YOUTH.

Sweet songs of old ! they thrill to-day,
  With undiminished gladness,
Our hearts beneath their heads of gray
  And under brows of sadness.

Again they bring the bounding joy
  We knew among the heather
When, sunny girl and ardent boy,
  We roved and sang together.

What Ponce de Leon sought in vain,
  Youth's sparkling, never failing fountain,
We find in every witching **strain**
  Of lightsome deeds by vale and mountain.

Oh youth behind the mask of years !
  Oh subtle singing rare magician,
When e'er thy voice the spirit hears,
  She conquers age and scorns transition.

Away the latter sorows flee
  And hither troop to take their places,
The radient eyes the fleckless glee
  Of garnered days and gathered graces.

In every note a glory lives ;
  In every cord pure love vows **tremble** ;
At every call the singing gives
  A thousand happy thoughts assemble.

To age we give the meed of age,
  But when the tuneful breeze is blowing
Affection leaves the wrinkled cage,
  And, eagle like, **her** pinions showing,

Outsoars the dusk, the gray of grief,
  The changing winds of seasons rolling
To revel in the high relief
  Of spheres beyond the world's controlling

Thrice blesséd be the **songs of old,**
  And blesséd be the tongues that sing them,
And blesséd be the hearts that fold
  Their sweetness when the minstrels bring them.

In 1878 Mr. McLean published a small volume of his poems. The principal poem in the collection is the one entitled "Tom Moore." This was written for and read by the author, at the celebration, by the St. Patrick's Society of Brooklyn, of the ninety-ninth anniversary of the poet's birth. According to the "argument" the poem proceeds to disclose a council held in Elysium by Irishmen before the birth of Moore, at which, Heaven having signified a willingness to grant their country whatever single gift they should agree upon, it was resolved to ask for a poet, who should win the admiration of the world and glorify the Emerald Isle. In the course of the debate the qualities and purposes of his song are determined by various speakers. It is also shown that the misapprehensions of this life **so cease in the** light **of** the upper world that **old enemies** find themselves one in sympathy. Taken altogether the poem **is** certainly a very able and spirited one. It is, of course, too long for quotation **here** and it has to be read through to thoroughly appreciate its many beautiful passages and similies. Among the smaller **poems in the** volume "A Glimpse of April Sun" is particularly **fine.**

> Hail, gladsome gleam of April sun !
>   Thou glance from Nature's kindly eye ;
> Bright pledge of boisterous weather done ;
>   Fair flowery fragrant prophecy.
>
> Thy **radiance to the** bluebird shows
>   The gentleness he loves to sing,
> When winds that wanton with the **rose**
>   Forsake the rose to fan his wing.
>
> The various creatures of the woods
>   Are gladdened by thy early **grace,**
> As I am glad when angry moods,
>   Pass cloud-like from an old **friend's face.**

Socially, Mr. McLean **is one of** the best **of** men. He is possessed of a warm, confiding and generous nature, and he has won the esteem and friendship of all parties **with** whom he has come in contact. While he is the author of nearly one hundred poems, not one of which **he** may be ashamed to own, still he is extremely modest in his own estimation of his poetical abilities, and it is seldom that his poems when printed for the first time have the proper signature attached to them.

DANIEL McINTYRE HENDERSON.

Here too dwells simple truth; plain innocence;
Unsullied beauty, sound unbroken youth;
Patient of labor, with a little pleased;
Health ever blooming, unambitious toil;
Calm contemplation and poetic ease.

THE west of Scotland has been the birthplace of many eminent poets, and among these Mr. Daniel McIntyre Henderson, the subject of our present sketch, is destined to occupy a prominent place at no distant date. He was born at Glasgow on the tenth of July, 1851, but in 1861 his family removed to Blackhill Locks, a short distance from the city, and a place where there was little or no society. The situation, however, had its charms for our youthful poet. He was compelled to walk to and from the city each day, first for educational, and later on in life for social and literary advantages, and he attributes to this largely the fact that the thoughts of a naturally reflective mind began to shape themselves in rhyme. As with nearly all modern Scottish poets, Burns became his earliest model, and many of his boyhood's musings were inspired by reading and studying certain poems of the master bard. As soon as his education was finished he was sent to learn the wholesale drapery business, but he soon left this occupation, and after filling one or two other positions became bookkeeper to the Scottish Permissive Bill and Temperance Association. Since that time he has taken an active part in all temperance and religious movements, and some of the beautiful hymns now sung in our churches are from his pen. We append a specimen of his religious poetry, written in his mother-tongue :

OH, LIPPEN AN' BE LEAL.

(A Paraphrase).

Oh, lippen an' be leal !
  The Father's bairns are ye—
A' that He does is weel,
  And a' that's guid He'll **gie** !

The birds they ken nae cark,
  They fear nae cauld nor weet—
His e'e's ower a' His wark,
  They dinna want for meat.

Think o' the bonnie flow'rs,
  Wi' slender, gracefu' stem,
Drinkin' the summer show'rs—
  The Father cares for them !

The lilies o' the field
  At God's ain biddin' bloom ;
His bosom is their beild,
  His breath is their perfume.

And if He minds the flow'rs,
  And decks them oot sae braw,
He'll care for you and yours—
  Then trust Him wi' your a'.

The Father's bairns are ye—
  A' that He does is weel,
And a' that's guid He'll gie—
  Oh, lippen an' be leal !

Mr. Henderson composed a considerable number of poems before coming to this country, and it is to be regretted that none of these have been preserved. He tells us that when he resolved to leave Scotland he also resolved to " quit rhyming," as he had reached the conclusion that **he** was not a poet, a wonderful conclusion, by the way, for one of the rhyming fraternity to reach. Landing in Baltimore in 1873 he obtained a position as bookkeeper with Messrs. R. Renwick & Sons, the well-known furniture manufacturers, with whom he still remains. Memories of home soon revived the poetic spirit, and in 1874 appeared " Flowers frae Hame," an exquisite lyrical piece, which was at once set to music by the late Mr. Archibald Johnson, of New York, and became decidedly popular. Soon afterward appeared his "Scotland Mine," a poem which proved that however much he had become attached to the land of his adoption, his heart still beat loyally toward the land of his birth.

> Oh, Scotland mine, my mother-land,
>   How grand, how fair art thou ;
> The sunbeams play about thy feet,
>   The lightnings round thy brow.
> How stout of arm, how fierce of speech,
>   In battle and in storm ;
> But to thy children, bosom-nursed,
>   How tender-souled and warm.
>
> My mother-land, how bare thy form,
>   How wild thy heart of flame,
> Till kindly snows and mists and dews
>   With gentlest soothing came:
> And now in nature's greenest robe,
>   A queen I see thee stand ;
> The fairest, grandest child of earth,
>   My own, my mother-land.

In 1880 Baltimore celebrated its sesqui-centennial. A feature of the occasion was a parade of the Scottish societies, with delegates from New York, Philadelphia and other cities. Mr. Henderson contributed an ode in connection with the event which was widely copied and favorably noticed. An epistle, also written about this time to the late Mr. David Kennedy, the Scottish vocalist, was greatly prized by him, especially the verses :

> We want to hear the guid auld sangs that carry back the mind
> To the faces and the friendships, and the hame scenes o' lang syne
> We want to hear the Doric braid and lauch and greet by turns
> As ye sing the sangs o' Tannahill and oor ain brither Burns !
>
> Sae ye'll come back, Davy Kennedy, and mak' oor hearts rejoice
> Wi' your cheerie face, your cantie ways, and the music o' your voice,
> And if the warl' could spare you, we'd keep you for a year,
> And you'd hae concerts nichtly, and we'd a' be there to hear.

Of a different nature, and rich in humorous sentiment, is Mr. Henderson's now famous epistle to Mr. Andrew Carnegie. It was written

a few years ago and published in the New York *Scotsman*, from
whence it was copied into quite a number of American and British
newspapers. There is certainly a great deal of truth and honestly
deserved praise compressed in the verses, and we doubt not that Mr.
Carnegie looked upon the poem as one of the kindliest compliments
ever paid to him.

EPISTLE **TO ANDREW CARNEGIE.**

Oh, Andrew Carnegie, it's weel to be you !
To hae siller and sense is the lot o' but few !
Ye hae gear and the grace for guid to employ it,
And leisure ye hae and the heart to enjoy it—
　　　　Lang life to ye, Andrew Carnegie !

Auld Scotland, oor mither, is prood o' your birth,
As **she** blesses her bairns abraid ower the earth ,
And America's prood ye hae fa'en to her lot,
Her typical man, and oor typical Scot—
　　　　Lang life **to** ye, Andrew Carnegie !

Ye ken what hard wark is, ye've earned **you ain bread,**
And wrocht your way up wi' **your hands and your head,**
And true to yoursel' through it a' ye hae been ;
Though your wallet grew fat, your heart didna grow lean ;
　　　　Lang life **to** ye, Andrew Carnegie !

And noo, through your bounty, your ain native toun
Has its storehouse o' knowledge, and's prood o' the boon,
And hearts are made glad ilka side o' the **sea,**
By the heart that can feel, and the han' that can **gie**—
　　　　Lang life to ye, Andrew Carnegie !

It's oh to be you, to sae cannily slip
Awa' roun' the warl' in a cosey bit ship,
Or merrily rattle owre Britain's braid lan'
Wi' the wale o' guid chiels in a snug four-in-han' !—
　　　　Lang life to ye, Andrew Carnegie !

I vow, should the fates or the fairies decree,
That anither, and no my ainsel' I maun be,
Gin mine were the choice, takin' a' things thegither,
I'd be Andrew Carnegie, withoot ony swither !
　　　　Lang life to ye, Andrew Carnegie !

In 1876 Mr. Henderson re-visited Scotland and while there was
united in marriage to Miss Alice Ashcroft, a refined and talented young

lady who has since proved herself well worthy of the love which he
bestowed upon her. "Their American home," to use the words of
another well-known author, "now rings with the music of children's
voices." Death, however, once crossed their happy threshold and
robbed them of one of their treasures. Note the resigned, yet hopeful and Christian spirit in which the following verses are written, in
connection with the event.

> Rest thee, rest thee, bonnie doo,
>   In the Faither's keepin';
> Nocht shall fear or fret thee noo
>   In the kirkyard sleepin!
> Rest thee, bonnie bairnie rest,
> Wakin's waefu', sleep is best.
>
> Rest thee, rest thee, bonnie doo,
>   White, white is thy plaidie,
> Sae He gie'th snaw like 'oo',
>   Warm and lown to hide thee!
> Rest, my bonnie bairnie, rest,
> Wakin's waefu', sleep is best.
>
> Rest thee, rest thee, bonnie doo,
>   Bide the simmer bringin'
> Gowan's white and bell's o' blue,
>   And the birdies singin'.
> Rest thee, bonnie bairnie, rest,
> Wakin's waefu', sleep is best.
>
> Rest thee, rest thee, bonnie doo,
>   Aye we'll mind oor dearie.
> A' the gowden simmer through,
>   A' the winter dreary.
> Rest thee, bonnie bairnie, rest,
> Wakin's waefu', sleep is best.
>
> Rest thee, rest thee, bonnie doo,
>   Sair has been oor sorrow,
> Oh to greet the bairn we loe
>   In Heaven's gleesome morrow.
> There, my bairnie, wakin's blest,
> There, my bairnie, wakin's rest.

The same sad occasion also gave rise to an incident which tended
in some measure to soothe the feelings of the bereaved parents :

OUR NEIGHBOR'S PITY.

That day our little one lay dead,
　And we were sad and sore of heart,
And all the joy of life seemed fled,
　Our neighbor sought to ease the smart.
Oh ! strange, sweet power of sympathy !
　That grief should find assuagement thus !
Our sorrow seemed the less to be,
　The more we thought, she pities us !

And then she said, how blest was she,
　Since God had still denied her prayer,
Nor set a baby on her knee ;
　For such a gift meant such a care !
Our pain was stilled by sad surprise ;
　New feelings in our heart did stir,
We looked into our neighbor's eyes,
　And pitied her—and pitied her.

Mr. Henderson is a studious reader of nearly all kinds of literature.
The life, character and writings of the late Dr. David Livingstone con-
stitute him his nineteenth century hero. Carlyle, however, is his
favorite prose writer, and Browning and Lowell his favorite poets. His
own poems are carefully and skillfully written, and show that he is
possessed of a cultured literary taste. His style is natural and unrestrained, and the characteristics of a true son of song are manifested
in all of his writings. Many of his pieces have a soft, melodious
cadence with them which is very pleasing. Take for instance his
piece entitled " A Song of Love."

Love's season is but brief,
　　So they say,
It opens like the leaf,
　　To decay ;
Ah ! well, I only know
The long years come and go
But 'tis leaf time with Love alway !

A silver cloud is Love,
　　So they say,
That floats a while above,
　　Then away ;
Ah ! well, the years have brought,
Their freight of care and thought,
Yet I build in the clouds to-day.

Uncertain as the sea,
　　So they say,
Love ever will be free,
　　Well-a-day !
The years have come and gone,
Life's ebb and flow go on,
But the sea is the same for aye.

If loves do fade e'er long,
　　As they say,
Yet Love is true and strong,
　　And will stay.
The leaf and cloud and tide
Through all the years abide—
Is not Love longer lived than they ?

Among the various sonnets which Mr. Henderson has composed, the one entitled "Thomas Carlyle" is decidedly the best. It is a scholarly production, and bears on its face the imprint of the work of a master. There have been numerous sonnets published on the same subject, but the present is the finest that has come under our notice so far :

THOMAS CARLYLE.

(Buried at Ecclefechan).

Yes, it was meet that there he should be laid ;
　The great and wise beside the good and just—
　They were his kindred ! Nature's "dust to dust."
The final law had honor when they made
His bed, not with the chisel, but the spade,
　Not in the Abbey, but the kirkyard lone.
　His mother-mould takes tenderly her own,
And o'er him spreads her green, all sheltering plaid.
God made from out the dust of Scottish earth
　A man whose spirit was th' Almighty's breath :
　The moorland breezes shouted at his birth,
And blew brave music through him till his death !
Knox, Wallace, Burns,—priest, patriot, and bard,
Woke once again, sleep now in yon kirkyard.

With these few selections from the poetical writings of Mr. Henderson we take our leave of him. That he is possessed of true poetical gifts none will dispute, and we refer those of our readers, who desire to obtain a collection of his writings, to the volume just published by Messrs. Cushings & Bailey, Baltimore, entitled " Poems, Scottish and

American." Reviewing this **work** *The Critic* (**New York**), says: "Happy the poet that is **born in Scotland.** Perhaps it is because 'the interesting' abounds there; from whatever cause a natural grace **and** ease, a true feeling for the music of verse, a close sympathy with nature, and a warm humanity, seem the birthright of the singer sprung from Scottish soil. All these characteristics are to be found in **the** collection of 'Poems, Scottish and American,' by D. M. Henderson. It is a pleasure to meet a little book so sincere, so satisfying within its limits. The poet longs, under the bright Southern sky, for the **song** of the skylark, entering the Holy of Holies in the far blue above; **he** notes, with the **keen** eye that reads the sweet meanings of nature, the significance **of** the giant poplar 'maimed, but a giant still,' 'rustling a **thankful psalm,**' as it aspires to heaven from the feverish turmoil of the city. **Perfect in** its way is the tenderness of 'Rest thee, Bonnie Doo,' a lullaby to the bonnie bairnie warm-folded under the 'white plaidie' of winter by Him who giveth snow like wool. Worthy of a compatriot of Burns are the simple song 'Jeanie, lass, I lo'e thee,' and the arch lines 'Seekin' Sympathy.' In a loftier tone is the poem on Carlyle. It is not needful that we should have an unqualified admiration for that teacher, in order to appreciate **the** ring of Mr. Henderson's verses."

DR. JOHN M. HARPER.

Such sweet, such melting strains!
Their soft harmonious cadence rises now,
And swells in solemn grandeur to its height!
Now sinks to mellow notes—now dies away—
But leaves its thrilling memory on my ear!

SWEET as the note of a bird in the wildwood, strongly imbued with patriotism, fervent in religious sentiment, eloquent in thought, pure in expression, and noble in purpose; such form a few of the characteristics of the muse of Dr. John M. Harper, the Canadian educationist and author. Many of his principal poems are of considerable length, displaying both skill and talent in their construction, while glittering through all of them, like stars in a clear midnight sky, are metaphors of rare and striking beauty. His themes, as may readily be inferred, embrace a wide variety of subjects, and we hesitate somewhat in deciding as to which of his pieces are the most suitable to include in our brief sketch, the better to enable our readers to form a just estimate of his intrinsic merits as a poet. In his poem, entitled "In Memoriam," for instance he says:

Man's strength is weakness in the face of God's;
  His stinted powers are weaker than his will;
He plans; and yet his boldest plan forbodes
  The human weakness that may not fulfil.
'Tis near his loved ones dying that he knows—
When seeking strength from every hope that blows,
  When all the tendrils of his being thrill—
That God is fate, and death his messenger,
That Christ of perfect peace is still the harbinger.

Ephemeral shine the brightest of our joys,
  Amid the clouds that float across our sky;
They're but the golden star-dust heaven employs
  To beautify man's life and destiny.
A shadow here is but no shadow there:
There is no light where all is bright and fair:
  Joys quenched reveal the living joys that lie
Around us—while a light as sweet as dawn
Plays peaceful round the shadows of the hope that's gone.

Lines like these are not the idle musings of a mere rhymist, they are the finely conceived ideas of a cultured imagination and intellect, in other words they are the work of a true poet. Among **Dr.** Harper's finest efforts are a group of poems artistically tied together under the poetical title of "Lays of Auld Lang Syne." Such poems as " The Burgh's Bells," "Sacrament Sunday," "Auld Jeames and his Crack," " Johnstone Landward," and many others are included in the group, the whole forming as fine a collection of Scottish **poetry** as one would wish to read. The introduction to the group is as follows:

> My native land, a debt of song **I** pay,
> A debt of love, that lieth on my soul,
> When memory draws the veil of bygone day,
> And olden music greets the lifting scroll.
> **A** tribute to thy freedom's faith I bring:
> The piety that scents thy glebe I sing;
> Thy purple hills whose silver mists unroll
> The waving gold of dawn; thy pleasant plains
> And hawthorn banks and braes where hamlet
> **meekness reigns.**

The first mentioned poem of this group is after the manner of Burns's " Twa Dogs," and consists of over four hundred and fifty lines, which run smoothly and harmoniously from the beginning to the end. The preface to the poem explains the purpose of the writer **thus:** " A little while ago the lieges of Johnstone, in discussing the **true** owner- ship of the fine bell that hangs in the steeple of the **parish** church, were found indulging in that warmth of expression **which** seems to arise so naturally in discussions over local affairs. In this case there were two well-defined parties, the one claiming, from facts connected with the purchase of the former occupants of the steeple, that the present bell is the property of the town, the other claiming that its ownership is vested solely in the trustees of the church. Now that the storm is over the following verses have been written with the simple intention of crystallizing the discussion. If the Doric or Scot- tish dialect be, indeed, dying out, as some declare it is, the writer, in making use of it as a literary medium, can only urge, as an excuse for his temerity, the fact that much of the discussion must necessarily have been conducted in Lowland Scotch." The poem then opens with a description of the vale of Cart, and from this we obtain a pretty fair idea of our poet's descriptive powers:

'Twas at the gloaming of a springtide day,
While sunset's golden locks were fringed with gray
Beyond the western slopes of Cartha's vale,
Beyond the isles that echo ocean's wail,
While yet o'erhead the silvery shadows fell
To shroud the glory of the day's farewell—
I sought the silent path whose slope commands
The view of burgh built on Houstoun's lands—
To spend an hour with nature in repose
Or weave a silken thought in rhyme or prose.
The moon, all radiant at the sun's retreat
In time drew near her beauty's zenith-seat,
And threw her modest veil around the scene
That peaceful glowed amid the electric sheen.
The giddy stars like courtiers unrestrained
Danced on the floor of heaven, chaotic-stained,
As if they thought their merry rays alone
Shed light enough to lustre midnight's throne.

Amid the silence of midnight the prologue of the poem is rung out by the new bell in this manner:

With a brave-hearted roll my tongue dares to toll
  And dirl a dread of the past ;
With the present still here, I shall ring out a cheer
  That no memory-cloud shall o'ercast ;
Neither grumble nor groan, neither malice nor moan
  Shall hinder my cheer-ringing mirth,
In the morn of my pride, all care I'll deride
  As I roll out the joy of my birth.

Let other bells weep generations asleep,
  As for me I shall ever ring joy ;
As I throb in my steeple, I'll stir up the people
  Full moments of mirth to employ.
So hurrah ! as I swing, as I joyously ring
  The burghers their lives to fulfil,
Let me banish all fear as their spirits I cheer
  With tones that all honest hearts thrill.

Afterward there appear before the poet's vision the ghosts of the two old bells discussing the new bell and its prospect in life. The following is a good example of the pith of the Scottish dialect, and illustrates to what a wonderful extent Dr. Harper is master of his mother tongue:

> Guid e'en, auld grannie, neebour mine,
> I needna speer what gars ye whine,
> Or glower sae angry thro' your mutch
> As if the steeple were some witch—
> As if ye'd grip'd yon gommeril's throat
> And chirt frae him his dying note ;
> For truth to tell, his giddy bouncing
> Would set auld Job himsel' aflouncing,
> But ne'er ye fash your thumb, guidwife,
> He's but a menseless nyaffin cuif,
> A trashtrie-trifler fu' o' win',
> That kens nae glory save in din.
> For us, our day is past, 'tis true,
> For lang's the time since we were new ;
> But then experience is nae vice
> Gin sense it bring as virtue's price ;
> And if auld age has cracked us baith
> Or forced us else to don ghost's graith,
> Our record's guid and weel worth hearing
> By a' that hae for guid a caring ;
> While as for boastin' Tam up yonder
> He'll nocht be but a nine day's wonder.

The two old beldames converse for some time in the most friendly manner, until disagreeing upon some point of local history their conversation breaks out into angry words. The last of the ghost's words are very human :

> Ha ! ha ! you drab, wha's angry noo ?
> Mayhap ye've gi'en my grunt a grue ;
> You wise folk canna bear defeat
> But burn your temper wi' its heat,
> Tam yonder's daft, but ye are crazy,
> Philosophy hath made ye hazy !

And the piece winds up with the writer's words:

> No more I heard beyond a dreadful *whish*
> As if the ghosts did then their anger push
> To close attack. An eerie moment passed,
> And then I shuddering rose, downcast
> With fears, and shivering in the midnight cold,
> Determined ne'er again to be so bold
> As wander near the haunts of spirit bells
> That show the weakness human hate reveals.

Glancing over the smaller poems in the group, "To a Sprig of Heather" comes peeping forth, sweet in its simple beauty, and charming us with its fragrance of other days.

> My bonnie spray o' pink and green,
>   That breathes the bloom o' Scotia's braes,
> Your tiny blossoms blink their e'en,
>   To gie me glimpse o' ither days—
> The days when youth o'er-ran the hills,
>   A-daffin' wi' the life that's free,
> 'Mid muirland music, and the rills
>   That sing their psalm o' liberty.
>
> Your wee bit threads o' crimpit fringe
>   Ance shed their fragrance in the glen,
> Whaur silence hears the burnie bringe,
>   And o'er the the scaur its prattle sen':
> And now your bonnie flow'rets blink,
>   To mind me o' the burnie's sang,
> To move my heart perchance to think
>   O' mirth that thro' the bygane rang.
>
> E'rewhile the hillside breezes kiss'd
>   The dew-drops frae your coronet,
> Or made you smile as thro' the mist
>   The peep o' day dispelled the wet :
> And now your bloom's the token sweet
>   O' freenship in a brither's heart,
> That smiles to see our cares retreat,
>   When freenship acts a brither's part.

Nor must we overlook another little poem which is hidden behind the "Sprig of Heather." It is entitled "Woo'd and Wed," and it is seldom that we come across a piece so brief and yet so daintily clothed in the sweet language of the true poet. This, with the former piece and many others of our author's lyrics, has been set to music.

> The east wind blustered in her ear,
>   The daisy shuddering drooped her head,
> Such wooing pinched her heart with fear,
>   She closed her eye and said
> "No lover true would think to harm
>   A wee bit thing like modest me ;
> I'll crouch me down and keep me warm
>   Till summer sets me free."

*   *   *   *

The zephyr whispered though her hair,
  The daisy blushing coyly smiled,
She thought to say, " How do you dare ?"
  His sighs her thoughts beguiled.
He kissed her crown, and crimson lips,
  Her tresses trembled on his crest,
But dew-drops stained her petal tips
  When Æol drove him west.

⁎   ⁎   ⁎   ⁎

The bloom of autumn woo'd her heart,
  The daisy gave her heart away.
Such loves as theirs true joys impart,
  Their life was golden day,
No thought how long such love could last,
  'Twas his upon her heart to lie,
Her matron hopes no shadow cast
  That love would ever die.

Among Dr. Harper's more serious pieces **we** have a special liking **for** the one entitled " The Old Graveyard." There is something of the quaintness and pathos of Wordsworth embodied in each verse, the **poem** altogether being full of those human sympathies that **make** the world of one kin. We append **it** herewith:

THE OLD GRAVEYARD.

The summer's day is sinking fast,
  The gloaming weaves its pall,
As shadows weird the willows cast
  Beyond the broken wall,
And the tombstones gray like sentinels rise,
To guard the dust that 'neath them lies.

The whispering breezes solemn bear
  A requiem knell-intoned,
As the steeple's throbs alarm the air,
  And through the valley sound,
To bid the weary seek repose,
When dies the day at twilight's close.

Then silken silence murmurs rest,
  And the peace that reigns supreme
Seems but awaiting God's behest,
  To wake it from its dream,
While yet it soothes the hearts that weep
Lament for those that lie asleep.

The moon, deciphering virtue's claims
    To deeds of duty done
Illumes anew the graven names,
    That time hath not o'ergrown,
Though the deeds of all are in the book,
Where time hath never dared to look.

Five generations slumber here,
    Beneath these crowding mounds,
And still their spirits hover near,
    As memory makes its rounds—
When widowed love here finds retreat,
And sympathetic echoes meet.

The first to find their rest were those
    Who saw the hamlet's birth,
When hum of industry arose,
    To blend with rural mirth—
When progress first beheld its dawn,
Near by the river's virgin lawn.

But now the glebe a surfeit knows
    Though scarce a century old,
And undisturbed the rank grass grows
    Above the tear dewed mould,
While men in thousands claim it theirs,
Where lie their kindred and their tears.

And oft 'tis here we learn to die,
    As sorrow sifts the soul,
When love's sweet longings seem to sigh,
    And with our grief condole—
To make us feel what joy it is
To know that death makes all things his.

For if tradition reads its lore
    In lines of dismal light,
Our higher hopes the tints restore
    To dissipate the night—
To courage us to think of death
A change beatified by faith.

Among our poet's sonnets, of which, by the way, there are a very great number, we come upon many that are of the very highest order of merit. Such, for instance, are the following:

TO THE **TRUE POET.**

Sweet as the sheen the dew-drops sip at dawn
  Thy purity of song hath laved my heart,
The rhythm of its light hath inward shone
  To bid the shadows from my soul depart.
As soars the lark beyond the fragrant mead
  To bear the breath of wild flowers to the skies,
  'Tis his to greet the sphere that purifies
Earth's sweetness with its own; and scattering seed
  Of scented truth upborne upon the wing
Of song, 'tis thine to seek an upper light
  Beyond life's clouds, while we upgazing sing
A timid greeting to thy venturous flight,
And long to bathe our being in the air
Where none but thee and such sweet singers dare.

LAW AND LOVE.

How pleasant 'tis to watch the sweet-mouthed tide
  Wave over wavelet kiss the golden sands,
Where, coyly moored, the dancing skiffs deride
  Its silvery crest or where the chubby hands
Of childhood dare its frolic and embrace—
  To find too late its foam a sackcloth wreath.
Even so in life, when charmed with virtue's face,
  We often learn how danger lurks beneath
For venturous love that heeds not law's restraint.
  When morning's sweetness, noonday steals away
And night distils from beauty's breath the taint
  That marks the bloom of nature, nature's prey,
'Tis then we ask why law hath love betrayed
Or why in vain our love to law hath prayed?

Dr. Harper is President of the Quebec St. Andrew's Society, an association which has long and faithfully performed its mission of caring for the needy. He is the author of several odes and poems in connection with the anniversary of their patron saint, and these have been highly spoken of and are warmly received by his countrymen everywhere. We give as a specimen of his work in this connection one of his poems which is written in the Doric and entitled:

ST. ANDREW'S DAY.

St. Andrew's Cross—nae Cross of Fire
That bids the sons of Celtic sire
    Their claymores furious draw—
With sympathetic scroll unfurled,
Hath borne its summons roun' the world,
    To greet us ane and a';
For Scotland yet anither year
    Hath added to her fame,
And friends forgather far and near
    In honor of her name ;
    And cheerfu' nor fearfu'
        Of hindrance to our mirth,
We time then our rhyme then
    In honour of her worth.

A-lowe with symphonies of hame
Our modest daffin' thinks nae shame
    To woo the winsome past ;
Our noblest joy's an honest pride
In sires, whase deeds heroic guide
    Our faith still firm and fast ;
The liberty our forbears prized,
    Though wounded oft and torn,
Now wears content its scars, baptized
    With tears for those forlorn,
    And binds a', to kinds a'
        A helping hand to len'—
    To strengthen and brengthen
        The britherhood of men.

To haud our hearts in humble vein
Fate whiles may single out our ain
    To sere with sorrow's fire,
Or, in disdain, may make a ba'
Of some puir brither, gin he fa'
    In Clootie's treacherous mire ;
But Scotia ne'er can lose her pride,
    Though fate should seem her foe,
Gin Scotsmen share, whate'er betide,
    Their joy with ithers' woe,
    To pray for, ilk' day for
        The weaker of our kind,
    Sustaining, ne'er paining
        The broken hearts they bind.

The echoes of a strife at times
Blends discord with the Sabbath chimes
    Of some sweet highland glen,
When lording's heel presumes to bruise
The liberty that aye embues
    God's bairns to make them men ;
But manhood dares its pœan raise
    To sanctify the strife,
And puts to shame the tyrant's craze
    That mars the sweets of life ;
        For blot ne'er, true Scot ne'er
            Shall thole upon the shield
        That broadly and proudly
            Protects the puir man's bield.

A tribute to our patron saint !
Love for the hearts that never faint
    In doing deeds of love !
Their pibroch is compassion's call
That sweetens hate and poortith's **thrall:**
    Their gospel's from above :
Theirs is the anthem Andrew taught—
    Fair virtue's **holiest hymn ;**
Theirs is the love that life begot
    When liberty burned dim .
        Our pride then may bide then
            By Scotia's proudest aim—
        To care for and dare for
            The love that hallows hame.

The subject of our sketch also holds the honorable position of Vice-President of the Quebec Literary and Historical Society. He has paid many a glowing tribute in verse to the genius of Burns, and we regret that these addresses are generally of so lengthy a character that we are unable to reproduce one here. We presume that it is unnecessary for us to refer to his love for "The Land of the Tartan." He reveres its every nook and corner, and is an authority on all matters pertaining to its history, customs or literature. The land where the sword of freedom has flashed in the hands of Wallace and Bruce, where the voices of Knox, Guthrie and Chalmers have rung out with gospel **truths** that have echoed around the world, the birthplace of poets, philosophers, statesmen and hundreds of intellectual celebrities, shall only become obliterated from his thoughts when life itself becomes extinct:

Hurrah for auld Scotland, **the land o'** the heather,
  Whase fragrance has scented our hearts fond o' hame,
Tis meet when her bairns in their friendships forgether
  To lilt the sweet memories that halo her name.

Hurrah for auld Scotland, the land **o'** the thistle,
  Whase motto we hold **as** the shield o' her fame;
Let us sing mid our cheer o' the men and the muscle
  That flushed freedom's **foes wi'** terror and **shame.**

Yes, hip, hip hurrah! for the land o' our forbears,
  Whase brave deeds bedizzen ilk muirland and glen!
Let us think o' their hardships mid life's many warfares,
  And face all our foes like brave-hearted men.

John Murdoch Harper was born at Johnstone, in Renfrewshire, **on** the tenth **of February,** 1845. He was reared amid comfortable **sur**roundings and early gave evidence of being in possession of bright intellectual **qualities.** He **received** the rudiments of his education at the parish **school, from whence he went to** the Glasgow E. C. Training College, **which** he entered as a Queen's **scholar of** the first rank. **He** left Scotland **for Canada** in 1867, and after several years' residence in his adopted land became a graduate **of** Queen's University. A few **years later the degree of Doctor of** Philosophy was conferred upon him by the **Illinois University.** Since that time **he has** devoted himself to educational **pursuits, and he has** achieved both honor and distinction throughout the Dominion **of** Canada as an instructor and head **of educational** institutions. He is at **present** Inspector of Superior Schools **for** the Province of Quebec, **having** been for several years Rector of the Quebec High School, and for a season interim Professor of Mathematics in Morrin College. He is **also** Secretary of the Board **of** School Commissioners and Superintendent of **the** Quebec City Schools.

He has **written and** compiled various school text **books** and in connection with general literature he is the author of historical and biographical sketches, **essays, novels,** etc., **all of** which have been published from time to time. **He** was for many years editorial writer for no less than three weekly newspapers, and he is now literary editor of the *Educational Record* of Quebec. Encomiums of a flattering nature have frequently been passed on his powers as a lecturer and public **speaker. He numbers among his personal** friends many prominent authors and scholars of the day, and with one of his sonnets of sympathy to a brother poet we will conclude our sketch:

A MOTHER'S CROWN.

Inscribed, with warm sympathy, to Duncan MacGregor Crerar, on the occasion of his mother's death.

A psalm of sympathy our hearts intone
　　To soothe the wail of sorrow's anthem weird
That wrings the soul of filial love.　She's gone!
　　She sleeps the sleep fair virtue never feared,
Howe'er the solemn change draws tears from him
　　Who was not near to see her fall asleep.
The lamp of love and sweetness ne'er waxed dim
　　That lit the chamber of her life, when deep
Within her children's souls she sought to plait
　　The golden threads of truth—to beautify
With woof of faith the yawning warp of fate,
　　And on it fresco flowers that never die.
Her sleep immortalizes love.　The crown
　　She wears, eternal shines a wreath of light.
The lustre of her saintship streameth down
　　In diamond rays to drive away our night
Of doubt—to beckon us from frailty's fears,
And melt in love the mist of mortal tears.

ROBERT WHITTET.

> While he lives,
> To know no bliss but that which virtue gives,
> And when he dies, to leave a lofty name,
> A light, a landmark on the cliffs of fame.

WHEN Robert Whittet in 1882 published his "Brighter Side of Suffering and Other Poems," he added a work to the poetical litera- ture of America which will perpetuate his memory for many years to come. Taken in whole or in part, it is a beautiful and finely conceived production, and it deserves special consideration at our hands, as it forms the longest poem so far issued by a Scottish American poet. Rich in metaphorical language, it is also sweet in expression, while a deeply religious sentiment, and a quiet, philosophic pathos pervades its every page. "In point of composition," says a well-known Scot- tish writer, "it has all that spontaneity and unbroken connection which are true indications of a full emotional nature, and a mind cul- tured to a fine vocal utterance. * * * The most casual reader cannot fail to be struck with the range of subjects suggested in every page of Mr. Whittet's book, his wealth of imagery, his keen moral perception, and above all, that fine spiritual eye that sees good in everything, and marks his principal work as one of a kind which we not only enjoy as a rich intellectual treat, but as one that tends to lighten the burdens of life, by painting in colors of unfading bright- ness the better side of human suffering."

The poem which gives the title to the work occupies two hundred and fifty-one pages, and is divided into seven chapters. Chapter one is entitled "Suffering in Nature," and, after describing the various beauties of nature, shows how these only attain a higher type of beauty by passing through the process of decay. Chapter second is devoted to "National Liberty, the Fruit of Suffering," and illustrates how liberty, both **civil** and religious, have been secured through suffering. Chapter three refers to "Suffering **in** the individual life of man," which, being universal, creates a common sympathy. Chapters four and five deal with "Suffering in individual experience;" chapter six with "The highest conception of suffering"—suffering for others—and chapter seven is a summary of the whole, and proves that the suffering **and** unsatisfactory nature of the present life implies a better life to come. As none are exempt from suffering, so none are forgotten in God's arrangements to enjoy the fruit of suffering in a future state of perfect happiness.

It will **readily** be seen from this brief synopsis of the **work that it is** one of considerable importance. It is of too lengthy a nature to **allow of** our making sufficient quotations from it that would convey to the reader a true idea of its meritorious character, **and we** will therefore content ourselves with one extract from chapter **four.** Here the author demonstrates how God's purposes **are** accomplished **alike in** the babe and in the life of three-score-and-ten:

> **But** ah! what varied ends, what varied years,
> Are strangely meted out as each one's line!
> The baby life, that, **like a** sunbeam's glint
> Is cast one moment o'er the household heart,
> As if the angelic messengers who brought
> Tarried one moment at the open door
> Until a greeting and a parting—both
> Enwrapped in one fond kiss—were given, **and then**
> Took back the gift that hope had thought would stay!
> And our fathers, bent with reverent age,
> Have only had a larger handful given
> Of that unmeasured time they've but begun—
> The first gray dawn of immortality;
> Their guardians but a little longer wait,
> **To let** earth's greetings be enjoyed awhile,
> And farewell be a little oftener said:
> But yet infinite wisdom, that can find
> Its ends accomplished **in each** atom's breath,
> Whose cloud-capped mountains are of sand-grains built,
> And ocean but a dew-drop multiplied,
> Has furnished all He first designed within
> The babe's short span, or three-score years and ten.

Mr. Whittet dedicates his work to "My wife, whose loving self-sacrifice has met and warded many of our mutual sufferings, and to our children, whose dutiful affection has been a solace in seasons of care and anxiety." In a pleasing prefatory prelude, which another poet characterizes as being " musical as the warble of a wild bird at the dawn," he says:

One linnet's note the more or less
    Within the wildwood's minstrelsy,
Can neither raise nor aught depress
    The sense of joyous revelry.

And yet each linnet from the **spray**
    His swelling notes melodious flings,
And pipes his own sweet roundelay
    Heedless of how **another sings.**

He has a song 'tis his to sing.
    And that he sings right earnestly,
And waiteth not for anything
    To urge his heart to minstrelsy.

The skylark sings where bliss belongs,
    That song an ampler field be given;
Takes to the clouds his seraph songs—
    Throws half to earth and half to heaven.

And some sweet songster, near **alight**
    On thorny perch, amid the throng,
Gives to the passing heart delight,
    And cheers it with a joyous song.

So are the songs that poets sing
    Within secluded quiet retreat,
But single echoed **notes, that bring**
    Their quota for **a choir complete.**

Each pipes his own peculiar strain,
    On artful lute or simple reed,
And sings, and sings, and sings again,
    To satisfy his own heart's need.

Yet may some raptured thought out-reach
    Far, far the poet's dream above,
And some faint wavering heart beseech
    To deeds of grace, and hope, and love.

To sing has given one heart employ,
    And thus did end enough fulfil;
But if, resung, another's joy
    Is more enlarged, 'twere better still.

And so, self-pleased, I give the song
  That's kept my own past clear and bright,
If that, perchance, some other tongue
  May lift **the lilt,** and find delight.

Interwoven in "The Brighter Side of Suffering" are smaller **poems** of great beauty and worth. We give as a specimen of these **the one** entitled:

HOME LOVE.

Oh! love is like a summer day,
  When sunny pleasures crowd;
When brightest shines the silver ray
  Nearer the thunder cloud;
But mother's love and father's care,
  Where'er our footsteps roam,
Still make our hearts the sunshine share
  Of love, sweet love at home!
    O home-love! sweet home-love!
    There's no love **like home-love;**
    Though all else may faithless prove,
    Lealty's aye in home-love.

O'er the prairie waste the wanderer
  Plods with laggard step alone;
On the billow toss'd, the mariner
  Treads his watch, even starlight gone;
And from whence, to such ones weary,
  Can a sweeter comfort come,
Than to know that hearts sit dreary,
  For their sakes, far, far, at home?
    O home-love! sweet home-love!
    There's no love like home-love;
    Wander where our footsteps may,
    We cherish still our home-love.

The bustling world to some is joy,
  Or dreams of golden gain—
What loved ones gone would deem a toy,
  Perhaps esteem as pain!
When to the mind, 'mid care and strife,
  No resting-place can come,
The balm for every ill of life
  Is surest found at home.
    O home-love! sweet home-love!
    There's no love like home-love;
    The sweetest rest for aching breast
    Is the couch of home-love.

As where the purest light is given
  The brighter are the flowers,
So when the life is likest heaven
  The purest joy is ours;
And thoughts of highest bliss are bound
  By heaven's unclouded dome,
And most of heaven on earth is found
  Around the hearth at home.
    O home-love! sweet home-love!
    There's no love like home-love;
    The purest—best—the sweetest zest,
    Is surely found **in** home-love.

But ah! beside the love of heaven,
  Earth's best we dare not name,
For there the lovers' hearts, unriven,
  Are changeless and the same;
But still earth's dearest, tenderest ties
  Nearest to heaven's standard come,
Where'er the barb of grief and sighs
  Are solaced best—at home!
    O home-love! sweet home-love!
    The purest love is home-love;
    Though all else may faithless prove
    Faithful aye is home-love.

Passing from "The Brighter Side of Suffering" we find that the rest of the volume (one hundred and thirty-three pages) comprises a collection of poems by the author on various subjects. Among them, 'Foibles," "The Kirk and State," "A Union Question," "Thought," "After the Funeral," "The Ingle Side," "The Daisies," and numerous others, are all readable and talented compositions. There are also a few sonnets displaying considerable merit. Take the following one for instance:

MY BOOKS.

I have had friends whose friendship died away,
And some, diseased by selfishness, a **day**
Was all their little life of love; some wane
Or wax as circumstances move; the main
Of all are fickle as the cloud-swept skies,
Or mists that o'er the mountain-tops arise;
But I have friends within my own home bower
Whose love no season withers: yet, no flower
Can match their sweetness; their's is far above
The wayward constancy of human love:
They are my teachers unto truth sublime,
And give for patterns hero-men of time;
Right noble friends are they—my books—whose bloom
Sheds joy o'er life from manhood to the tomb.

In addition to his English poems, Mr. Whittet has wisely included in his volume a number of his pieces that are written in the Doric. They are all of a graceful and tender character. Referring to them in his preface he says: "To his friends on the American side of the Atlantic the writer owes an apology for having inserted so many pieces written in the Scottish dialect. He trusts they may deem it a sufficient excuse that, though resident among them a good many years, and the recipient of many kindnesses, yet the recollections of the old home and the friends that are very dear, and the idiom of his boyhood still remains the most expressive, and he loves it and everything Scottish with all the stubborn tenacity of his countrymen. He has, however, toned down much of the peculiar orthography, that they may be the more easily intelligible to the American reader." We quote as a specimen of these Scottish musings:

THE FROZEN BURN.

O whare is the wee brook that danced through the valley,
 Wha's murmur at gloamin' sae sweet was to me?
Or whare are the gowans that decked a' the alley,
 And gae us, when bairnies, in summer sic glee?

O cauld cam' the rude blast that blew frae the wild hills,
 And keen bit the hoar frost and fierce drave the snaw,
And they plucked a' the sweet flowers that busket the wee rills,
 And sealed up the burnie's wee wavelets and a'.

But spring soon will come wi' its buds and its blossoms;
 The waving young leaflets will clead ilka tree,
The birdies' sweet love note will thrill frae their bosoms,
 And this snaw-covered desert an Eden will be.

The wee flowers will peep up their heads by the burnie,
 And its waters will dance in the sunbeams again,
Ilk thing that has life in't will flourish and charm ye,
 When the life now entombed shall have burst its ice-chain.

Sae man, like the burnie when summer is glowing,
 Glides on in his rapture, free, lightsome and gay;
But life has its winter, and toward us 'tis flowing,
 And soon will its rude breath freeze us in the clay.

But there is a summer the soul kens is comin',
 When life to those temples anew will be given;
Then fret nae, but cheer ye, and comfort your gloamin'—
 The grave has but planted the flowerets for heaven.

The volume concludes with a series of **poems,** entitled " Sabbath Day Communings." These are the outpourings of a sincerely Christian spirit, and **they** form as fine **a** collection of short religious **pieces as** we have ever **read.** The concluding one is as follows:

HOME SHOULD BE BEAUTIFUL.

God has reserved for us a home—
His heaven—when earthly things are done,
Its golden streets, its rainbow dome,
He keeps secure till life has run;
And while time's gliding moments **roll**
Ceaseless to the glorious goal,
He girds us daily with His love;
He's made our earth a joyous bower,
Full plenishéd with fruit and flower,
And over all revealed—(that **we**
May strive to copy faithfully)—
The pattern of His home above!
Then be it ours, while life is given,
To make earth's home like that of heaven!

Mr. Whittet is a native of Perth, where he was born in 1829. On **completing his education he was sent to learn** the printing trade, **and after working for some years in Aberdeen** and Edinburgh returned to **Perth, where he set up in business for himself.** Though in this reasonably **successful, yet the strain of** excessive competition was always a **jarring element to his sensibilities, and induced** a desire for relief **which developed into a determination to** emigrate and seek a quieter **life in rural occupation in** this country. In 1869 he purchased a plantation of some four hundred acres in Virginia, **close** by the old city of Williamsburg, and in scenes made historic by the struggles of the first settlers on this great continent; but the **venture** proved—as one less possessed of the sentiment **of an ideal life** might have expected—a disaster, and he regretfully retreated to his old occupation, in the city **of** Richmond, where he still labors, mostly in printing and publishing, **under** contract, the papers **and** literature for **the** Sunday-schools of **the** Presbyterian Church **South.** This business has since become **more largely developed, and Mr. Whittet is now** well known through**out the South as the senior partner in** the publishing firm of Messrs. **Whittet & Shepperson. He is** a warm-hearted Scotsman, and he has **won** his **way to the front by his** energy, perseverance and sturdy Scottish independence. **He** has been blessed with poetical gifts of the highest order, and he holds an unquestionable right to the title of a **true poet.**

WILLIAM MACDONALD WOOD.

> Though gay as mirth, as curious though sedate;
> As elegance polite, as power elate;
> Profound as reason, and as justice clear;
> Soft as compassion, yet as truth severe.

THE Brooklyn *Daily Times* has enjoyed a prosperous **career since** it was established in 1848. Its present editor, Mr. William Macdonald Wood, is a native of Edinburgh. **He** was born in 1847. His father, James Wood, followed the occupation of a printer, and **seems** to have been possessed of a deeply religious nature, as we learn that, while not an ordained minister, he frequently officiated as a preacher of the gospel in Kirkcaldy. His mother, Susanna Macdonald, was descended from an ancient Highland family. She was a woman of strong intellectual faculties, and our author is said to have inherited many of her distinguished qualities. Mr. Wood, after receiving what in those days was considered an excellent education, began the battle of life on his own account by becoming an apprentice to a publishing firm in his native city. Life, however, in Edinburgh seemed too slow for his ideas. At the age of twenty-one he emigrated to this country, and after travelling somewhat extensively through the South settled in New Orleans. Here **he** readily obtained **employment,** and shortly **afterward** began contributing a series of articles **on** various subjects **to the** *Edinburgh Review* which attracted considerable attention and brought his name prominently before the literary celebrities of the time then domiciled in the Scottish metropolis. He does not seem to have taken kindly to Southern life, however, although one of his friends writes that "the balmy, delicious climate and summer pomp of the South still lingers pleasantly in his memory." In a few years he came North and took up his residence in Brooklyn. Obtaining a minor position on the *Times*, his abilities as a journalist were soon recognized, and he was rapidly advanced until at length he was offered and accepted the post of managing editor. Mr. Wood composed verses from his

boyhood, and many of his early musings evince considerable talent
and skill.   Take as a specimen of this:

ACHILLEA MILLEFOLIUM.

Not by the sounding name that science wrote
  For thee, fair Yarrow, do I hold thee dear;
Yet that is precious, even as mothers gloat
  O'er honors that their darling children wear.

Fair child of summer! with thy thousand leaves
  Bordering with living green the dust brown street,
While through the emerald fringe thy blossom weaves,
  Thick clustering stars for beauty's garland meet.

In many a land—beneath the tropic's blaze,
  On Northern hills where snow-fed torrents foam—
Thy flowers have answered back my wearied gaze
  And thrilled me with soft memories of home.

And that dear stream, in whose song-honored name
  Thou, Yarrow, art baptized and consecrate;
Its steep, birch-shadowed banks remembrance claim
  Where rock-throned Newark sits in lonely state.

Oh, fairest stream! Not broader in thy course
  Than Bushkill Creek, by amorous willows kissed,
And given to gloom and darkness at the source
  By flowerless crags enveiled in tearful mist.

Fond memory hears thy hidden music rise
  Through dense wove branches from the deep ravine,
While Newark's silent towers before me rise
  (Not like its Jersey antitype, I ween).

Even there, as here, my wayside blossoms gleam,
  Flinging their odors to the hill-born gale,
Drinking their glory of their patron stream,
  And giving beauty to the birchen dale.

As in the shell the land-bound sailors hear
  The sullen roaring of the distant sea,
So Yarrow's glen, St. Mary's lonely mere,
  Are pictured, Yarrow, in thy flowers to me.

And if thy flowers, neglected and unsought,
  Are crushed beneath the ploughman's heedless tread
True lover hands shall strew, with tender thought,
  Thy blossoms o'er the summer's dying bed.

As might be expected from one whose abilities have secured for him the responsible position of editor of a daily newspaper, Mr. Wood's writings prove that he is possessed of highly cultured literary tastes. His poems display marked strength, a fanciful imagination, quiet humor, and keen descriptive powers, while, in addition to these, we find a spirit of true Christian piety hovering over and beautifying the whole of his work. Although the largest number of his pieces are written in the English language, he has given us quite a few which prove that, however cosmopolitan he may have become in his ideas, he still retains a warm place in his heart for his "auld mither tongue." The following lyrical production is a good illustration of this:

OLD AND NEW.

O dinna sing thae jingling sangs
   That tempt the graceless feet,
Wi' solemn words in daft array,
   Like guisers on the street;
But to the grand auld measures
   That fill the kirks at hame,
Sing the sweet sangs that David sang
   To strains that he micht claim.

At least let thae licht sangs be still
   On the holy Sabbath day,
Nor thrum sic evil dancin' rants
   When to your God ye pray,
Ill do sic wanton thrains
   Become the holy name,
O sound His praise in the grand old strains
   That fill the kirks at hame.

O grannie, let the bairnies sing
   As fit their lichtsome mood,
Nor let the gloom O Sinai cloud
   Their gowan-busket road,
Sweet were the auld kirk anthems,
   Where lyart elders knelt;
Yet thinkna heaven disdain'd to hear
   The laverock's gladsome lilt.

Aft have our torn an' tempted hearts
   Thrill'd to the psalmist's lyre,
An' kenned the sins an' griefs our ain
   That did his strains inspire;

But the sangs that pleased the Master,
  When this cauld world He trod,
Were the glad hosannas o' the weans
  That hailed Him as their God.

Bethink ye how our faith was wrocht
  In persecution's fires
When on the covenant anvil stern
  God fashioned out our sires
The hills that drank their life-bluid
  Echo their **martyr** psalms,
Each misty moor their children till
  Their **ragged faith embalms.**

But they have fa'en **on summer days,**
  Thae slips o' the auld tree;
Tho' covenant bluid is in their **veins**
  Nae covenant fires they dree
Theirs are lauchin' blossoms,
  The fragrant sweet-blown flowers
O' the faith bedewed wi' martyr bluod
  On Scotland's heathery moors.

Then, grannie, let the bairnies sing
  As suits their gleesome mood;
Nor let our Sinai cloud the path
  Their God wi' flowers has strewed.
When David's waes beset them
  Like us, his psalms they'll sing;
But let the loud hosannas rise
  That hail the children's king.

Among our author's various poems we also find a number of what we might term domestic pieces. These are written in simple and choice language, easily understood and long remembered. While they contain some very thoughtful and touching passages, they also possess the rare feature of never soaring into impossibilities. Such a one is "Wedded Love." It was written many years ago, but it has stood the test of time, and remains one of Mr. Wood's most admired pieces.

WEDDED LOVE.

Tradition says, **when** Stradivarius wrought—
  The idol of Cremona's golden days
  When Art's inspired evangels hymned his praise
And as a shrine his dingy workshop sought—

The Master, slowly fashioning piece to piece,
　　Surveyed with doubt and self-distrustful shame
　　The unaccorded and untempered frame
Till Time's acclaim gave to his doubts surcease.

But still he wrought, with patient, tender skill,
　　Singing his soul into each instrument,
　　And, as the mellowing seasons came and went,
These, ripening, grew responsive to his will.

For, wedded part to part in union strong,
　　Veined through with throbbing tides of harmony
　　The parts forgot their old identity,
Merged in one glorious avalanche of song.

So, wife **of** mine; returning seasons prove
　　That year by year our hearts the closer grow,
　　The old self fades as round our spirits flow
The all suffusing symphonies of love.

Eight years ago, O dearer life of mine!
　　Alone with God we stood and joined our troth,
　　Alone, though loving kinsfolk hailed our oath,
No presence felt **we, love, save mine and thine.**

We loved, as youth and maiden love, **when all**
　　Of heaven is essenced in the loved one's smile,
　　Nor conscious doubt, nor dream of hidden wile
Bade its dark shadow o'er our nuptial fall.

Yet, looking back across those happy years,
　　Seemeth not, loved one, fondly as we stood
　　On that March day, our love unripe and crude,
Waiting the mellowing touch of mingled tears ?

Heart grows to heart, and soul to soul, alone
　　When touched by common joys and common woes,
　　But self dies hard, and struggles as he goes
Though fading into bliss before unknown.

Our thoughts, O wife, are but the thought of one;
　　Our tears have flowed, our smiles as one flashed forth,
　　The years but prove to each the other's worth,
And true **love ripens with each** rising sun.

Probably the finest of all Mr. Wood's productions, however, is his poem on the famous Scottish divine, Thomas Guthrie, who died in 1873. The subject afforded him considerable scope for the exercise of his poetical powers, and he certainly made good use of the same. There is not a verse in the poem which could not stand as a true picture of Dr. Guthrie in some phase, and altogether they form, in our judgment, one of the finest eulogies ever pronounced on this noble and God-serving hero.

THOMAS GUTHRIE.

Here is one whom ye may mourn,
A man, whatever title others claim,
This ever shall his name adorn—
In every fibre of his burly frame;
In his broad, vehement speech, ablaze with thought
In every noble work his strong hands wrought,
Staunch, stubborn manhood, fit expression sought.

What was he? this gray-haired man,
Lying so still, though wet with burning tears,
Washed with orphan tears, yet wan—
Scarred with the hurricanes of storm-filled years?
An iron veteran, battle-worn and grim,
Yet love bends over him with soft eyes dim,
And hosts of homeless children weep for him.

He was a prophet of the Lord,
His lips aglow with coal from God's own altar,
And all the gold of fashion's horde
Was vain to tempt his steps to swerve or falter
From the steep path alone by duty lighted,
Bravely he went to seek the souls benighted,
Till even his tempters followed him delighted.

A man of wondrous eloquence,
Melting proud schoolmen with his glowing zeal,
And shaping intellect and sense,
As on his forge the workman shapes the steel;
Yet, scorning, like the Galilean Chief, the praise
And costly offerings of the host he sways
And caring more the outcast poor to raise.

Even as his wandering Master took
Lepers and thieves and others in His care,
Unheeding Pharisee's rebuke,
So Guthrie trod dark alley and vile stair,
And vice shrank withered from his words of fire,
And men, uplifted, shunned the drunkard's mire,
And the neglected children found a sire.

Honor to Thomas Guthrie's name!
His hearty voice is heard no more on earth,
But we are richer with his fame,
And heaven is richer with his love and mirth.
Write on his tomb that Scotland never gave
To earth a **man more** noble, kindly, brave,
Than this who rests from toil in Guthrie's grave.

Among the other notable poems of this talented Scottish poet we might mention "My Joy is Taken," "The Gaelic Race," "The Children's Festival," and his much admired tribute to the genius of John Howard Payne, the author of that imperishable lyric, "Home, Sweet, Home." One of his most cherished aspirations is the desire to compose a set of words to the air of Yankee **Doodle,** as he considers that by its audacious aggressive unconventional measure, this air constitutes itself the true American national anthem. He has "tried **his** hand," as he says, on this once **or twice,** with more or less **success.** The following will give an idea of **his work** in this direction:

Hail, O Fatherland, **to thee!**
  Hail, thou restless **giant!**
Marching on **from sea to sea,**
  Strong and self-reliant.
Laurelled with a hundred years
  Whence no shames assail thee,
Proudly still with songs and cheers
  We, thy children, hail thee.

With a thousand tongues we come
  In one anthem blended;
Faction's feeble voice is dumb,
  Ancient feuds are ended.
Gothic force and Gaelic fire
  Mingling here unhindered;
One and all we hail thee, sire,   -
  Clasping hands of kindred.

Hail to thee, America!
  Lift thy banner stainless;
Land of freedom, land of law,
  Kingless land and chainless.
Lo! the nations far that bear
  Brand of fetters feudal,
Lift their hearts in hope to hear
  The song of Yankee Doodle.

Mr. Wood commands the respect of a very large circle of literary and other friends. In his pleasant home at Manhasset, L. I., the surroundings of which he likens to "a region transplanted from the Lothian uplands," he lives at peace with the world, and serene and happy in the midst of his family and his books. Mr. Thomas C. Latto writes that "under a very gentle exterior there is a true manliness, a tender feeling, a warm love of country, native and adopted, and a genial wit and humor that would hardly be suspected by those who do not know him thoroughly." He has never ventured on the publication of a volume, but it would afford his numerous friends a sincere pleasure were they to see the announcement made that he was about to issue a collection of his poems in book form.

ANDREW WANLESS.

Whose song gushed from his heart,
As showers from the clouds of summer
Or tears from the eyelids start.

MR. WANLESS is a deservedly popular Scottish poet. He has now
been before the public as an author for upwards of forty years, and
during that time he has published many beautiful and valuable poems
that will live and be admired long after the present generation has
passed away. On the publication of his second volume of poems, he
presented a copy to Her Majesty, Queen Victoria, and in due time
received the following acknowledgment of the same. "Lieut. Gen.
Sir T. M. Biddulph has received the Queen's commands to thank Mr.
A. Wanless for sending his volume of Poems and Songs, which Her
Majesty has been graciously pleased to accept. Buckingham Palace,
Septemper 2, 1876." Mr. Wanless is now getting well on in years.
In an epistle to his friend, Mr. James McKay, of Detroit, he says :

"I'm getting unco auld and stiff,
And glow'ring ower life's dreary cliff;
'Twill no be lang or I play whiff,
    And close my e'en,
And sail awa in death's dark skiff
    To the unseen.

"Yet still I needna grunt and grane,
I'm no just in the warld alane,
I've wife and bairns to ca' my ain,
    And when I dee
Nae stranger cauld wi' heart o' stane
    Will close my e'e!"

In a short autobiographical sketch of our author, to which we have
had access, we find him saying:—"I was born in Longformacus, Berwickshire, May 25, 1824. This is near the classic Tweed and among

the Lammermoor hills, the scene of Sir Walter Scott's 'Bride of
Lammermoor.' The same locality is also mentioned in the 'Heart of
Midlothian,' when Jennie Deans, on her visit to London, informed
the Duke of Argyle that she had an aunt residing in Longformacus,
'Wha was a grand maker of ewe-milk cheese.' My father studied and
graduated from the famous University of Edinburgh. He was the
parochial teacher of the parish in which he lived for more than fifty
years. I have a vivid recollection of his intense grief when the tidings
of the death of Sir Walter Scott first reached him. He was an ardent
admirer of the wonderful ability of the famous 'Wizard of the North.'
The mind of my mother, however, was strongly tinctured with Cal-
vanistic doctrines, and she regarded the matter in a very different
light. 'Houts, guid man,' said she, 'he's weel awa'. He was just
fillin' the heads o' the folks fu' o' downright havers!'" Young Wanless
was sent to school at an early age, and received the usual education
which was supposed, at that time, to fit a lad for almost any business
calling. He gives us a pleasant glimpse of his boyhood days when he
says, "My keenest pleasure, in early life, was found in wandering
about my native land, visiting romantic haunts and burnsides. I was
always of a studious and retiring disposition, enjoying the society of
nature more than that of man. As I said in rhyme years afterwards:

> ' When floods cam' gushing down the hill
> And swelling wide the wee bit rill,
> As sure as death—I mind it still—
>   In some lone nook,
> I'd stand and learn poetic skill
>   Frae nature's book.

> 'A snow-drop on its bielded bed
> Would raise its modest virgin head,
> My very heart to it was wed
>   With nature's chain;
> And tears o' joy would o'er it shed,
>   I was sae fain!

> ' And when the bonnie spring would come,
> When bees around the flowers would bum,
> And linties were nae langer dumb
>   The woods amang,
> 'Twas there, wi' them, I learned to hum
>   My wee bit sang.'"

After leaving school Mr. Wanless was sent to Dunse where he entered upon a seven years' apprenticeship as a bookbinder. On completing his term of service he removed to Edinburgh, where he procured a position as foreman in a large bookbinding establishment. "In Edinburgh," he tells us, "I frequently met and conversed with Professor Wilson (Christopher North), Hugh Miller, Robert Chambers, Francis Jeffrey, Lord Cockburn, and many other famous literary and scientific men of their day. I also attended the School of Arts, where I acquired a knowledge of French and various other fancy accomplishments which have never been of practical benefit. My mind then, and pretty much ever since, found room only for contemplation of the songs of the old Scotch Bards."

In 1851 he emigrated to Canada, and taking up his residence in Toronto entered into business on his own account as a bookbinder. This turned out an unfortunate adventure for him, as his shop was burned one day and he was left without a penny. While in Toronto he contributed a large number of poems to the press, and published a volume which was warmly received by the public, and is now entirely out of print. In 1861 he removed to Detroit, where he once more set up in business, this time as a bookseller. Since then he has been successful in all respects, and is now one of the best known and most respected citizens of Detroit. "My career in this city is too well known to justify elaboration," he writes. "I have lived a quiet, peaceful life, and sincerely trust I have made few enemies. I have gradually surrounded myself with a large collection of old books, both standard and miscellaneous in character. I have seen many changes in the city, and have seen those whom I had learned to love drop out of the long race one by one. In 1873 I published another volume of poems which met with such favor that a second edition was demanded a year later. I have travelled extensively in this country and in Canada, reading before Scotch audiences. I have now a book in manuscript which is nearing completion, which I have called 'The Droll Book of Original Scotch Anecdotes.' I possess a remarkable memory for the folk lore with which I was familiar during my early years. I should have told you that I have been married twice and have a family of six children, all bonnie lasses." From his comfortable home in Detroit he has sent forth the majority of his finest poems. One of these, "Our Mither Tongue," was read before the St. Andrew's Society, Detroit, November 30, 1870. It at once achieved popularity both in America and Scotland, and to day is probably one of his widest-known pieces.

OUR MITHER TONGUE.

It's monie a day since first we left
    Auld Scotland's rugged hills—
Her heath'ry braes and gow'ny glens,
    Her bonnie winding rills—
We lo'ed her in the by-gane time,
    When life and hope were young,
We lo'e her still, wi' right guid will,
    And glory in her tongue!

Can we forget the summer days
    Whan we got leave frae schule,
How we gade birrin' down the braes
    To daidle in the pool?
Or to the glen we'd slip awa
    Where hazel clusters hung,
And wake the echoes o' the hills—
    Wi' our auld mither tongue.

Can we forget the lonesome kirk
    Where gloomy ivies creep?
Can we forget the auld kirk yard
    Where our forefather's sleep?
We'll ne'er forget that glorious land,
    Where Scott and Burns sung—
Their sangs are printed on our hearts
    In our auld mither tongue.

Auld Scotland! Land o' mickle fame!
    The land where Wallace trod,
The land whose heartfelt praise ascends
    Up to the throne of God;
Land where the martyrs sleep in peace,
    Where infant freedom sprung,
Where Knox in tones of thunder spoke
    In our auld mither tongue.

Now Scotland dinna ye be blate
    'Mang nations crousely craw,
Your callants are nae donnert sumphs,
    Your lasses bang them a'
The glisks o' heaven will never fade,
    That hope around us flung—
When first we breath'd the tale o' love
    In our auld mither tongue.

O ! let us ne'er forget our hame,
  Auld Scotland's hills and cairns,
And let us a' where'er we be,
  Aye strive " to be guid bairns,"
And when we meet wi' want or age
  A-hirpling owre a rung,
We'll tak' their part and cheer their heart
  Wi' our auld mither tongue.

Mr. Wanless's poems have a genuine ring that is not to be mistaken. They are deep in thought, exquisite in fancy, tender in sentiment, rich in humor, and not a few of them are of a very pathetic nature, although it must be admitted that it is only on rare occasions that he introduces anything of a gloomy or sorrowful character. Probably the best of all his pieces, in this connection, is **the** one entitled " My Bonnie Bairn," which we herewith append. It is a very touching piece of poetry and will always be ranked **as** one of his finest inspirations.

MY BONNIE BAIRN.

In my auld hame we had a flower
A bonnie bairnie sweet and fair,
There's no a flower in yonder bower
That wi' my bairnie could compare.

There was nae gloom about our house
His merry laugh was fu' o' glee;
The welfare o' my bonnie bairn
Was mair than worlds wealth to me.

And aye he'd sing his wee bit sang,
And o' he'd make my heart sae fain,
When he would climb upon my knee
And tell me that he was my ain.

The bloom has faded frae his cheek
The light has vanished frae his e'e,
There is a want baith but and ben
Our house nae mair is fu' o' glee.

I'll ne'er forget the tender smile
That flitted o'er his wee bit face,
When death came on his silent wing,
And clasp'd him in his cold embrace.

We laid him in the lonesome grave,
We laid him doon wi' mickle care;
'Twas like to break my heart in twain,
To leave my bonnie darling there.

The silent tears unbidden came,
The waefu' tears o' bitter woe,
Ah! little, little, did **I** think,
That death would lay my darling low.

At midnight's **lone** and mirky hour,
When wild the angry tempests rave
My thoughts—they **winna** bide away—
Frae my ain bairnie's **wee bit grave**.

The lyrical productions of our author **are all** refined and musical.
"**The** very language, **as he uses it**," said the *New York Scotsman*,
"makes him tender, brave, superstitious, patriotic and charitable. It
has a charm to him, and he casts its spell over his readers. In many
points he resembles Burns, in the pathos of his love songs, in his sub-
mission to and communion with the mysterious influences of nature,
and in his tender regard for the humbler forms of life." Among his
finest productions are "Home Recollections," "A Sabbath Morning
in Scotland," "Sandy Gill," "Lammermoor," "Turning the Key,'
"The Creelin'," "War and Peace," "Caledonian Games on Belle
Isle," inscribed to J. B. Wilson, Esq., "Tam and Tib," "Nan o'
Lockermacus," "The Second Sight," "Jean and Donald," "Craigie
Castle," "The Lang Tailor o' Whitby," his epistle "To A. H. Wingfield, Esq." (the author of the beautiful ballad, "There's Crape on the
Door") and "The Scott Centenary," a poem which has many admirers,
and which has been extensively re-printed by the British and Canadian
press. At the time when it was first published the *Edinburgh Scots-
man* remarked that a single line in it, viz., "And Scotland lives in
Bannockburn," contained a whole volume.

THE SCOTT CENTENARY.

A hundred years have rolled away,
This morn brought in the natal day,
Of one whose name shall live for aye.

Beside the clear and winding Forth
Was born the " Wizard of the North,"
The muses circled round his bed
And placed their mark upon his head;

And Nature sang a grand refrain
As Genius claimed his wondrous brain,
For every bird in bush or brake,
Beside the silv'ry stream or lake,
Sang blythly on their leafy throne,
In honor of the "great Unknown!"

The thistle raised its drooping head,
The lark forsook his heather bed,
Shook from his wing the dewdrop moist,
And on the golden cloud rejoic'd;
The classic Tweed took up the lay,
The Yarrow sang by bank and brae,
And Ettrick danc'd upon her way.
The daisies by the crystal wells
Smiled sweetly to the heather **bells;**
And rugged craig and mountain dun
Exulted he was Scotia's son!

Time sped, **and from that brilliant brain**
There issued many a martial strain;
He sang of knight and baron bold,
Of king and clown in days of old,
Though dead and gone, and passed away—
Forgotten in the mould'ring clay—
We read, we **trow,** his magic brain
Brings back the dead to life again!
He sang of men who ne'er would yield
In border fray or battle field.
Yes! on the page of endless fame
He wrote of many a deed and name;
How patriot heroes dared to die
For God, for right and liberty!

We see the beacon on the hill,
The slumb'ring earth no more is still,
For borne upon the midnight gale
The slogan's heard o'er hill and dale,
The din of battle and the cry
That echoed through the vaulted sky,
As warriors fell and rose **and** reel'd,
And died on Flodden's fatal field!

The minstrel loved auld Scotland's hills,
Her gow'ny braes and wimpling rills,
He loved the land that gave him birth—
A land beloved o'er all the earth;

There stood the brave in weal or woe,
Who never crouched to foreign foe—
Who stood in battle like a rock,
And snapped in twain the **tyrant's yoke!**

O ! Scotland, thou art dear to me!
Thou land of song and chivalry!
There Scott and Burns and many more,
Did pencil nature to the core—
There Wallace held the foe in scorn,
And Scotland lives in Bannockburn!
And every patriot, far or near,
In foreign land, or Scotia dear,
In castle proud, or lowly cot,
Reveres the name of WALTER SCOTT.

Mr. Wanless, from his very earliest years, has been strongly imbued
with a love for the ancient traditions and folk-lore of his native land,
and he has skilfully woven a few of the former into very tender
ballads. **Nearly all of his pieces are** written **in the** Scottish dialect.
He possesses an intimate knowledge of the Doric, and he uses it in
all its purity and simplicity. **Among** the few pieces which he has
composed in **connection** with **American** subjects, his poem on the late
Gen. Ulysses S. Grant, was both timely and appropriate.

When reason was banished, and **treason arose,**
And brother 'gainst brother dealt death-dealing blows,
And the words came as one from the lips of the brave—
" The flag of our fathers forever must wave; "
And a hero arose in the midst of our woe,
" Forward! " he **cried " we must** vaquish the foe; "
But there's gloom on the earth, and there's gloom in the **skies,**
And the light burns dim in the room where he lies.

The foe is advancing—every effort they **strain,**
But back they are hurled again and again,
And the shout of the Victor is heard in the air:
" While Liberty **lives we shall never despair ;"**
And the hero looks round on the death-striken field,
" **We must conquer** or die, but we never will yield,"
But **there's gloom on** the earth, and there's gloom in the **skies,**
And the light burns dim in the room where he lies.

The sword's in the scabbard, the warfare is o'er,
May the din of the battle be heard never more;
And now through the length and the breadth of the land,
May brother meet brother with heart and with hand;
May the past be forgot and may bitterness cease,
And the watchword be ever: "Come let us have peace!"
But there's gloom on the earth, and there's gloom in the skies,
And the light has gone out in the room where he lies.

No sketch of Mr. Wanless and his writings would be complete without referring specially to his patriotic feelings and unconquerable love for the land that gave him birth. His muse has been used for no mercenary purposes, but simply, as he informs us in the preface to one of his published volumes, "To recall the scenes of our early years, to bring up in imagination the braw lads and bonnie lasses that we forgathered with in the days of the lang syne, and attempt to describe, on this side of the Atlantic, the wimpling burns, the gowany braes, the bonnie glens, the broomy dells, and the heather-clad mountains of our native land: the land where Wallace and Bruce wielded the patriotic sword, and where Ramsay, Burns, Scott, Tannahill and many more sang the songs of love and liberty." Nor do the feelings of the gifted Bard become in any way changed while age begins to twine the white locks around his venerable forehead. Only a few weeks ago he composed the following :

WHA DARE MIDDLE ME?

Scotland! how glorious is the theme,
  That in the days by gone,
Your patriot sons undaunted stood
  And battled for their own.
Time after time the foe advanced
  Your rights to trample down,
To blot your name forever out,
  And grasp your royal crown.

Your sons could never bow the knee,
  Nor brook the tyrant's chains,
Nature had written on your hills—
  "Here freedom ever reigns."
Sons of the brave! your hearts were one,
  That Scotland must be free,
Now far and near the cry is heard—
  "Wha dares to middle me?"

Forward! see Scotland's gallant sons
   Dash on to meet the foe,
Their strong right hand grasps freedom's sword
   And freedom guides the blow.
Their bows are bent, their swords are keen,
   And with their matchless might,
Strongly they stand to crush the wrong,
   And battle for the right.

The battle rages fierce and fell,
   Till o'er the deadly fray,
The welkin rings—"the victory's won!"
   Scotland has won the day.
While heather blooms on Scotland's hills,
   And while her thistles wave,
Freedom will flourish on her soil,
   And guard the warrior's grave!

Every verse of this song burns with intense patriotism for the land of his birth, and it is entitled to stand side by side with Henry Scott Riddell's immortal song " Scotland Yet." The Scottish language is peculiarly adapted to touch and enoble the finer feelings of our nature. In view of this, and in conclusion, we quote from our author's writings the two following kindly and homely lyrics, the last of which, it may be stated, appeared in a late issue of the *Detroit Free Press:*

ROBIN.

I hae a bird, a bonnie bird,
   And Robin is its name,
'Twas sent to me, wi' kindly words,
   Frae my auld Scottish hame.
And when it cam' unto my hand
   It looked sae dull and wae,
Nae doot it miss'd the flow'ry glen,
   The burnie and the brae.

There's mair than you, my bonnie bird,
   Hae cross'd the raging main,
Wha mourn the blythe, the happy days,
   They'll never see again.
Sweet bird! come sing a sang to me,
   Unmindfu' o' our ills;
And let us think we're ance again
   'Mang our ain heather hills.

The joyfu' hours o' nameless bliss,
  O, come ye back to me;
My love, my lost, again we meet
  Aneath the trysting-tree.
O, sing to me, my bonnie bird,
  And ilka note o' thine
Will conjure up the gladsome days—
  The joys o' auld lang syne.

COME HAME.

My love, my beautiful, my own,
  I'm sitting a' **alane;**
O, how I long to hear your step
  And welcome you again.
There's neathing now looks bright to me,
  The sunshine's left my ha',
There's nae ane now to cheer my heart
  Since ye hae gane awa'.

The sun's gane doon ayont the hill,
  And night steals slowly nigh—
'Tis gloomy night, the weary winds
  Around me moan and sigh.
My love! at midnight's silent hour
  I saw thee come to me,
I saw thee in thy youthful bloom
  Come tripping o'er the lea.

I woke to find it but a dream,
  A vision of the night—
Come hame, come hame, my darling, come,
  Come hame my heart's delight.
O, come again, my life, my love,
  And fill my heart with glee,
The whisp'ring winds no more will sigh
  When ye come back to me.

ALEXANDER H. WINGFIELD.

Over the harp, from earliest years belov'd,
He threw his fingers hurriedly, and tones
Of melancholy beauty died away,
Upon its strings of sweetness.

"IN these days," writes Mr. Wingfield, "the notion prevails that
poetry, like miracles, has ceased, and it requires a certain amount of
courage for an individual unknown to fame to come forward and say,
varying the memorable expression of a great painter, that he too is a
poet. This is the age not only of mechanical invention, supposed to
be the very antithesis of poetry, but—more dreadful still—of criticism;
the terrors of which makes timorous poets pause. Homer and Milton
stood in no dread of reviewers; though, to do justice to our own time,
it must be added that they were at certain disadvantages for want of
publishers. We are most of us conscious of a belief that poetry was
to be looked for as a matter of course in days gone by, when shepherds
piped by the banks of classic streams, and when scholars assembled in
academic groves; or when in more recent times our own poets found
inspiration by lake and mountain, around some

'Sweet Auburn, loveliest village of the plain,'

or in meditative quiet and solemn stillness of the country churchyard.
But can poetry be born amid the noisy rattle of the loom, the birr of
wheels, the clang of hammers, the screaming whistle and thundering
rush of the locomotive?" In answer to this we unhesitatingly reply
yes, and in confirmation of our opinion we have only to point to the
volume which Mr. Wingfield published a few years ago, a volume that
is replete with poems and lyrical pieces of a very high order of merit,
and all of which were composed amidst the din and clatter of the
Great Western Railway boiler shop at Hamilton, Ontario. There are,
indeed, many excellent specimens both of Scottish and English verse
in this volume, and each piece seems to have been composed with a
special purpose in view which necessitated their being carefully thought
out before being committed to the world. Mr. Wingfield, however,

is very **modest in regard to** the merit of his different poems. **"If** there be poetry in them," he says, "it is such as comes from homely, natural inspiration, unaided either by varied reading or literary leisure. **As I have** really felt, or believed, **or** imagined, so have I written; and **whatever** faults of expression there may be in my efforts, there is **no** failure in honesty **of** intention. Having neither read much **nor** travelled far, nor been able to put the world of nature and of history under contribution, I have found my subjects chiefly among **the** familiar scenes and every-day experiences of my own humble walk **in** life; taking such color and impression of them as residence in a **busy** city like Hamilton could not fail to present." **His** muse has **thus** dwelt on various subjects and to show the kindly nature of the man and his feelings toward **even the** smallest of God's creatures, we **pre-** sent **our** readers with **his well-known** address of **welcome to the** sparrows:

Ye're welcome, wee sparrows, ye're welcome to **me;**
You mak me as happy as e'er I can be ;
When I hear you chirp, chirpin', an' see ye sae tame,
You **just** aye look to me like kenn'd faces frae hame.

There are some canna bear ye, an' say that ye steal,
An' fecht wi' your neebors at times like the deil;
An' they hope ye may meet wi' a' sorts o' ill luck,
But I like ye—ye're emblems of true British pluck.

D'ye ever turn hame-sick at nicht when at rest
(The lot of an exile is ne'er very blest);
D'ye think o' the **times** ye've had fleein' aroun'
Wi' the cronies you left, baith in kintra an' toon ?

D'ye e'er min' the hedge-rows, whaur often at e'en,
Ye hae woo'd your blithe mates near whaur Burns woo'd his Jean;
An' ye heard the sweet sang o' the lark in the morn,
As he rose up dew-winged frae his nest 'mang the corn?

D'ye min' the green hawthorns an' red-shinin' ha's,
That you feasted on aft by the auld castle wa's ?
I doubtna, wee birdies, ye whiles mourn like me,
For the hame ye hae left far awa owre the sea.

Ye gar me think o' days when a bairn at the schule,
I hae hunted an' chased you wi' hearty guid-will;
When ye fleed frae my steps away up on the trees,
I hae staned you wi' **vigor—I winna tell lees.**

I hae harriet your **nests wi'** the rest **o'** my chums,
An' hae often enticed ye wi' wee bits of crums
To come down frae your young ones, baith early an' late,
An' then trapp'd ye wi' glee wi' three bricks and a slate.

But those times are changed noo—altho', to my min',
I have never seen happier anes e'er sinsyne;
For the wrangs I hae dune ye in life's early day,
Fain, fain wud I noo wi' some kindness repay.

I am wae when I think o' the lang winter days
Ye'll be happin aroun' on your wee, frozen taes;
Guid kens whaur ye'll get **your bit** pickin's **ava,**
When the earth is laid under **its mantle o' sna'.**

I'm no blest wi' owre much ; I've but little to spare ;
Yet, there's naethin' I hae but wi' you I wud share ;
If ye e'er fin' your way whaur my wee hoosie stan's,
You are aye sure o' something at least frae my han's.

Thro' the cauld winter days may ye meet wi' nae harm ;
May ye aye fin' a beild to jouk in frae ilk storm ;
May the raven's Provider tak care of ye a',
Till the blithe simmer comes an' the **winter's awa.**

Mr. Wingfield **expresses his sentiments in clear** and chaste language,
and while through many of his poems there runs a rich vein of innocent
humor, or of manly independence which makes them enjoyable at all
times, still, it is in his serious pieces we think that his poetical powers
are displayed to the greatest advantage. All of these musings are
simple and full of words of sympathy. They are written from the
heart, and they appeal directly to the heart, and in no instance do we
discover in their composition a mere straining after effect. Take his
"Crape on the Door," for instance. It has truly been said that who-
ever could compose lines like the following was capable of greater
efforts, and we yet look for something from Mr. Wingfield that will
place his name among the poets who have achieved a world-wide
fame:

CRAPE ON THE DOOR.

There's a little white cottage that stan's 'mong the trees,
Whaur the humming-bird comes to sip sweets wi' the bees,
Whaur the bright morning-glories grow up o'er the eaves,
And the wee birdies nestle among the green leaves.
But there's something around it to-day that seems sad—
It has'na that look o' contentment it had;
There is gloom whaur there used to be sunshine before;
Its windows are darkened—there's crape on the door.

There is crape on the door—all is silent within;
There are nae merry children there making a din;
For the ane that was merriest aye e' them a'
Is laid out in robes that look white as the sna'.
But yesterday morn, when the sun shone so bright;
Nae step bounded free'er—nae heart was mair light;
When the gloamin' cam' round, a' his playing was o'er,
He was drowned in the burn—sae there's crape on the door.

Nae mair will he skip like a lamb o'er the lea,
Or pu' the wild flowers, or gang chasin' the bee;
He'll be miss'd by the bairns when they come hame frae schule,
For he met them ilk day coming down o'er the hill.
Beside his wee coffin his lone mother kneels,
And she breathes forth a prayer for the sorrow she feels;
Her puir widowed heart has been seared to the core,
For not lang sinsyne there was crape on the door.

Her sobs choke her utt'rance, **though** she strives, but in vain
To stifle her grief, or her tears to **restrain;**
Yet she lovingly murmurs, " I winna repine ;
Thy will be done Father ; Thy will and not mine;
Though my trials are great, yet I winna complain;
For I ken that the Lord has but ta'en back His ain,
To dwell wi' the angels above evermore
Whaur there's nae sin nor sorrow, nor crape on the door."

Among our author's other serious pieces, "The Last Farewell,"
" The Widow's Wail," "Wee Tot," "Our Wee Jeannie" and " Not
Lost, but Gone Before," are all poems of a beautiful and touching
nature, and prove that he is possessed of a tender and Christian heart.
The last named piece was composed on the death of a favorite child,
and as it has been considerably spoken of we reprint it here:

NOT LOST, BUT GONE BEFORE.

We've nae wee Lily noo, Maggie,
  We've nae wee Lily noo;
Death's laid his cauld, damp, icy, han'
  Upon her bonnie broo,
That broo whaur gowden curls played,
  Aboon her een o' blue.

'Twas destined sae to be, Maggie,
  'Twas destined sae to be;
That God should tak' awa the gift

He gied to you and me ;
'Twas hard to part wi't ; sorrow's aye
A bitter thing to dree.

She looked some like yoursel, Maggie,
    She looked some like yoursel ;
How much I lo'ed her, nane but He
    Wha kens our hearts can tell.
We will not murmur at His will,
    He doeth all things well.

We'll miss her unco sair, Maggie,
    We'll miss her unco sair ;
But she has gane whaur grief and pain
    Will never reach her mair ;
Whaur flowerets bloom and shed perfume
    In Heaven's garden fair.

We will not mourn her noo, Maggie,
    We will not mourn her noo;
She isna lost, but gane before—
    Just hidden frae our view ;
She's better aff than she could be,
Were she still here wi' you.

We'll meet wi' her again, Maggie,
    We'll meet wi' her again,
When we hae passed thro' death's dark vale,
    And crossed o'er Jordon's plain ;
'Mang ither lammies in Christ's fauld
    We'll see our ain wee wean.

Passing from Mr. Wingfield's serious pieces, we come upon many
displaying a humorous sentiment, to which is not unfrequently combined a little well-directed satire.   There is not a word or a line in
any of these pieces, however, that could offend the taste or hurt the
feelings of any one.   This in itself is deserving of note.   "That he
has penned nothing," says the *Hamilton Evening Times*, "that can
lower or vulgarize life in any of its relations, nor even pandered to
irreligion or sensuality, is something to feel honestly proud of, for, in
these days of sensationism, even poets of mark not unfrequently
sacrifice morality and purity in their craving for a certain kind of
popular sympathy."   A good specimen of his humorous writings is:

A SHILLIN' OR TWA.

Friendship has charms for the leal an' the true,
There's naething can beat it the hale warl thro',
But ye'll gey aften fin' that the best friend ava
Is that white-headed callan a shillin' or twa',
Eh, **man,** it's a fine thing, a shillin' or twa,
Hech, man, it's a gran' thing, a shillin' or twa',
It keeps up your spirits, it adds to your merits,
If ye but inherit a shillin' or twa.

It's surprisin' how much you'll be thocht o' by men,
You'll get credit for wisdom altho' ye hae nane,
Tho' ye'r but a dunce ye'll be honored by a',
When they ken that ye hae a bit shillin' **or twa.**
Eh, **man, it's a fine** thing, a shillin' or twa,
Hech, man, it's a gran' thing, a shillin' or twa,
Ye'll ne'er ken what it means to want plenty of frien's
Gin ye glamour their e'en **wi'** a shillin' or twa.

But it alters the case when your pouches are toon,
An' your credit's a' gane an' nae wab in the loom,
Be sure then ye'll get the cauld shoulder frae a',
If ye ask for the lend o' a shillin' or twa.
Eh, man, it's a fine thing, a shillin' or twa,
Hech, man, it's a gran' thing, a shillin' or twa,
But there's no mony then that will haud out their han'
An' say, "here, my man, there's a shillin' or twa."

There are some that for siller wud swap their auld shoon,
There **are** some that wud cheat for't it and ne'er ca't a **sin,**
An' there are some sae devoid o' morality's law,
Wud shake han's wi' the deil **for a shillin' or twa.**
Eh, man, it s a fine thing, a shillin' or twa,
Hech, man, it's a gran' thing, a shillin' or twa,
To become rich an' great, an' hae flunkeys to wait,
When ye drive out in state aff your shillin' or twa.

But we scorn the fause loon that for vain worldly pelf
Wud wrang ither folks to get riches himself,
Aye live an' let live, an' do justice by a',
An' may you ne'er want for a shillin' or twa.
Eh, man, it's a fine thing, a shillin' or twa,
Hech, man, it's a gran' thing, a shillin' or twa,
I've aften been scant o't, and weel ken't the want o't,
But now, Gude be thank't for't, I've a shillin' or twa.

From a poet like **Mr.** Wingfield we naturally look **for** many pieces chronicling the deeds or extolling the virtues of his native land, and our expectations in this respect are largely realized.   He is continually **singing** of her hills and glens, woods and streams, people, history and religion.   While he says:

> Oh, Canada! I lo'e thee weel!
>   Altho' nae son o' thine
> Within thy wide domain there beats
>   Nae truer heart than mine.

Yet the home of **his infancy is ever in his** thoughts, and **it** seems impossible for him to **resist the temptation to** write about her.   Here is one of his numerous pieces **on this subject:**

THE CALEDONIAN.

> There's a land where the heather and thistle wave,
>   Where the foot of a slave ne'er trod,
> **Where the blue bells** bloom o'er her martyrs' grave
>   **And** hallowed is that sod.
> There's a land whose sons are staunch and brave,
>   Whose hills are lofty and grand,
> Whose shores are kissed by the blue sea **wave,**
>   And Scotia is that land.
>   'Tis an honored place that same proud land,
>   The home of the Caledonian.
>
> **There's a land whose bards have struck their lyres**
>   To none **but the** loftiest strains,
> Whose inspiring tones would call forth fire
>   From the dullest coward's veins.
> There's a land where noble Wallace fell,
>   The first in freedom's van,
> Whose name still sounds like a magic spell—
>   And Scotia is that land.
>   'Tis teaming with heroes that mountain land,
>   **The** home of the Caledonian.
>
> All other lands the palm must yield
>   To Scotia's daughters fair;
> And in the tented battle-field
>   Her sons are foremost there;
> Her tartan-plaided warriors
>   Have climbed the steeps of fame;
> Their daring deeds the wide world o'er
>   Have earned a deathless name.
>   'Tis a nation of heroes—deny it who can,
>   The home of the Caledonian.

> The Scotsman need not blush to own
>   The land that gave him birth
> For her name is known from zone to zone
>   As the noblest spot on earth.
> Should the foot of a foe e'er dare to tread
>   On that little land of the free,
> The thistle would raise his stately head
>   Saying "You mauna meddle wi' me."
>   It's a sturdy plant that guards our land
>   The pride of the Caledonian.

Alexander **H.** Wingfield was born in 1828, at Blantyre, Lanark-shire, Scotland, **in a** house situated a few doors from the one in which Dr. Livingston, the celebrated African **traveller,** first **saw** the light. His parents removed to Glasgow **when** he was **six weeks** old, and he received little or no education, **as** he was **sent to** work in a cotton **factory** before he had reached his tenth birthday. He may therefore claim, and deserves' credit for being in **all respects** a self-made man. In 1847 he emigrated to America and settled **in** Auburn, N. **Y., but** three years later he went to Hamilton, **Ont.,** where he worked as a mechanic for eighteen years on **the** Great Western Railway. For the past eleven years he has held **a** responsible position in the Canadian Customs Department. His **name** is now a familiar one throughout **Canada.** That his muse had long been appreciated by the public may **be** surmised **when** we state that within **ten** days after the first copy of his book was ready the expense of **the** whole work was paid out of the sale of it, and the entire edition, consisting of fifteen hundred copies, was disposed of in the short space of seven weeks. The book is now **out of** print, and stray copies are eagerly picked up at advanced prices wherever they are offered for sale. He does not seem to have composed much of late, and in concluding our sketch we would say to him in the words of his illustrious friend, Mr. Andrew Wanlass:

> "Though grief has racked you to the core,
> Take up your harp—sing as in yore;
> Ye still hae monie joys in store—
>   I hope and pray
> That crape may ne'er hang on your door
>   For monie a day!"

MALCOLM TAYLOR, JR.

I've scanned the actions of his daily life
With all the industrious malice of a foe ;
And nothing meets mine eyes but deeds of honor.

MALCOLM TAYLOR, JR., poet and dramatist, is a native of Dundee, where he was born in 1850. Coming to this country with the other members of his family in his tenth year, he was given a careful education, and his boyhood glided peacefully into manhood surrounded by all the pleasures and comforts of a happy and moral home. On completing his studies he was sent to learn the plumbing trade, but this proving distasteful to him, he abandoned it and entered into commercial engagements which suited him better.

There are few Scotsmen in this city better known or more respected than Malcolm Taylor, senior, the father of our poet. He is blessed with very fine musical qualities, and his singing of many of the old Scotch songs is a rare treat even to those persons who do not hail from the land of the mountain and the flood. Previous to his selecting a home for his family in the new world he was precenter of one of the principal churches in Dundee, besides being leader for many years of the Dundee Choral Union.

Our author at an early age gave ample evidence of possessing true poetic gifts. His mind, even at school, was completely wrapped up in poetical matters, and his sole ambition at one time was to become a great poet. We have had the pleasure of reading a number of his early musings, and there is no doubt that they display genuine talent, not only in their versification, but also in their ideas and general construction. They are bright and musical, and always of a pleasing character. Take the following one, for instance. It was written in his fourteenth year and published in a well-known New York weekly newspaper:

LOVE'S QUESTIONING.

Do you love me? Tell—
  Does your heart swift beat
And your bosom swell
  When I talk so sweet?
Does a sudden thrill
  Of estatic bliss
Your whole body fill
  When our lips they kiss?

Do you love me? Tell—
  In your memory
Does there always dwell
  Pleasant thoughts of me?
Do hours like days seem
  When I am not nigh?
Of me do you dream
  When in sleep you lie?

Do you love me? Tell—
  Do you love sighs heave
When I say farewell?
  And then when I leave,
Do you linger still
  The doorstep upon,
Watching me until
  From sight I am gone?

Do you love me? Tell—
  When you hear the chime
Of a marriage bell,
  Long you for the time
When we too shall stand
  At the altar's side,
Linking hand in hand,
  Having love's knot tied?

Do you love me? Tell—
  Love me fond and true?
In your looks I spell,
  What tells me you do;
But, just to be heard,
  Whisper in my ear
That one simple word
  I so long to hear.

Do you love me? **Tell—**
  Why still are you **dumb?**
Known the answer well,
  But yet let it come.
Do you love me? Speak—
  Darling now confess!
Ah! that blushing cheek!
  Your reply is—" Yes."

Nor was it in his English compositions alone that Mr. Taylor, through his early efforts, gave promise of one day attaining a prominent position among the poets. He seems to have written many pieces in his mother tongue which obtained considerable popularity for him among his countrymen. Here is a little Scottish lyric which he composed in his fifteenth year and which proves that even at that age he possessed an intimate knowledge of the Doric:

BONNIE GIRZIE O' GLENBRAE.

Leeze me, lassie, but I lo'e thee,
  And my thochts run like a sang,
As the burn adoon the corrie,
  Louping wi' sheer joy alang.
Gin ye knew their sang by hairt, love,
  And would lilt the simple lay,
Oh, how happy wad it mak' me,
  Bonnie Girzie o' Glenbrae.

'Mang the lave thee only lo'e I,
  And my hairt is like a bloom,
As a gowan on the haugh-side,
  Bursting wi' love's pure perfume;
Wad ye wear my modest posy
  On thy bosom, blest for aye,
It would yield its inmost spirit,
  Bonnie Girzie o' Glenbrae.

Wad ye sing my thochts, my dawtie,
  Yours wad lilt fond symphony;
Wad ye wear my hairt-bloom ever,
  Yours wad fellow-blossom be;
Sweet wi' joy and love enduring,
  Song and bloom wad blend alway,
Livin' melody and fragrance—
  Bonnie Girzie o' Glenbrae.

On comparing the above pieces **with any** of our author's more recent productions **we** will **at** once notice the advancement which he has **made.** He has certainly cultivated his talents very carefully and the result is that his muse is now vigorous, inspiring and scholarly. **In** addition **to** this there is a love of nature and a purity of feeling embodied in and adding a lustre to all of his later work that is not to be found in any of **his** earlier compositions. Take a poem entitled " Hyacinth," which **he composed a few years ago and** we will **readily** note the difference: .

> In the body-bulb buried low, and hid
>   From the glint of human eye, and sun,
> **Like a** lifeless corse 'neath a coffin-lid,
>   Longing to rise, with freedom won,
> Lies the Hyacinth, awaiting the birth
>   From a dormant state, which is as death,
> Till Nature's Christ comes on the earth,
>   And resurrects it with living breath.
>
> As a vague, dim hint of a day **to come,**
>   In time now looms, from the dark, dank mold,
> A tip of green, striving, slow and dumb,   .
>   With feeble force its powers to unfold;
> And soon on the surface spread vernal arms,
>   That embrace the air and caress the light,
> Till the centre stalk feels life's fond charms,
>   And rises in majestic might.
>
> **Then a** cluster of stars shoot into view,
>   Petaled Pleiades to gem the ground,
> And lend their sheen of tender hue
>   To illume the varied scene around;
> Whilst the eyes and lips of the budding head
>   The smiles and breath of love give free,
> On the air the wealth of its soul to shed,
>   To live in the mind eternally.
>
> Thus the poet's soul, innate and **cold,**
>   Awaits the call of Nature's God
> **To** burst from its gyves of human mold,
>   And peer above the insensate sod.
> First, looming up, one struggling thought
>   Finds expression, as the hint of green;
> Then his mind, with ardent feelings fraught,
>   Aspires to reach to heaven serene.

Soon his fancies teem to a budding head,
  And crown his brain, as a group of stars,
Their lustre rare around to shed,
  To charm the sense in rhythmic bars;
While his thoughts, like arms, stretch wide apart,
  The sum of love and life to embrace,
And his lips and tongue give voice to his heart
  In a song that time cannot efface.

Mr. Taylor revisited Scotland in 1874, and while there contributed numerous articles and poems to the *New York Scotsman*. One of the latter, a lengthy poem, entitled "Mountain Musings," appeared in serial form and was universally admired. Another lengthy descriptive poem which he composed in the Highlands, entitled "In the Wilderness," was published in *Human Nature*, a well-known London literary magazine, and commanded a great deal of praise from the critics of the English metropolis. A brief excursion through Ayrshire further inspired his muse and called forth a very fine poem on Robert Burns, from which we make two extracts:

Now let me, with my pen's weird wand, forsooth,
  Waive by the windings of his young life path,
  The petty trials he had, as each child hath,
Till soon we see him as a reaper youth;
When, bending low beside some winsome Ruth
  To bind with wheaten gyves the levelled swath,
  Or gathering up the golden aftermath.
He tried to sing the love he felt in truth;
  Then woke the poet's spirit in his form,
Moved was his hand to touch the latent chords
That longed to give expression fair in words
  To what his heart felt in affection warm;
And as he told his love in lilted line
He wooed the willing Coila, muse divine.

       *   *   *   *   *

And now behold him, Fashion's pampered child!
  The Pet of wealth! The social board around
  His favored friends did reverence profound,
While he, with his own songs, the time beguiled
Till, with that Circe, Pleasure's draught grown wild
  Our laverock Rab soon had his sad rebound
  And, faulty, fell back to the common ground,
To sink from sight, in poverty exiled;

But though was smirched with shame in touching dross
The form that housed his soul, above mere pelf;
Yet crushed not was the better part of self;
　From human failings suffering no loss
His songs lived on and lingered, still sublime,
Throuh all the echoing corridors of Time.

In 1878 Mr. Taylor was united in marriage to Mrs. R. E. Scher-
merhorn, an accomplished lady who had already won distinction for
herself as the first lady attorney of the city of Rochester.　During the
following five years he resided at their magnificent house, Cascade, on
the beautiful shore of Owasco Lake, in central New York.　While
located here he ventured into the dramatic field, and many of the
plays which he has since written have met with phenomenal success.
His "Auld Robin Gray," a dramatization of the celebrated ballad of
that name, was pronounced by Mr. James H. Stoddart, the eminent
actor, to be one of the finest Scotch pastoral plays that he had ever
read.　The above, with some of his other dramas, such as " The
Afflicted Family," " Rags and Bottles," and "Aar-u-a-goos " have been
published, and are played with great success throughout the United
States each season.　Through the channel of his dramatic writings
our author gradually drifted into the theatrical profession, and he now
holds a prominent and resposible position in one of the best paying
theatres in central New York.　While cultivating the good graces of
Thalia and Melpomene, however, he did not altogether forget his old
love.　While he may have neglected his muse for the time being, yet
the following recently composed sonnets will prove that she still
lingers within his reach willing to be wooed by him at all times:

LOVE'S SUMMER.

You ask me am I lonely?　Not at all
　Though thick the dun October clouds may loom
　And wild winds cry around the wail of doom
That summer's vernal foliage finds its fall,
I mourn not, having thee.　If, like a pall,
　The storm does gather close about, in gloom
　To shroud me, livened by the June-like bloom
That seems to spring up at thy cheery call,
The earth, that otherwise would serve to load
　My heart with heaviness, at prospects sad,
　Now seems a very paradise, so glad
My spirit is.　With thee to walk the road,
　Though knowing that it led to regions dark,
　Still would I on such journey fain embark.

And why? Because the light from out thine eyes
  Makes shining bright the scene with sunny smiles,
  And thy rich laugh, like bird-trill, still beguiles
The passing hour with music, while fast flies
Each feathery warbler unto warmer skies,
  Each blush-rose that my word-warmth without wiles
  Brings into bloom upon thy cheek, **denials**
To no great purpose, as fair flowers apprize
Me that my **love** finds soil within thy breast;
  Hence in thy presence summer ever stays,
  Since smile, and laugh, **and** blush, always
Are sun, and bird, and flower to me most blest,
  And this is why, **in seasons** dark or bright,
  I in thy company still find **delight.**

Among Mr. Taylor's poems not already referred to, "A Four-Leaf Clover," "Six Kisses," and "The Violet's Death" are worthy of special mention on account of their meritorious character. The two latter are poems of considerable length, but they contain many noble passages, together with numerous lines of genuine poetry. His verses addressed to **"Auld Kirk Alloway" are** in excellent taste and will always **be kindly remembered by Scotsmen** in connection with this illustrious old ruin.   We quote a few verses:

The wild rose decks your broo in spring,
Aroun' your form the ivies cling
Like memories dear, while linties sing
  Their leal love's praise,
As Rab did his, meandering
  On Doon's green braes.

    *   *   *   *

Your wa's still stan', though roofless lang,
And wi' carse, crumblin' cild nae strang,
Sin' syne your bell in peal has rang,
  Fu' mony a wight
Has joined the dust frae whence he sprang,
  An' gane frae **sight.**

    *   *   *   *

As lang's the lays the ploughman sung
To chords o' Coila's lyre, love-strung,
Repeated are by human tongue,
  Fame to prolong,
Ye will be known foremaist among
  The kirks o' song.

When time is done, the poem divine,
Ilk age a verse, ilk year a line,
In nae ae stanza will there shine
  A brichter name,
Than his, wha gied ye, ruined shrine
  Your storied fame.

Sae fear nae, though **you're fallin' fast**
Ye will be to oblivion cast,
For while the mind o' man does last,
  In comin' day
Ye'll live in glory o' the past,
  Kirk Alloway!

It will readily be seen from these specimens of the poetical writings of Mr. Taylor that he possesses all the qualifications of a very fine poet. He is just entering upon the prime of manhood, and we feel confident that if he would concentrate his powers upon some one subject he would yet produce a poem worthy of his youthful ambition, and which would entitle him to rank among the most eminent of Scottish poets.

ALEXANDER M'LACHLAN.

> Creative Genius ! from thy hand
>   What shapes of order, beauty, rise,
> When waves thy potent, mystic wand
>   To people ocean, earth and skies !

ALEXANDER M'LACHLAN holds a prominent position in the circle
of Scottish bards who have made for themselves a home in the new
world.   A native of Johnston, in Renfrewshire, Scotland, he was born
in the year 1820.   His father, a mechanic to trade, was possessed of
considerable poetic talent, and the son at an early age became strongly
imbued with his spirit and soon established a reputation for himself in
the neighborhood as a writer of rather intelligent verses.   His education, however, amounted to very little, and it certainly speaks well for
him now that he is in nearly all respects a self-educated man.   As a
boy he was fond of reading, and he early acquired a thorough acquaintance with history and general literature.   His father died while returning from a visit to Canada, leaving a widow and four small children
unprovided for.   Alexander was first sent to work in a cotton factory,
but soon left this occupation and became a tailor's apprentice.   While
a young man he took an active interest in the Chartist movement, and
many of his early efforts in verse were full of sympathy and encourage-
ment for those who were struggling for more freedom.   In 1840 he
emigrated to Canada and went to work on a farm.   He was thus
engaged for many years, during which time, however, he gave vent to
his thoughts and reflections in poems of so beautiful and valuable a
character that they stamped him as no ordinary man, and sent his
name ringing throughout the Dominion.   In 1855 he was induced to
publish a small collection of his poems.   It met with a ready sale and
was followed in 1858 by another volume entitled " Lyrics," which was
also accorded a favorable reception.   Three years later appeared his
" Emigrant and Other Poems," and in 1874 " Poems and Songs," a
large 8vo volume, containing nearly all of his poetical writings up to
that date.   The opening poem in the last named volume is entitled

"God," and is probably the finest piece of poetry which Mr.
M'Lachlan has written. It at once gives us an idea of his powers as
a poet, and, as one writer remarks, "is equal in grandeur and sublimity to the best efforts of the **greatest** Anglo-Saxon or Celtic poets."
We quote a few stanzas:

God of the great old solemn woods,
God of the desert solitudes,
    And trackless sea:
God of the crowded city vast,
God of the present and the past,
    Can man know Thee?

God of the blue sky overhead,
Of the green earth on which we tread,
    Of time and space:
God of the worlds which Time conceals,
God of the worlds which Death reveals
    To all **our race.**

From out **thy wrath the earthquakes leap**
And shake the world's **foundation deep,**
    Till Nature groans:
In agony the mountains call,
And ocean bellows throughout all
    Her frightened zones.

But when thy smile its glory sheds,
The lilies lift their lovely heads,
    And the primrose rare:
And the daisie decked with pearls
Richer than the proudest earls
    On their mantles wear.

These thy preachers of the wild-wood,
Keep they not the heart of childhood
    Fresh within us still?
Spite of all our life's sad story,
There are gleams of thee and **glory**
    In the daffodil.

And old Nature's heart rejoices,
And the rivers lift their voices,
    And the sounding sea:
And the mountains old and hoary
With their diadems of glory,
    Shout, Lord, to Thee!

The mysterious in nature seems to be a fascinating subject for our author, and one at which his muse loves to draw inspiration. On such occasions his writings are eloquent and profound and they display a large amount of sound philosophical reasoning. He is extremely earnest in purpose and no one can fail to observe the sincere longing with which his heart is filled for a knowledge of the unseen. There is a great deal more than poetry in his verses entitled "Mystery":

> Mystery! mystery!
> All is a mystery,
> Mountain and valley, woodland and stream;
> Man's troubled history,
> Man's mortal destiny
> Are but a phase of the soul's troubled dream.
>
> Mystery! mystery!
> All is a mystery!
> Heart-throbs of anguish and joy's gentle dew,
> Fall from a fountain
> Beyond the great mountain,
> Whose summits forever are lost in the blue.
>
> Mystery! mystery!
> All is a mystery!
> The sigh of the night winds, the song of the waves:
> The visions that borrow
> Their brightness from sorrow,
> The tales which flowers tell us, the voices of graves.
>
> Mystery! mystery!
> All is a mystery!
> Ah, there is nothing we wholly see through!
> We are all weary,
> The night's long and dreary—
> Without hope of morning O what would we do?

In another poem, entitled "Who Knows?" we have verses similar to the following:

> From deep to deep, from doubt to doubt,
> While the night still deeper grows;
> Who knows the meaning of this life?
> When a voice replied, Who knows?
>
> Shall it always be a mystery?
> Are there none to lift the veil?
> Knows no one aught of the land we left,
> Or the port to which we sail?

Poor shipwrecked mariners driven about
By every wind that blows;
Is there a haven of rest at all?
And a voice replies, Who knows?

O why have we longings infinite
And affections deep and high;
And glorious dreams of immortal things,
If they are but born to die?

Are they but will-o'-wisps that gleam
Where the deadly nightshade grows?
Do they end in dust and ashes all?
And the voice still cried, **Who knows?**

No poet was ever blessed with a finer conception of the **beauties of** external **nature,** however, than the **subject** of our sketch. He has a happy faculty **for describing rural** scenes, and his poems **entitled** "Spring," "Indian Summer," "Far in the Forest Shade," "**The** Song of the Sun **" and** "The Hall **of Shadows "** are replete with descriptive passages of **the** very highest **order of merit.** Mingling with his poetry is the rich perfume of buds and **blossoms, the** warble of the birds, the murmur of the brook, **the hum of insects and** the **rustle of** autumn leaves. He loves **them all with the love of** a poet, and his muse is ever **ready** and delights **in** proclaiming their beauties, whether in the field or the forest, the highway or the hillside. The following may be **taken as** a specimen of his descriptive pieces:

MAY.

O sing and rejoice!
Give to gladness a voice,
Shout a welcome to beautiful May!
Rejoice with the flowers,
And the birds 'mong the bowers,
And away to the green woods away!
O, blithe as the fawn
Let us dance in the dawn
Of this life-giving, glorious day!
'Tis bright as the first
Over Eden that burst—
O, welcome, young, joy-giving May!

The cataract's horn
Has awakened the morn,
Her tresses are dripping with dew

O hush thee, and hark!
'Tis her herald the lark
That's singing afar in the blue,
It's happy heart's rushing,
In strains wildly gushing,
That reach to the revelling earth:
And sinks through the deeps
Of the soul till it leaps
Into raptures far deeper than mirth.

All nature's in keeping!
The live streams are leaping
And laughing in gladness along;
The great hills are heaving,
The dark clouds are leaving,
The valleys have burst into song.
We'll range through the dells
Of the bonnie blue bells,
And sing with the streams on their way
We'll lie in the shades
Of the flower-covered glades,
And hear what the primroses say.

O crown me with flowers,
'Neath the green spreading **bowers,**
With the gems and the jewels May brings;
In the light of her eyes,
And the depth of her dyes,
We'll smile at the purple of kings.
We'll throw off our years,
With their sorrows and tears,
And time will not number the hours
We'll spend in the woods
Where no sorrow intrudes,
With the streams, and the birds, and **the flowers.**

Home and the affections also claim a particular niche in our author's heart, and **he** has given us many very fine poems on **these** subjects. He begins one:

" Where'er we may wander,
Whate'er be our lot
The heart's first affections,
Still cling to the spot
Where first a fond mother,
With rapture has prest,
Or sung us to slumber
In peace on her breast."

But the finest specimen of all, is his well-known poem entitled, "Old Hannah," a poem so real and yet so exquisite in construction and finish that no one but a true poet could have conceived and written it.

OLD HANNAH.

'Tis Sabbath morn, **and a** holy balm
  Drops down on the heart like dew
    And the sunbeams gleam
    Like a blessèd dream
  Afar on the mountains blue,
Old Hannah's by her cottage door,
  In her faded widow's cap;
    She is sitting alone
    On the old gray stone,
  With the Bible in her lap.

An oak is hanging above her head,
  And the burn is wimpling by;
    The primroses peep
    From their sylvan keep,
  And the lark is in the sky.
Beneath **that shade** her children played,
  But they're all away with Death,
    And she sits alone
    On that old gray stone,
  To hear what the Spirit saith.

Her years are o'er threescore and ten,
  And her eyes are waxing dim,
    But the page is bright
    With a living light,
  And her heart leaps up to Him
Who pours the mystic harmony
  Which the soul can only hear:
    She is not alone
    On the old gray stone,
  Tho' no earthly friend is near.

There's no one left to love her now;
  But the eye that never sleeps
    Looks on her in love
    From the heavens above,
  And with quiet joy she weeps;
For she feels the balm of bliss is pour'd
  In her lone heart's deepest rut;
    And the widow lone
    On the old gray stone
  Has a peace the world knows not.

There are no weak of frivolous pieces to be found in Mr. M'Lachlan's latest volume. There is life and energy and strength, and true poetry in all **that he** writes, and it proceeds from him naturally and gracefully **at all** times. He **has had** the highest encomiums passed **on** his powers **as** a poet by men **who** were well able tó judge of his abilities. **Says** the Rev. Dr. Dewart:—"As long ago **as** 1864, in **my** ' Selections from Canadian Poets', I said of Mr. M'Lachlan: ' It is no **empty laudation** to call him **the Burns of** Canada. **In** racy humor, in **natural** pathos, in **graphic portraiture of** character, he will compare favorably with the great peasant **bard** ; while in moral grandeur and beauty he frequently strikes higher notes than ever echoed **from the harp of** Burns.' After **nearly a quarter of a century I am prepared to stand by this estimate still."**

No notice of our author would **be** complete without referring to **his lyrical pieces.** These embrace many **that are written** in the Scottish **dialect, and which** have added considerably to his fame **as a poet. There is a wealth of poetic feeling** and language, simplicity **and** tenderness **in such** songs as " Lovely Alice," " My Love is Like the Lily Flower," and " Mary White," that is **not to** be met with in the Scottish song of to-day. We quote the following as a specimen **of** his Doric. The title has long since **become a** familiar **proverb with the Scottish people :**

WE'RE A' JOHN TAMSON'S BAIRNS.

O, come and listen to my sang,
  Nae matter wha ye be,
For there's a human sympathy
  That sings to you and me;
For as some kindly soul has said—
  All underneath the starns,
Despite of country, clime and creed,
  Are a' John **Tamson's bairns.**

The higher that we sclim the tree
  Mair sweert are we to fa',
And, spite o' fortune's heights and houghs,
  Death equal-aquals a';
And a' the great and mighty anes
  Wha slumber 'neath the cairns
They ne'er forgot, though e'er so great,
  We're a' John Tamson's bairns.

Earth's heroes spring frae high and low,
   There's beauty in ilk place,
There's nae monopoly o' worth
   Amang the human race;
And genius ne'er was o' a class,
   But, like the moon and starns,
She sheds her kindly smile alike
   On a' **John** Tamson's bairns.

There's nae monopoly o' pride—
   For a' wi' Adam fell—
I've seen a joskin sae transformed,
   He scarcely kent himsel'.
The langer that the wise man lives,
   The mair he sees and learns,
And aye the deeper care he takes
   Owre a' John Tamson's bairns.

There's **some distinction, ne'er a doubt,**
   'Tween Jock and Master John,
And yet it's maistly in the dress,
   When everything is known;
Where'er you meet him, rich or poor,
   The man o' sense and barns,
By moral worth he measures a'
   Puir auld John Tamson's bairns.

There's ne'er been country yet **nor kin**
   But has some weary flaw,
And he's the likest God aboon
   Who loves them ane and a';
And after a' that's come and gane,
   What human heart but yearns,
To meet at last in light and love,
   Wi' a' John Tamson's bairns.

Among the poems not already referred to, "**The Halls of Holy-**rood," "Martha," "The Settler's Sabbath Day,' "**Napoleon on St. Helena**," "Wilson's Grave" and "Up and be a Hero" prove themselves the work of a master poet. In each instance the diction is pure, **the** rhyme easy and flowing, and the ideas original and choice.

"His 'Britannia' and 'Garibaldi,'" says Dr. Daniel Clark, "stir us as would the clarion notes of a bugle call on a battlefield. His 'Lang Heided Laddie' shows his quiet humour, versatility, and good-ntended sarcasm. His 'Balaclava' does not lose by comparison with

Macaulay's 'Lays of Ancient Rome,' or Aytoun's 'Historic Ballads of Scottish Chivalry.'"

One other poem, which we are unable to quote on **account** of its length, deserves special mention, viz: "Old Adam." This is one of his most admired productions. The description of the old man, his peculiarities, sympathies and **desires,** are all graphically **set** forth, and form a picture which is **at once interesting** and true to life.

> "**He was** nae thing that **stood apart**
>   Frae universal nature:
>   But had a corner in his heart
>   **For every living creature.**"

In conclusion we would allude to the fact that at a public **meeting recently** held in Toronto it was unanimously resolved, as a **mark of** respect to the genius of Mr. M'Lachlan, to purchase and present him with the valuable farm upon which he now resides. And surely the **poet is** worthy of **such** distinguished recognition at the hands of his admirers. The **talents** entrusted **to** his keeping have been nobly employed, **and have** yielded an abundant harvest. He has accomplished **the work he** was sent to perform, and after he passes to **his reward, his good** works will keep his memory revered and honored **among the sons of** song on earth.

WILLIAM MURRAY.

I live not like the many of my kind ;
  Mine is a world of feelings and of fancies ;
Fancies, whose rainbow-empire is the mind—
  Feelings, that realize their own romances.

WILLIAM MURRAY was born on the twenty-fifth of May, 1834, at
Finlarig, Breadalbane, Perthshire, in an old-fashioned house close by
the old castle of Finlarig, built by Black Duncan, head of the then
house of Breadalbane. His father, Peter Murray, held the position of
head gardener to the Breadalbane estates for a period extending over
thirty-five years. He was an intelligent, straightforward, God-fearing
man, and to this day is kindly remembered by all who knew him. He
early noticed the bright faculties with which his son was endowed, and
he spared no expense in providing him with as careful and as complete
an education as was to be procured in the Highlands of Scotland at
the time. Shortly after finishing his studies our author resolved to
strike out in the world on his own account, and emigrating to Canada
found himself occupying a subordinate position in a mercantile
establishment in Toronto just as he was entering upon the twenty-
first year of his age. He has always been industrious and earnest,
and fortune has showered her favors on him, as he is now well to do
in every sense which that term implies. He has been connected for a
great many years with the well-known and extensive dry goods house
of Messrs. A. Murray & Co., Hamilton, Ontario. Mr. Murray's birthplace is situated in one of the most picturesque positions in the Highlands, and his muse takes a special delight in winging her way back
and describing the magnificent and historical scenes amid which he
first saw the light. In this connection his poem entitled "My
Birthplace," and inscribed to Mr. Even MacColl, is perhaps the finest
of all his productions. It contains numerous lines of true poetry,
together with many beautiful similes, the diction is good and pure,
while as a descriptive poem it will compare favorably with the work

of many of the author's brother bards. We make the following
extracts from it :

When first my eyes awoke to light,
The Grampian hills were full in sight;
The Dochart and the Lochay joined,
Repose in deep Loch Tay to find.

   *   *   *   *

Not far beyond lies Fortingall
The scene of many a bloody brawl;
But chiefly, here the Roman shield
Was driven shattered from the field:
Here Cæsar's chivalry first felt
The metal of the Highland celt,
And with his finger in his mouth
Enquired the shortest passage south!

Now, rise with me to yonder hill,
Watered by many a crystal rill,
Covered by Scotia's darling heather,
With here and there a hill bird's feather,
And fox glove's mazy tangled knots,
Holding its own until it rots,
And, to the sportsman ever dear,
The grouse and blackcock crouching near,
The lark rejoicing up on high,
The eagle swooping through the sky.
But best of all to grazier's eye,
The hardy black sheep passing by,
Nibbling away with sharp white teeth
Their perfumed provender, the heath,
And never deem their journey high
Till hidden in the misty sky.

   *   *   *   *

But worse than blameful would I be,
Were human friends forgot by me—
Those friends who cheered my early years,
Increased my joys and soothed my fears,
Who nursed me, taught me and caressed me,
And when I left them, sighed and blessed me!
However primitive their talk,
Unstudied and untrained their walk—
Altho' they wore the simple plaid
Which their own thrifty hands had made,
And were content with Highland bonnets,
Highland whiskey, Highland sonnets—

They were a noble race of men
Whose like we ne'er shall see again—
Their faults I hardly wish to hide,
Their virtues I admire with pride.

*   *   *   *

Yes, while I here, far from **these** scenes,
May value all that money means,
A something says, with thrilling tones,
"In Scotland you must lay your bones."

Another very fine poem by Mr. Murray is the one entitled "Rob Roy," written for the *New York Scotsman* some years ago. This is a composition of considerable length, but it **is** well written, the interest is sustained throughout, and it conveys to us a graphic picture of the life and times **of this** celebrated Highland chieftain :

As he proudly stood arrayed
In his graceful kilt and plaid,
With a power to be obeyed
   In his kingly face,
The MacGregor looked the head
   Of a noble race.

Noble race it truly was,
Notwithstanding Saxon laws,
And the chief who leads its cause
   Rules it heart and soul.
See him! every breath he draws
   Claims supreme control.

True, bold Rob, in hours of sleep,
Sometimes captured Lowland sheep
Which the owners couldn't keep,
   Lacking strength and skill;
Or some cattle he might sweep
   From some Lowland hill.

He believed that sheep and cattle
Gave a kind of charm to battle,
Which improved a hero's mettle
   And (which wasn't worse)
While they helped his nerves to settle,
   They improved his purse.

'Twas the simple ancient plan
Taught by every genuine clan,

To recover from each man
  What the other lost;
Nor did one or other scan
  Closely what it cost.

*   *   *   *

Clansmen all, the story's told,
Many years have come and rolled
Since we first in Scotland old,
  With a boyish joy,
Heard of all the doings bold
  Of the brave Rob Roy.

Thank the Lord the times are changed;
Every wrong has been avenged;
On the side of right are ranged
  People, Crown and Law—
All from each, no more estranged,
  Strength and glory draw.

Celt and Saxon now are one,
Fights and feuds are past and gone,
And o'er Scotia's mountains lone
  Shedding peace and joy,
Queen Victoria fills the throne
  Of the bold Rob Roy.

Although frequently pressed by his friends to publish a collection of his poems in book form our author, thus far, has refrained from doing so. This is not the result of a want of confidence in himself or a fear as to what the verdict of the public might be at such a step. It is simply because he lacks ambition, or more properly speaking perhaps, is too unassuming in regard to his own merits. While he admits in a recent poetic epistle addressed to the writer that—

" We rhymers richly relish praise,
And when a nurse like you displays
    In such attire,
The bairns which from our brains we raise,
    We go on fire—"

still it is a well-known fact that, while he is the author of a sufficient number of poems to fill two good-sized volumes, many of his pieces have appeared in magazines and newspapers without his name or even his initials being attached to them. He has been actively engaged in business for many years, but in the midst of this busy portion of his life he has had moments of genuine inspiration, moments in which an irresistible force has compelled him to lay bare his heart and feelings in poems, epistles and lyrical pieces of acknowledged merit. He writes in a graceful and easy style and his muse generally alights on subjects which are interesting as well as instructive. His poems are skillfully worked out and contain thoughts and expressions which prove that he possesses a fine literary taste. His "Caledonians and the Romans," "Epistle from St. Andrew," "Our Ain Snug Little House," "Canada to Uncle Sam" and "The Scottish Plaid" are very creditable productions in all respects and will always be accorded a loyal welcome by admirers of the Scottish muse. The last-named piece contains no less than forty-six verses and illustrates the mastery which our author still retains over his native Doric :

> The plaid amang our auld forbears
> Was lo'ed owre a' their precious wares,
> Their dearest joys wad be but cares
>   Withoot the plaid.
>
> And when the auld guidman was deid,
> 'Twas aye by a' the hoose agreed,
> That to his auldest son was fee'd
>   His faither's plaid.
>
> Ah! gin auld plaids could speak or sing,
> Our heids and hearts wad reel and ring
> To hear the thrillin' tales that cling
>   To Scotia's plaid.
>
> To hear hoo Scottish men and maids,
> 'Mang Scotland's hills and glens and glades,
> Baith wrocht and focht wi' brains and blades
>   In thae auld plaids.
>
> The star o' Scotland ne'er will set,
> If we will only ne'er forget
> The virtues in our sires, that met
>   Aneath the plaid.
>
> Amang the Scottish sichts I've seen
> Was ane that touched baith heart and een;
> A shepherd comin' oure the green
>   Wi' crook and plaid,
>
> And i' the plaid a limpin' lamb,
> That on the hill had lost its dam,
> And, like some trustfu' bairnie, cam,
>   Row'd i' the plaid

Anither sicht I think I see,
The saddest o' them a' to me—
The Scottish martyrs gaun to **dee**
    I' their auld plaids.

But let's **rejoice,** the times are changed,
The martyrs hae been a' avenged—
An English princess has arranged
    To wear the plaid.

In addition to the poems referred **to, Mr. Murray has** written many pieces which gives us a glimpse **of himself** and his daily life. These evince true poetic talent and **can be read** with pleasure and profit by all. We can readily trace **his own disposition** and character, for instance, in the following verses :

MY FRIEND.

Reserve for me on earth
    The man to call my friend;
In whom both mental worth
    And heavenly wisdom blend.

The man who has a heart
    To sympathize with grief,
And break misfortune's dart
    With counsel **and** relief.

The man whose voice will never
    Unrighteousness defend,
But scorneth to discover
    The weakness of a friend.

The man who stamps to dust
    Vile slander ere it grows,
And who is true and just
    Alike to friend and foes.

The man who worlds can trace,
    And yet in whom we find,
Combined with cultured grace,
    Humility **of mind.**

The man who's not ashamed,
    Though lord of every school,
However wise and famed,
    To own himself a fool.

> Or, in a word, the man,
>   Beneath affliction's rod,
> Or, high in fortune's van,
>   Who glorifies his God.

Standing apart, so to speak, from his other pieces, and beautiful in their workmanship and design, are the numerous religious poems and paraphrases which our author has composed from time to time. These form a cluster of fine spiritual thoughts, and serve to show that the seeds of piety which were implanted in his heart in youth-time have retained their possession and are now bearing good fruit. We quote as a specimen of these religious musings the one entitled:

RETURN A GENTLE ANSWER.

A SERMON IN RHYME.

"A soft answer turneth away wrath,"—Proverbs.

> "Return not ill for ill," be thine
>   To imitate thy Lord divine;
> Though wrathful lips provoke, let mine
>   Return a gentle answer.
>
> The world may sneer: "perchance," it says,
> "Such softness suited earlier days.
> We now must study 'manlier' ways—"
>   Return a scornful answer.
>
> Receive not lessons from the world,
> Its wrath but rises to be hurled
> Where baffled pride's dark champion gnarled
>   Receives his awful answer.
>
> The Master's lessons are the best,
> And they alone will stand the test
> When death, each mortal's final guest,
>   Demands his solemn answer.
>
> "Reviled, He ne'er reviled again,"
> Not even from dread Calvary's pain,
> Where innocence for guilt was slain,
>   Escaped a vengeful answer.
>
> Is thy reward of little worth?
> Grasp if thou canst its glorious girth;
> Who are the heirs of this wide earth?
>   "The meek?" is Christ's own answer.

And " Blessed-God's own children!" those
Who barter benefits for blows,
And peace establish among foes:
    Their actions are their answer.

When angry words arise, forbear
To fan the flame of fury there,
And show the scorner that you dare
    Return a gentle answer.

Withhold the fuel from the flame,
And soon its fierceness will turn tame;
So wrath unfed by angry blame
Will soon to reason answer.

And haply he who was thy foe,
Receiving winsome words for woe,
Ashamed, with gratitude may glow
    To thee for thy kind answer.

Meek, mild, yet manly in thy life,
Assist to lessen sin and strife,
Allay contention's tumults rife
    With th' oil of a soft answer.

And on thy happy head shall fall
The joy which shall belong to all
Who at the blessed Master's call
    Are ready with their answer.

Acrostics, as a general rule, are of little value to anyone, but our author who seems to have a particular liking for this fantastic style of composition, has written a few which are worthy of perservation. Such, for instance, is the one

TO WILLIAM EWART GLADSTONE.

On the occasion of his visit to the Earl and Countess of
Breadalbane, at Taymouth Castle, Oct. 1883.

Welcome to Taymouth, grandest of grand men!
I liken thee to a Breadalbane ben,
Leaving the hillocks at thy feet below,
Looking abroad beneath a crown of snow.
In thee Breadalbane honors all who claim,
A share in thine and Britain's matchless fame.
Monarchs their merits still may faintly plead.

England's great Gladstone is a king indeed.
William the Norman conquered with the sword,
A greater William conquers with a word,
Resistless as the thunderbolt that cleaves
The storm cloud which around Schihallion heaves.

God bless thee, noble champion of right!
Lions nor Launcelots can withstand thy might.
Angels in legions are upon thy side,
Demons and dastards from thy halberd hide.
Scotland remembers whence thy brilliant blood,
The Highlands claim thee from before the flood.
O'er all the rolling world thy fame resounds,
Nor even can the bards define its bounds,
Enjoy Breadalbane's famous house and grounds.

Mr. Murray has been elected for a succession of years as one of the Bards of the Hamilton St. Andrew's Society, and is now senior Bard of the Caledonian Society. As such it becomes his pleasant duty each year to present to those associations original poems in connection with the anniversary of the birthday of Robert Burns, St. Andrew's day, etc. These compositions, of course, contain a great deal of what is merely of local interest, but there are also embodied in their lines many happy and patriotic allusions to Scotland which are especially pleasing to those who hail from the "Land of Cakes." Among the smallest poems which we have met with on the Ayrshire Bard is the following:

A LINE ON BURNS.

His like we ne'er again will find,
　Such kings have no successors;
But of the treasures of his mind
　All nations are possessors;
And while the vault of heaven glows
　And earth endures below it,
So long resplendent lives and grows
　The fame of Scotland's poet.

On December 1, 1888, Mr. Murray addressed the following words of welcome to His Excellency, The Right Honorable Lord Stanley of Preston, Governor-General of Canada, on the occasion of his first visit to Hamilton, Ontario:

A WELCOME TO HIS EXCELLENCY.

Welcome to Hamilton, Lord Stanley! First,
  Because you represent our Gracious Queen—
The first and best of sovereigns—who has nursed,
  What Earth's old orb till now has never seen,
A family of free nations, blest with all
  That loyal hearts can ask or love bestow;
Ready to rally round her throne at call,
  And guard her empire 'gainst its fiercest foe.

And, secondly, we welcome you because
  You are yourself entitled to esteem,
As one of that great race whose lives were laws
  To knights and nobles, and whose glories gleam
Not only in old England's mightiest wars,
  But also 'mong her Senate's brightest stars.

In conclusion, we would state that while Mr. Murray has never tasted of matrimonial joys his lot in life is by no means an unhappy one. He enjoys a large circle of friends, is respected by all, and is ever ready to lend assistance wherever and whenever required. He is the author of many poems which deserve to be better known than they now are, and we hope that he will yet be induced to place a collection of his writings in a permanent form before the public.

MAJOR·GEN. DONALD CRAIG McCALLUM.

> He drew his light from that he was amidst
> As doth a lamp from air which hath itself
> Matter of light, altho' it show it not.

DONALD CRAIG McCALLUM was a native of Johnstone, in Renfrewshire, and was born in 1815. His parents originally came from Campbellton in Argyleshire, and his father followed the occupation of a tailor. In 1832 the entire family emigrated to America and took up their residence at Rochester, N. Y. Our author first mastered the tailoring trade, and then, for some reason, becoming dissatisfied with it, crossed over to Canada and went to work to learn the trade of a carpenter with a firm at Lundy's Lane. During the term of his apprenticeship we learn that "he attended night school and made great progress in geometry and mathematical studies generally. He gave much of his leisure time also to the study of architecture, and soon became a capable and skilful designer." Having completed his apprenticeship and studies he returned to Rochester, where he successfully conducted a business on his own account for a number of years. In 1851 he invented what is known as the "inflexible arch truss bridge," and was afterwards engaged in superintending the construction of various bridges and railroads. During the war he was made director and general manager of military railroads with the rank of Colonel, United States Army, and history will always shed a lustre on his name on account of the valuable services which he rendered to the nation at that period. We quote the following from Mr. John Laird Wilson's excellent biography of him :—" It had become evident to all that a great struggle was about to take place at Chattanooga. Stanton was anxious that there should be no failure, and that Grant should deal Bragg a final and crushing blow. To make matters more secure it was deemed advisable to reinforce Grant. The great question, however, was how to get the troops transferred from the Rapidan to Stevenson, Ala., in time to be of service. It was a distance of twelve hundred miles. It was the opinion of General Halleck that the task was next to impossible—that the transfer of so many men with all the appurtenances of war could, certainly, not be accomplished in less than six weeks. McCallum was sent for and appealed to. The transfer, he thought, might be accomplished in seven days. Halleck pronounced it impossible. It could not be done! McCallum made his conditions. He must have absolute control of the railroads and be permitted to seize engines and cars wherever he could find them. The conditions were granted. The trains were set in motion, and within the time specified the task was accomplished. As a feat of military railroading that transfer of the Eleventh and Twelfth corps of the Army of the Potomac stands unparalleled in history. McCallum's services on this occasion were rewarded with the rank of major-general. His services were equally conspicuous and equally valuable during the Sherman campaigns, and it is not too much to say that but for McCallum and his department the march to the sea might have proved a failure." One is scarcely prepared to believe after reading the above that General McCallum was a poet of no mean order of merit. Indeed, many of his poems are of a very high order of merit, and entitle him to an honorable niche among the more prominent of the minor Scottish bards. There is something manly and real and thoughtful in all that he has written, and his muse never alighted on anything which she did not beautify and make more valuable. In 1870 he issued a small volume of his poems, and this has long since been out of print. The volume opens with the following quotation from one of Mr. James Russell Lowell's beautiful poems:

It may be glorious to write
    Thoughts that shall glad the two or three
High souls like those far stars that come in sight
    Once in a century.

But better far it is to speak
    One simple word which now and then
Shall waken their free nature in the weak
    And friendless sons of men.

To write some earnest verse or line,
    Which seeking not the praise of art,
Shall make a clearer faith and manhood shine
    In the untutored heart.

Following these lines are many very fine poems, not a few of which have already acquired considerable popularity. "The Water Mill," for instance, is known in all English-speaking countries, and is no doubt the poem on which the author's reputation as a poet will last. The General was very proud of this production, and was frequently pained by seeing weak and frivolous imitations of it, bearing the same title, and going the **rounds** of the **press.** We quote herewith the poem from the author's copy :

THE WATER MILL.

Oh, listen to the water mill, through all the live-long day,
As the clicking of the wheel wears hour by hour away.
How languidly the antumn wind doth stir the **withered leaves**,
As on the field the reapers sing while binding up the sheaves.
A solemn proverb strikes my mind, and, as a spell, **is cast,**
" **The mill will** never grind again with water that is past."

Soft summer winds revive no more leaves strewn o'er earth **and main;**
The sickle never more will reap the yellow-garnered grain.
The rippling stream flows ever on, aye, tranquil, deep and still,
But never glideth back again to busy water mill.
The solemn proverb speaks to all with meaning deep and vast,
"The mill will never grind again with water that is past."

Oh! clasp the proverb to thy soul, dear loving heart and true,
For golden years are fleeting by and youth is passing too.
Ah! **learn** to make the most of life, nor lose one happy day;
For time will ne'er return sweet joys, neglected—thrown away;
Nor leave one tender word unsaid—thy kindness sow broadcast,
"The mill will never grind again with water that is past."

Oh! the wasted hours of life that have swiftly drifted by;
Alas! the good we might have done, all gone without a sigh,
Love that we might once have saved by a single kindly word—
Thoughts conceived but ne'er expressed, perishing unpenned, unheard,
Oh! take the lesson to thy soul, forever clasp it fast,
"The mill will never grind again with water that is past."

Work on **while yet the sun** doth shine, thou man of strength and will,
The streamlet ne'er doth useless glide by clicking water mill;
Nor wait until to-morrow's light beams brightly on thy way,
For all that thou can'st call thine own lies in the phrase " to-day."
Possessions, power and blooming health must all be lost at last,
"The mill will never grind again with water that is past."

Oh! love thy God and fellow-man—this comprehendeth all,
High Heaven's universal plan, here let us prostrate fall;
The wise, the ignorant may read this simple lesson taught,
All mystery or abstruse creed compared therewith are naught.
On! brothers on! in deeds of love, for life is fleeting fast.
"The mill will never grind again with water that is past."

Embodied in the General's compositions are many very fine descriptive passages which prove him to have been a keen observer and an intense admirer of the beauties of external nature. Here and there in his poems we come upon many notable word pictures which photograph themselves upon our minds and make us wish that he had devoted a few more of his leisure hours to this particular style of composition. In his poem entitled "The Warning Voice," for instance, we find the following lines wedged in between a mass of theological and philosophical facts and reasonings :

    "'Twas early autumn:
The rustling leaves arose and fell upon
The gentle winds, resplendent in decay,
More beautiful in death than life were they;
O'er rugged rocks the streamlet wildly dashed,
Anon, in ripplings o'er its pebbly bed,
Sighed to the sombrous woods its plaintive song."

From what is perhaps the most peculiar of all our author's pieces, "The Madman's Reverie," we quote the following as a specimen of his command of language and force of expression :

Ha! ha! prate not to me of hope,
While damnéd souls in darkness grope!
Who ne'er hath seen blest happy hour,
That fate did not o'ertake, devour!
Yea! followed on as demon would
A soul condemned, bereft of good!
Relentless as his brother Death
To claim his own! List what he saith:

"When born, thy fate was in me bound,
I've followed thee the world around,
I've shown thee pleasure, but to dash
It from thee with swift thrilling crash!
Ha! curses on thy lips I hail
As glorious triumphs! Do not fail
To gorge thy soul in gloom and hate,
This is thy doom—thy curséd fate!"

Quite a large number of the General's compositions display a high moral tone of thought, and as religious poems are excellent creations. They contain suggestions which appeal to our better feelings, and no one who reads them can for a moment doubt that he was a man who honored his Maker in sincerity and truth at all times. Many of these poems are in manuscript only, but from among those printed in the volume referred to we select the following **as a** specimen of the whole :

BE KIND TO THE **ERRING.**

Be kind to the erring, the humble, the meek,
'Tis coward alone who would trample the weak,
Ye know not how deeply the past they deplore,
In charity cover their sins evermore.

Be kind to the erring, the lowly, the sad,
Oft circumstance ruleth, whose chain driveth **mad;**
Ah! boast not thy virtue, but con thy heart o'er,
Communion with self crusheth pride evermore.

Commune with thyself, think how reckless thou art,
Enriching thy coffers to wither thy heart,
Take warning by thousands on yonder dark shore,
Remember thy soul must exist evermore.

Love good for good only, nor measure thy gain,
Such motives are sordidly selfish and vain,
Strewing blessings all round thee, with heart gushing o'er
Flowing on to the ocean of love evermore.

Religion is nothing, pretensions are vain,
If works are still wanting, ah! where is thy gain ?
As bark cast away on some desolate shore—
As wreck on the deep thou art gone evermore.

Thy days fleet away as a meteor's gleam,
Flashing bright for a moment they fade as a dream;
Yea! dream though it be, yet on far distant shore
Shall in thunders re-echo the past evermore.

As flowers dost thou blossom, mere thing of a day,
As breath of the flower thou wilt vanish away;
Let love be thy motto this gloomy life o'er,
Then in sunshine of love wilt thou bask evermore.

Mr. Wilson, who has carefully read over General McCallum's unpublished writings, places a very high estimate on his powers as a poet.

" His works," he says, " are not mere jingles of meaningless rhymes. On the contrary, they are the outpourings of a soul in which poetry and philosophy are strangely and wonderfully combined—a soul deeply in love with all that is true and beautiful and good, in harmony with all that is noblest, purest, sweetest in the universe of God. Mc-Callum wrote poetry for the same reason that the lark sings—he could not help it. He wrote poetry not because he wished to be a poet, but because he was obedient to the spirit that was in him." Among the finest of his published poems not already referred to are " The Creed of Life," " A Dream," " Soldiers Song of Freedom," " An O'er True Tale," " Solemn Thoughts," and " The Rainy Day." These are elevating, pure and poetic in every sense. As a specimen of his lyrical powers we quote one of the numerous songs which he composed in his mother tongue :

SONG—BESSIE DEAR.

O Bessie dear, I ne'er can tell
  The love I have for thee;
O meet me in yon fairy dell,
  Down by the hawthorne tree.
Down by the hawthorne tree, my dear,
  The warbling burnie rins;
O come, my dearie—dinna fear—
  The bravest heart aye wins,
  The bravest heart aye wins, my dear, etc.

Thy rosy lips, thy gowden hair,
  Doth haunt me all the while;
Thou drivest me to keen despair
  By thy sweet angel smile.
The lily in yon flow'ry dale,
  Nae purer is than thee;
The sparkling gem doth surely pale
  Beneath thy bonnie e'e.
  Beneath thy bonnie e'e, my dear, etc.

As magnet to the pole, my dear,
  Sae true's my love for thee—
Where'er I roam, be't far or near—
  On land or raging sea.
Then come my dearie—dinna wait—
  Thou'rt world and a' to me;
O meet me at the trysting gate
  Down by the hawthorne tree,
  Down by the hawthorne tree, my dear, etc.

" General McCallum had a commanding presence," writes Mr. Wilson. " In his younger years, with his long black hair falling in curls on his shoulders and his magnificent beard resting in wavy folds on his manly breast, over six feet in height, erect of stature, light and graceful in all his movements, he must have been a handsome and attractive man. Even in these later years he was a conspicuous figure in any company; and he was in the habit of receiving the respect which his presence commanded. Now that he is gone those who knew him best will miss him most. His memory will long be green in many a chosen circle ; but we shall not soon see his like again."

A day or two before the General passed away (December 27, 1878) Mr. Wilson called at his residence and was admitted into the sick chamber. The dying man knew that his end was fast approaching, and, taking hold of his friend's hand, he said : " John, after I am gone will you see that my memory is taken care of ?" " I will, General," answered Mr. Wilson, softly, and shortly afterwards withdrew. Nor was the promise forgotten ; and one of the most beautiful and tasteful of the many articles which Mr. Wilson continued to contribute to the *New York Scotsman*, even after he had retired from the editorship of that paper, was the one on the life and work of his late friend, Major-General Donald Craig McCallum.

JOHN PATTERSON.

We live in deeds, not years—in thoughts, not breaths—
In feelings, not in figures on a dial;
We should count time by heart-throbs. He most lives
Who thinks most—feels the noblest—acts the best.

MR. JOHN PATTERSON, the subject of our present sketch, is the author of a number of beautiful poems and lyrical pieces. While he is by no means a voluminous writer of poetry, nor makes any claim to the title of poet, yet the various effusions which he has published from time to time prove him to be possessed of fine intellectual qualities and true poetic gifts. His muse is simple but melodious, full of feeling, pure in expression and deeply imbued with piety and a love for all that is noble and good. Mr. Patterson was born at Inverness in 1831. His father was a seafaring man, and his ancestors had followed the same occupation for many generations. The family consisted of four sons and three daughters, all of whom were early sent to school and received a good common English education. On completing their studies the sons were apprenticed to useful trades, the one selected for our author being that of a compositor or printer. He had no particular liking for this trade at the time, but he applied himself diligently to master it, and before the term of his apprenticeship had expired was complimented on his being a skilful and competent workman. At the age of twenty-two, and with a view of bettering his condition in life, he left Inverness and proceeded to Glasgow, where he took passage for New York. "I left Glasgow," he writes, "in the autumn of 1853, and after a passage of sixty-six days, in an old packet-ship, with about two hundred others, arrived at Staten Island. During the voyage typhoid fever broke out among the passengers, several of whom died and were buried at sea. About a week before we landed I was stricken with it, and on our arrival had to be taken to Quarantine Hospital, which was then on Staten Island, and where I remained for two months." On his recovery he readily obtained employment at his trade, and has been in comfortable circumstances ever since. Prosperity, however, never obliterated or dimmed the recollection of his boyhood's Highland home, and after an absence of nearly twenty years in this country, he composed the following lines in connection with it:

SWEET HOME OF MY YOUTH.

Sweet home of my youth, near the murmuring rills
That are nursed in the laps of the North Scottish hills,
Ere the gray streaks of morning the songster arouse
From his leaf-curtained cot to his matinal vows,
My thoughts cling to thee, and lovingly press,
Sweet home of my youth, on the banks of the Ness.

When the gay king of light doffs his gladdening crown,
And mantles the land with his evening frown;
When night's sombre cov'ring the earth's overlaid,
And nature is mourning the day that is dead,
Then lov'd thoughts of thee do I fondly caress,
Sweet home of my youth, on the banks of the Ness.

Though thy little flower-garden twice ten times has lost
Its bright summer garb since thy threshold I've cross'd;
Though Atlantic's wide waters our fortunes divide;
Still, not time nor space from my memory can hide
Or dampen the love I am proud to confess
For the home of my youth, on the banks of the Ness.

These lines were given a prominent place in the columns of the *New York Scotsman*, and commanded considerable attention from the readers of that paper. In 1856 Mr. Patterson was united in marriage to Miss Mary Gertrude Treanor, an amiable and intelligent young lady who crowned his life with happiness and comfort for eighteen years. She died in 1874, leaving him with a family of six children, three sons and three daughters. How deeply he mourned her loss may be surmised from the tender sentiments expressed in his poem, "Fireside Reflections," and from the fact that he has remained faithful to her memory ever since:

FIRESIDE REFLECTIONS.

Hopes are crushed and hearts are breaking
    Every day and every hour;
Prospects blighted—joys forsaking
    Those who knew their vital power.

Vacant chairs around the table—
  (Household gravestones grim and cold)—
Tell that death in garments sable,
  Entered homes that bloomed of old,

And stole away the sweetest flower
  In the family bouquet's vase;
Our kind Father's priceless dower—
  The jewel with the brightest rays.

Tones familiar hushed forever;
  Form belovéd absent here;
But on Mem'ry's mirror ever,
  Ever present, ever near—

Near where mildewed hearts are sinking,
  Whisp'ring words of hope and love:
If you'd be joys eternal drinking,
  Seek them only from above.

Another little poem composed about this time and entitled "To a Dead Pet Canary Bird," also displays the tender and sympathetic feelings possessed by our author. The little songster had been for many years a special favorite with Mrs. Patterson, and its death awakened many sad memories in the grief-stricken household:

TO A DEAD PET CANARY BIRD.

Alas! poor thing,
  No more thou'lt fling
To space or time thy notes away;
  Thy song, so sweet,
  Shall never greet
Expectant ears the livelong day.

When I was sad,
  To make me glad,
(A notion wove on Fancy's loom),
  Thy siren voice,
  With trills so choice,
Would help dispel the damp'ning gloom.

But deeper cause
  Than sensual laws
Endear'd to me that form of thine;
  Thou loved that one,
  Now dead and gone,
Whose life was long entwined with mine.

Her winning words
E'en little birds
Could never hear and timid be;
No covert net
Their footsteps met
When they alighted on her knee.

Prompt at her call
Thou'd forfeit all
The comforts of thy wire-bound **land**;
And food and drink
Seem'd best, I think,
To thee when taken from her hand.

Alas! alas!
All pleasures pass,
All earthly joys must have an end;
On Death's long scroll
All names enroll;
Man, beast, and bird all there are penn'd.

Each of our author's sons now occupies a position of **trust in** New York city. His eldest daughter, Mary Gertrude, acts as housekeeper, while the second one, Isabella Forbes, being a graduate of the Normal College of the class of 1884, is a teacher in one of the public schools of this city, and the third one, Catherine, having a particular taste for music, has acquired considerable success as a teacher of the piano-forte. Many of Mr. Patterson's musings are of a **religious character** and prove that he received a very careful religious **training in** his youth. **As a** specimen of these pieces **we** quote:

GOD HELP THE POOR.

God help the poor! when sleet **and snow**
Around their dwellings fold
Their cheerless garb, and rough winds blow
Into their homes so cold.

God help the poor! when children cry
For bread and there is none;
Oh! listen to their hungry sigh
And hear their feeble moan.

God help the poor! with hunger press'd,
When Want's repeated knocks
The bolted door of the wealth-caress'd
With haughty silence mocks.

God help the poor! whose naked feet
  Pursue their weary tread
Throughout the cold and dreary street
  In quest of daily bread.

God help the poor of every land,
  Of every sect and clime;
Supply, Lord, with Thy loving hand,
  Their wants from time to time.

God help the poor! for Thou art kind,
  Thy love doth never end;
In Thee, oh Lord, they'll always find
  An ever-faithful friend.

There are few more patriotic American citizens than our present
author, and yet he has a warm heart for everything pertaining to Scotland. He has been an active member of the New York Caledonian
Club for over twenty years, and in addition to this he contributes
occasional letters and poems to the home papers, thus keeping up his
connection and his interest in the welfare of the fatherland. In his
poem entitled "Dreaming," he says:

The love of a Scot for the land of his birth
  Is not like a skiff that's upset by a squall;
'Tis like the stanch ship that sails 'round the earth,
  And sets at defiance the Storm King's thrall.

'Tis a well-spring of joy in far-away lands;
  A bright ray of hope in a cycle of gloom;
A pyramid firm 'mid life's shifting sands;
  'Mong affection's green leaves a rose-bush in bloom.

"Dreaming" is one of the longest, and, in our opinion, the finest of
all Mr. Patterson's productions. Taken altogether it is an excellent
poem, containing numerous fine passages and many pleasing pictures
of home. It was first published in the *New York Scotsman*, and is
dedicated, "To George Gilluly, Esq., President of the Greenpoint
(L. I.) Burns Club, a townsman and school fellow of the author, as a
token and manifestation of the uniform friendship that has always
existed between them."

The cruelties inflicted by the late evictions throughout the Highlands of Scotland have not escaped the notice of Mr. Patterson. "I
was brought up," he writes, "at my mother's knee to believe that God

was just, that all men were equal in His sight, and that **He made the earth** for the children of men." **He was** greatly incensed some time since on reading the following extract from a lecture on the "Leckmelm Evictions" by the Rev. Mr. McMillan, Free Church minister of Ullapool: "To strike terror into their hearts, first of all **two** houses were pulled down, I might say, about the ears of their respective occupants, **without any** warning whatever, except one of the shortest kind. The first **was** occupied by **a deaf** pauper woman, about middle life, living alone **for** years in a bothy of her own, apart from the other **houses** altogether. * * * Act the second is this: **Mrs.** Campbell **was a** widow with two children. After the decease **of her** husband she tried **to support herself by serving in families as a serv**ant. * * * She returned **to Leckmelm in** failing health. Her father had died since she left, **and the house in** which **he** lived and died, and in which in all likelihood he reared his family, was now tenantless. Here widow Campbell turned aside for a while, until something else would, in kind providence, turn up. But the inexorable edict had gone forth to erase her habitation from the ground. Her house was pulled down about her **ears."** **This** latter incident formed the subject of one of our author's most **touching poems:**

WIDOW **CAMPBELL'S APPEAL.**

Wild cries of distress **from** the **Highlands are ringing**
   In the ears of humanity, plaintive but shrill;
As their echoes resound, in despair they are bringing
   To the warm heart of manhood a blood-chilling thrill.
A widow, in anguish, her dire case is pleading—
   Her weak knees impressing the **frost-bitten moss;**
But no look of pity, he listens, unheeding—
   The Laird of Leckmelm, in the county of **Ross.**

"To let me remain in the home of my fathers,
   Is all that I ask in the land of my birth;
And I'll save from the pence my industry **gathers**
   Enough for the rental you think it is worth.
Then change your decree, and I'll bless you forever,
   And your kindness for aye on my heart will engross—"
Her words might have softened his blood-hound, but never
   The Laird of Leckmelm, in the county of Ross.

"Look there!"—to the churchyard she pointed a finger—
   "It's there where my husband, my Donald, is laid,

And oft, while the shadows of evening linger,
   There mourning I sit by his grass-covered bed.
Oh, then, from his grave cause me not to be parted;
   To be near him, though dead, slightly deadens my loss."
All who heard were in tears but that stony-hearted
   Rich Laird of Leckmelm, in the county of Ross.

" Oh, stop for a minute! there's one plea remaining—
   If that is unheeded, no more will I say—
My children! my children!—my courage is gaining—
   My fatherless children you'll not drive away.
Your features bespeak that your heart has relented;
   Oh, thanks be to Him who has died on the cross."
" My fiat is published, nor have I repented,"
   Hiss'd the Laird of Leckmelm, in the county of Ross.

As a specimen of Mr. Patterson's intimate acquaintance with the Doric and the appropriate manner in which he makes use of it, we quote a few verses from his "Auld Rabbie Hard:"

There lived ae man in oor guid toon
Wham I, a 'cute, auld-farrant loon,
   Observit weel,
Whase creed an' deed were wide asunder,
An' are, nae doot, 'less Death did hinder,
   Divergent still.

This man was rich in warldly good,
An' he amang his cronies stood
   In estimation;
For base-born churls roun' rich folks bum,
As bees roun' hawthorn blossoms hum,
   In ev'ry nation.

Gie me the frien' that's nae amiss,
When Fortune taks her fareweel kiss
   An' coorts anither;
That frien' to me will aye be dear,
Tho' life's wee day be dark or clear,
   Aye dear as brither.

The carl was ca'd Auld Rabbie Hard,
Which was nae joke, if we regard
   His miser habits;
But when a wean—years lang gane hame—
The parson to him gied the name—
   Robert Grabbits.

*   *   *   *

When Rabbie up life's brae did lair,
An' on the way twal milestanes mair
    Had left behind,
He found himsel' a thrifty miller,
Wi' walie pouches fill'd wi' siller—
    An' mair to grind.

Siller, siller, was a' he socht,
An' when he got it, a' his thocht
    Was then to haud it;
His hainin', hairtless, selfish life,
E'en if I were the miser's wife,
    I couldna laud it.

Robert **Waters**, Esq., Principal of the West Hoboken public school, writes: "I made the acquaintance of Mr. John Patterson while I was yet a lad working, like himself, **at** 'the case' in a New York printing office, and, strange enough to me, he has remained all these years at **the** same business, while I have wandered away from the craft, running over various foreign countries and striking out into **an** entirely different sphere of life. * * * **I** never suspected him **of dabbling** in poetry until one day, while visiting him at his house, he said to me, 'What do you think of this? here are **some** rhymes which I have been stringing together,' and he read to me a poem written **in** the Scottish dialect, which I remember as strongly reminding me of Burns, **both** in **manner** and spirit, and which was so good that it at once gave me a higher opinion of the man. The poem showed me that he had some talent in the rhyming line, so I advised him **to study and try to bring to** bear whatever power lay in him. What **strikes me as a prominent** trait of the man is his over-humble **estimate of his own abilities, which** is the reason **that he has** always filled **so** humble a position **in the** world. But **in** this I am perhaps wrong, for what position in **the world** is, in reality, superior to that of an American workman? * * **But if** he has not been active in advancing his own interests he has not been backward in furthering those of others. I recollect it **was he** that first set me **agoing in** a literary or lecturing way, for when I returned **from** Europe he induced **me to** give an account of my wanderings to the Caledonians in the New York Caledonian club-house, and I well remember his glee and kindly greeting after my half successful performance was done. John Patterson has an open hand and a warm **heart to** every **Scotsman** that comes in his way, and **I am** only afraid

that his generous hospitality and brotherly kindness are not **always** appreciated as they ought to be."

Among Mr. Patterson's published poems not already referred to, " My Native Land," " Lines on First-footing Mr. Donald Grant," " Santa Claus," " The Coming Morrow" and " Christmas is Coming," are well worthy of **special** notice. **He has also** numerous pieces in manuscript, and we trust that he will continue to exercise his talents until he produces something that will entitle him **to** a prominent place among modern Scottish poets.

WILLIAM TELFORD.

As wine, that with its own weight runs, is best,
And counted much more noble than the rest,
So is the poetry, whose generous strains
Flow without servile study, art or pains.

MR. WILLIAM TELFORD, a respected resident for many years of Smith, Peterboro, Ontario, and a Scottish poet of more than local fame, was born at Leitholm, Berwickshire, Scotland, on the sixth of January, 1828. He was sent to school in his seventh year, but on account of a long and serious illness which prostrated his father and left him incapable of providing for his family as he had hitherto done, he was compelled to quit his studies at the age of ten, and join his brothers at work digging drains, we are told in winter, and rendering whatever assistance he could in a brick and tile yard in summer. "But the severe labor he was forced to perform," writes his biographer, "did not crush out his inspirations for mental improvement. He rose superior to his prosaic environments, and the words of the poet Gray, applied to genius, extinguished in undevelopment, could not be applied to him:

Chill penury repressed their noble rage,
And froze the genial current of the soul!

He triumphed over conditions which would have brought discouragement, or plodding content, with ignorance, to a less aspiring soul. Day after day, in the rare intermissions of arduous toil, he strove, though but a child, with the energy and determination of a man, to improve his mental condition. He had neither books nor means to procure them, and he had consequently to rely on the kindness of neighbors, who sympathised with his aspirations, and the scanty supply of books their cottage shelves contained, and in the long winter evenings he was to be seen sitting in the ingle-nook of his mother's cottage poring over some old volume. In prose, the books to which he had access were such works as Bunyan's 'Pilgrim's Progress,'

Baxter's 'Saint's **Rest**,' 'Man's Four-fold Estate,' 'Josephus' History,' 'Hervey's Meditations,' 'Afflicted Man's Companion,' and such works—one would think, the least alluring in their ponderous sanctity to the lively temperament of **youth.** In poetry, Burns was his chief delight, although Pope, Moore, Montgomery, Tannahill, and other poets were conned by him with diligent delight. In his younger years the knowledge of grammar was to him as a sealed book, and the first dictionary he bought was for the use of his eldest son in school." In 1850 Mr. Telford emigrated to Canada, and has followed bucolic pursuits with marked success ever since. During these **many years,** however, he has found constant enjoyment in the **companionship** of the muse. He has wooed her at all times and under all circumstances, although he says that he **never** lost one hour's work with poetry. When a poetic idea came to him in the day time, he brooded over **and** cherished it until the **evening** meal **was past,** when he would sit down and endeavor to weave it into a poem. A few months ago he collected his pieces together and published them in a large 8vo volume. **Nearly one** thousand copies of this book have already been **sold, showing** conclusively that the author has a large circle of friends and readers who appreciate his talents and worth. Mr. Telford introduces himself to his patrons in the beginning of the volume thus:

> Look not for language, lofty or refined,
> Within this book, you no such thing will find;
> I never stood in high school class or college,
> God, books and nature, true sources of my knowledge
> If high your learning, kindly condescend—
> Some pity show to your less learnéd friend;
> Your high attainments, use not to deride,
> While criticising lean to mercy's side.
>
> Education is seldom obtained by stealth,
> Learning requires no small amount of wealth.
> My humble parents wished and nobly tried,
> To give to me what poverty denied.
> Many bright gems lies buried in the dust,
> Many heaven-sent gifts for lack of learning rust;
> Many golden talents lie in heads obscure,
> Because the parents and the sons were poor.

Following these lines are numerous gems of poetry and song, both in the English and in the author's mother tongue, and of which he may justly feel proud. These are replete with beautiful ideas and suggestions and they embrace a large variety of subjects, both commonplace and otherwise. Take the following as a specimen of his serious writings. The thoughts embodied in the poem flashed through his mind one day while **he was** engaged in sowing grain in one of his fields:

I AM SOWING.

I am sowing, will I reap it?
  That is more than I can say,
Before these seeds can germinate
  I may have passed away.

I know my life is fleeting fast,
  Those hands with which I sow
May both be clasped in Death's embrace
  Ere the **first** green blade grow.

I am scattering, who will gather?
  'Tis a mystery dark to me;
Long before the full ear openeth
  In the cold grave I may be.

As I watch the small seed falling
  Upon the fruitful ground,
Ah, alas! while they are growing
  I may sleep beneath the mound.

I am sowing, yes, and trusting,
  But my hopes may all be vain;
Perhaps my hands will never bear
  The sheaves of golden **grain.**

I may sow, another reap it,
  'Tis the common fate of man;
Death regards no times nor seasons,
  But destroys each hope and plan.

It is seed-time now, when harvest comes
  Will I be there to reap?
Or will death, that dreaded reaper
  Close my eyes in their last sleep?

Will I reap? No man can answer,
  It is God alone that knows;
Mysterious all His ways and He
  Doth none to man disclose.

But there was a greater seed-time,
　　And we are the seeds then sown;
By God's own hand we sprang to life,
　　Sustained, perserved and grown.

There will be as great a harvest,
　　We must all be present then;
When His angels will be reapers,
　　And the grain the souls of men.

Many of Mr. Telford's finest productions have been inspired by the love which he possesses for the beauties of nature. Indeed this may be said to be a special characteristic of his muse as it asserts itself more or less in all of his writings. In addition to this his descriptive powers are remarkably keen. Among the poems in which those two qualities blend harmoniously together, and which we have read with sincere pleasure and profit, are "The Fall of the Leaf," "An Address to Spring," "The Scenery of Scotland," "The First Day of April," "The Pioneer's Retrospect" and "Thoughts on the Season of Death." We quote a few stanzas from the latter piece:

I would not die in Autumn, with all summer beauties past,
Faded foliage, leafless branches, swaying with the northern blast,
Hoar frost shining, chilling breezes, drizzling rain and blinding sleet,
Frost-nipped herbage, leaves of yellow, crisping underneath our feet,
Gloomy season, bright sun clouded, every leaf stript from the tree,
Herb and plant, bright flowers of summer, I don't wish to die with thee.
Some that loved me might feel anxious to strew garlands o'er their dead,
Alas! they find but withered flowers wherewith to grace my coffin lid.

Die in Winter! surely never! how I shudder at the thought,
Shall my life's decisive battle in the winter time be fought?
Not one glimpse of summer's beauty, not one beam of sunlit ray
Sent to cheer my spirit as it leaves its prison-house of clay.
As from the hearse to open grave move my pall-bearers sad and slow
In silence bear my lifeless body over wreaths of drifted snow,
Death brings its terror at all times—in winter it adds gloom,
To sleep the first night's sleep of death beneath a snow-clad tomb.

If I possessed the keys of death I would not die in Spring,
When nature bursts its wintery bonds and birds begin to sing,
The ice-bound lake begins to wave, the frozen streams to flow,
The radiant beams of April sun, the balmy breezes blow,
With bud and blossom, early flowers, burst forth to life anew,
The snow-drop white, the violet, shows its variegated hue;
Cut me not down, 'mid fresh bloomed flowers permit me just to stay,
To gaze upon their richest bloom before I pass away.

Oh, Thou that ruleth life and death, **supreme** on earth and sky,
Oh, grant to me my earnest wish, in Summer let me die,
Amidst all beauty earth affords, **each** field and forest green;
Nature in dazzling splendor, robed to brighten up death's scene;
Push wide my bedroom door ajar, **raise up the** windows **high,**
Let the sweet fragrance of the flowers blow o'er me as **I die;**
They tell me there are flowers above, fade not with heat **or cold,**
Then let me gaze **on those below** till brighter I behold.

Another portion of **our** author's numerous writings relate **to** Scotland, or are in connection with Scottish subjects, such as the **anniversary** of Robert Burns, St. Andrew's Night, **addresses to the Sons of** Scotia, the members of **the Peterborough, St. Andrew's Society,** etc. Many of these are strikingly **patriotic in their expression, while others** are overflowing with love **and** admiration for the old land. "A Nicht Like Hame," "Grand Here to Gather," "Auld Scotia as It was and is," "Help Your Brither Scot" and "The Land o' Cakes," are all noble poems in this respect. **The** following piece may be taken **as a** specimen. **It was** inspired by **a present of a** small bunch **of** heather **from** his friend, Mr. John **Cameron, and is one of the shortest of** his **compositions:**

SCOTIA'S HEATHER.

Yes he brought it. I have **got it,**
 Can you guess **what it might be?**
It's the heather John did gather
 On Auld Scotia's hills for me.

First he pu'ed it, then he viewed it,
 With its blossoms' varied hue,
Paper folded, therein rolled it,
 Saying, "Bill, this is for you."

When I took it, how I looket
 At the sprig I so well knew,
Silent blessed it, almost kissed it,
 For the sake of where it **grew.**

When I showed it, yes, they knew **it,**
 Every Scotchman which I met;
Fast they held it and they smelled it,
 O, its scent they won't forget.

We adore it, true Scots wore it,
 In their Highland caps of yore
Their foes feared it, as they neared it,
 Highland blood the heather bore,

Time has tried it, blood has dyed it,
  Yes the best in Scotland shed,
They prayed on it, and laid on it,
  Oft the martyr's dying bed,

You may prize it, or despise it
  As your inclination be
Don't annoy it or destroy it,
  'Tis a precious gem to me.

Yes, I have it, I will save it
  While its twigs will hang thegither
Time will move them, but I love them,
  Both Auld Scotia and her heather.

Conspicuous among Mr. Telford's longer poems are the following:
"Don't Mortgage Your Farm," "A Poor Scholar; or, My Own Diffi-
culties," "The Age of Sham," "A True Husband's Wish," "A Voice
From Behind the Plough;" his various epistles to the late Mr. David
Kennedy, the Scottish vocalist, and his two very excellent poems on
the late President Garfield. These poems exhibit considerable originality and power. They are not encumbered with any useless or
unnecessary lines, and the language used is at all times select and
appropriate. Take a few verses from one of the last-named poems
for instance:

Endowed with talents bright and numerous too,
Rapid expanding as in years he grew,
His youthful soul sought not an empty name,
Increase of knowledge was his greatest aim.

His plans and hopes oft left him in despair,
His means were scarce, he little wealth did share,
Bravely he struggled up life's adverse road
Till every barrier underneath he trod.

As wild waves wash the pebbles to the beach,
What he had learned he stood prepared to teach,
Not to gain honor nor to hoard up pelf,
But earn an honest living for himself.

But soon the teacher's rod he laid aside,
And grasped the sword to hold his country's pride;
His daring bravery, in command displayed,
A Major-General he was promptly made.

Onward he pressed with persevering tread,
Till earth's highest honors graced his noble **head**:
Esteem and favor, gained on every hand,
Placed him head ruler o'er his native land.

*　　　　*　　　　*　　　　*

The land he ruled is draped in mourning o'er
And great men wept that seldom wept before,
Their grief is light, though tears bedim their eyes,
Compared with those bound by endearing ties.

*　　　　*　　　　*　　　　*

Son, husband, father, ruler is no more,
His honored name shines brighter than before;
The name of Garfield and his tragic end
To men unborn, in history will descend.

The few specimens of Mr. Telford's muse which we have here presented to our readers are sufficient, we think, to prove that he is endowed with poetic gifts of a very high order. When we consider the disadvantages which he **has** had to contend with, chiefly arising from a deficient education, the many years of incessant and laborious toil through which he has passed; the trials, privations and griefs which have fallen to his lot, especially in the early years of his life ; when we consider these facts we cannot but wonder that he has had the inclination, or found the opportunity, to compose so many beautiful and meritorious poems as he has **done.** His life from boyhood **has** certainly been a busy and eventful one, but he has conquered all **obstacles and** is now in more than comfortable circumstances. While **we have not touched,** to any extent, on his religious musings, the few pieces of this nature which we have perused prove him to be a **sincerely** religious man and his writings altogether give evidence that he has always made the noblest use of the talents created in him.

JAMES D. CRICHTON.

He does alot for every exercise
A several hour; for sloth, the nurse of vices,
And rust of action is a stranger to him.

THE stamp of true poetry is imprinted on many of the poetical productions of James D. Crichton, the present Assistant Librarian of the
Brooklyn Library. A man inheriting literary tastes and talents from
each of his parents, possessing a classical education, besides being
endowed with fine intellectual qualities which manifest themselves in
all of his writings, he certainly gives promise of occupying in the near
future a conspicuous place among the lights of the literary world.
His muse, which is vigorous and scholarly, never becomes fascinated
with trivial subjects. When she casts her spell over him she inspires
him with nobler ideas on noble themes, and he sings in obedience to
her command in a lofty strain, and in language which is at once poetic
and choice and clear. A fair specimen of his poetry may be found
in his poem entitled " Longfellow," written in 1875:

LONGFELLOW.

True poet thou! No defter hand
    Hath swept the lyre since time begun,
    Poet and preacher both in one;
With Jove-like front, serene and grand
Thou towerest o'er the puny throng,
    The petty singers of our day;
    And not a heart but owns thy sway
That listens to thy witching song.

Not thine that false and slavish creed;
    The utterance of a selfish heart;
    Which bids the poet take no part
To stem the march of worldly greed,
Which bids the poet hold his tongue

Or only sing of trivial themes,
  Of idle fancies, sensuous dreams,
Or twist the right to seem the wrong;
Which bids him sell for man's applause
  His birthright of divine protest,
  Against all ills that stand confess'd
In the clear light of God's pure laws;
Which bids him bend to shams his knee,
  And give for jewels painted glass,
  And with unruffled features pass
A brother man in misery;
Such soulless creed thou dost despise,
  Thou dost not close thy loving heart
  To human woe, or sit apart
Lull'd in an " earthy paradise."

But like the old Miltonic psalm
  Still echoing down the aisles of time
  Thy teachings, simple yet sublime,
Hush **the heart's murmur into calm.**
The charm of truth is in thy verse,
  Of purpose strong and firm and high—
  Like finger pointing to the sky—
And oft thou lovest to rehearse
That man lives not for self alone,
  And that life is not lived again,
  And biddest us forget the pain
Nor for the past make idle moan;
So shall we rise on wings of love
  Giving our best to God and **man,**
  So shall we pass thro' life's **brief span,**
And servants here, be sons above.

Mr. Crichton was born **at** Edinburgh on the twenty-second of January, 1847. His father, Andrew Crichton, was a younger son of **a**
landed proprietor in Nithsdale. At the age of thirteen he walked to
Edinburgh, entered himself as a student at the university there, and
never cost his father a penny afterwards. Educated for the ministry,
he quickly perceived that in those days of patronage preferment was
slow and uncertain. He therefore wisely turned his attention to journalism, contributed to the various magazines of **the** day, became
editor of the *Edinburgh Advertiser*, and afterwards **of the** *Edinburgh
Evening* **Post.** He was also the author of numerous works (about
forty in all), biographical and historical—his histories **of** Arabia and

Scandinavia, published in *Constable's Miscellany*, are still standard—
and in recognition of his literary merits he received the degree of
LL. D. from the University of St. Andrew's. He died in 1855, when
our author was only eight years of age.

Mr. Crichton's mother was Jane Gordon, youngest daughter of the
Rev. John Duguid, Parish Minister of Evie and Rendall, Orkney.
Accomplished in classical literature, modern languages and mathematical lore, she was, he informs us, his earliest and best teacher; and to
her he is indebted for a love of nature and a knowledge of botany
which even yet makes the most solitary rambles both attractive and
instructive. He was educated at the Queen's Street (Edinburgh)
Institute, and when fourteen years of age passed to the Edinburgh
University. At that time it was intended that he should take out a
few classes preparatory to beginning the study of medicine. But the
loss of the little means which the family possessed, by a bank failure,
put an end to this scheme, and forced him to find employment, and
make a living for himself. His college course was thus interrupted
and finally broken off, as he was often absent in different parts of
Scotland, and even in Ireland, fulfilling engagements as a teacher.
Whatever spare time he could afford was devoted to study and striving
to acquire a knowledge of modern languages, so that he might be
enabled to enjoy the master-pieces of foreign literature in their own
tongues. In Edinburgh he latterly formed a good teaching connection
and was engaged in preparing pupils for the public schools. On the
death of his mother, in 1873, he went to London, where he was
employed for some years in private tuition. He was also engaged by
Dr. Charles Rogers, the Secretary and founder of the Royal Historical
Society, to prepare indexes of the Society's publications and to assist
him in the translation of Latin charters. He also prepared the first
catalogue of the Society's library. For these valuable services he was
admitted in 1879 a fellow of the Society. After a year's experience
in the bookselling establishment of the Messrs. Sotheran & Co., he
left England, and, with his wife and child, came to America. Here
he was first employed at the Brooklyn Library specially to compile a
catalogue of the German works. After the death of Mr. Noyes, the
late Librarian, he was appointed Assistant Librarian, a position which
he still worthily fills. As to his poetry he says that he has always had
a taste that way inherited from his mother, who sung in a sweet and
facile manner. Many of his musings contain both original and peculiar

ideas, and remind us very forcibly of the writings of the late gifted
Alexander Smith. Take "The Garden of the Muses," for instance:

THE GARDEN OF THE MUSES.

I was in Elfinland last night,
　If there be any truth in dreams;
The air was full of sunny light
　And music of a thousand streams.

I saw the muse's garden fair,
　Where poets are for plants set round;
My wand'ring footsteps halted there,
　Such glamourie my senses bound.

There Shakespeare towers, an aloe sweet,
　That bloom'd but once on stately stem;
Dante and Homer, compeers meet,
　Toss high their laurel'd diadem.

Dan Chaucer, as the ivy, twines
　Around the pedestal of time;
And northern bards like northern pines
　Rear stems carv'd o'er with runic rhyme.

A tuft of wormwood stands for Pope
　(Forgive vex'd shade, th' irreverent fun),
And Milton as a heliotrope
　Turns blue eyes open'd to the sun!

There Byron burns a passion-flower,
　And Spenser is a pensive pansy;
Keats morning-glory lasts one hour,
　Grave Herbert is a bunch of tansy.

There Shelley blooms without a stain,
　A lily by a crystal brook,
Hemans and Landon, violets twain,
　Cower modestly in mossy nook.

And Wordsworth as the woodbine creeps,
　And Lamb is hyssop for fair dames,
Hogg as a mountain-daisy peeps,
　Swinburne a tiger-lily flames!

But King of all the garden there,
　See Burns o'ertop the flowery throng,
And scatter fragrance on the air,
　The red red rose of Scottish song.

" Burns' Poems," it may here be remarked, was one of the first books placed in our author's hands as soon as he had learned to read. They of course charmed and delighted him, and many of the finest poems and songs were committed to memory. Ramsay, Scott, Hogg, Lady Nairne and Tannahill were also read and studied in many a ramble around the neighborhood of Edinburgh, and the beauties embodied in their compositions became indelibly imprinted on his mind. He thus—unconsciously perhaps—drank in a love for his mother tongue which has never left him, and which he makes excellent use of in many of his poems. As a specimen of these Scottish musings we quote the following :

SONG—THE EMIGRANT SHEPHERD'S LAMENT.

O gie me back my lowland cot,
My shepherd's plaid and lowly lot,
When ower the hills I used to stray
And herd the sheep the lee-lang day.

Wi' Hector rinnin' at my heel
Nae king on earth could happier feel,
My sceptre but a hazel wand,
My kingdom but a strip o' land.

Whiles in my dreams I see the loch,
The steadin' wi' its boor-tree haugh,
The auld gray hills like shrouded ghosts
O' giant and lang buried hosts!

How sweet at morn to see the mist
Roll aff the peaks the sunlight kiss'd.
How saft at eve the dew-draps fell
When Mary met me in the dell!

Wae's me that fate us twa has twined,
And I sair' strangers ower the sea;
Their hearts are leal, their words are kind,
But lass, it is'na hame to me!

Quite a large number of Mr. Crichton's poems are written in a soft, melodious measure, which certainly adds considerably to their merit. Especially is this the case with such pieces as have been inspired by the love of nature with which he is imbued. A good example of this quality may be found in his poem entitled

SUMMER.

Summer is coming to forest and fell,
   To river and mountain, to thorpe and lea;
The leaves are green in the woodland dell,
   There's a glitter of gold on the sunlit sea;
Nature thrills to the fairy spell,
   Hark to the bee, with its joyous **hum**
And the gladsome songs of the birds that tell
   Summer is coming, summer is come!

Summer is coming with bud and with bloom
   To chase from the earth cold winter's gloom
For though the promise of spring be fair,
   The chill touch of winter lingers there.
Summer is coming, her warm breath glows,
   The snow drop yields to the blushing rose,
There's a quicker pulse in the dancing rill
   And a brighter green on the sun-kiss'd hill!

Summer is coming, the children play
   In the grassy meadows the livelong day;
They gather the gowans and pansies fair,
   For a rustic posy to deck their hair.
And the speckled trout from the waters deep
   Pursues the fly with a bolder leap;
And the voices of Nature long hush'd and dumb
   Proclaim in their chorus, summer is come!

Among **our** author's **finest** productions not already noticed are "The Death of **Evrémonde**," "Roslin," "Auld Fir Tree," "Only a Faded Flower," "Power of **Love**," "Dreams" and "Man." These are all poems of a superior caste and entitle him to a prominent place among modern Scottish poets. The last named poem consists of ninety-six lines, and is a very creditable piece of work in all respects. We quote **a** few lines :

Say then, why was I born,
If that there be no morn,
No waking of the dead,
No life when this life's fled.
No light behind the gloom,
No sound beyond the tomb ?
It cannot be that man
Should live his little span

And all his joys and tears
And all the hopes and fears
Into his life that press
Should end in nothingness!
That man divinely plann'd
The work of God's own hand—
Should perish like the brute,
And lie quiescent, mute,
Returned to kindred earth
From which he took his birth.

Apart from his original compositions Mr. Crichton deserves special credit for the numerous excellent translations which he has made from time to time. These include Greek, Latin, French, Spanish, Italian, Norwegian, Danish, Swedish and German master-pieces. Many of them are of considerable length, and were they published together in book form they would make a volume which could not fail to be both interesting and valuable to the lovers of poetical literature. "Versification," he writes, "has been to me a solace in times of care and anxiety. I do not claim any merit for my own compositions, but in translations I have always tried to preserve the metre and give the spirit, and, as far as possible, the actual phraseology of the original." In our opinion the finest of all his work in this direction is his translation of "Lenore," from the German of G. Burger. This piece consists of two hundred and fifty-six lines and is undoubtedly the best translation ever attempted of this celebrated poem. We quote one of his shortest translations, to enable our readers to judge of his ability for this particular kind of work:

CUPID'S VISIT.

GREEK OF ANACREON.

In the lonely hours of midnight,
When the Bear was fast declining
To the right hand of the Herdsman,
And the many tribes of mankind,
Wearied out with toil, lay sleeping,
Eros came, and, standing outside,
Tapped upon the bolted door.

"Who is there," I cried, "that knocketh,
Breaking in upon my dreaming?"
And Love only answered, "Open—

I am but a child, so fear not,
Wet and weary, I am forcéd
Through the moonless night to wander."

Hearing this I took **compassion,**
And uprising, straightway opened,
Lamp in hand, the door. Before me
Stood a little winged urchin,
With a tiny bow and quiver.

Quick beside the hearth I **set** him,
And he chafed his palms together,
Wringing from his locks dank moisture,
But, where'er the cold was banished,
" Come," quoth he, "and let us find out
If the wet hath hurt my bowstring."

Saying this the bow he bendeth,
And within my heart his arrow
Like a gadfly sharply stingeth.
Then, with laughter loud upleaping,
" Friend," said he, "congratulate me,
For the bow is all uninjured,
But thy heart keen pain must suffer."

Mr. Crichton enjoys the friendship of many eminent men of **letters.**
Prominent among these is the venerable Scottish poet and song-writer,
Mr. Thomas C. Latto. To this gentleman the writer is **indebted** for
many of the biographical facts herein stated ; also for his **being the**
first to point out to him the valuable character and **the** numerous
beauties which adorn the writings of our present author.

DONALD RAMSAY.

For his **chaste** muse, employed by heaven-taught **lyre**,
None but the noblest passions to inspire;
Not one immoral, one corrupted thought,
One line which, dying, he could wish to blot.

MR. DONALD RAMSAY is a **notable example of** the many Scotsmen who **have risen** from the ranks through their intelligence and **perseverance, and now** occupy prominent **and important positions in the United States.** He is a native of Glasgow, **having been born there on March 12, 1848.** His father, Donald Ramsay, **was a** native of **Isley, and his mother,** Flora Cameron, **of Morvin, in** Argyleshire. Both **belonged to that thrifty,** hard-working class of people, so common in Scotland. His father served as a ploughman in his early years, but on his settling **in Glasgow he had** to **content himself** with **an** inferior position in **life, yet, strange as it may seem, managed** to bring up his little family comfortably **on a salary of fifteen shillings a** week. Mr. Ramsay's earliest recollections are of Glasgow Green and the buttercups and gowans which he was wont to gather there. Mingling with these **are the recollections of** the pleasant **walks** which his father was **in the** habit of taking him on Sabbath mornings along the banks of **the river Clyde, or out to** the well-known "Auld Ruglin Brig." The **latter place** seems to have **possessed special** attractions for him, as **many** years after he **had** emigrated to this country he made it **the subject** of his muse in a poem which displays considerable feeling, besides **giving us a** fair specimen **of his** descriptive **powers. We** quote the poem here, feeling assured that it will **prove interesting to such of our** readers as hail from the west of Scotland:

AULD RUGLIN BRIG.

The early home, the hawthorn tree,
The bridge that spans the river,
The green lanes where we used to be,
Shall be forgotten never.

And though I wander far and wide,
  My memory ne'er shall scorn
Auld Ruglin Brig, that spans the Clyde,
  In the land where I was born.

Auld Ruglin Brig, whose buttresses
  Are each a garden plot;
The wonder of my childish years,
  That sweet, delightful spot.
The echo, in the arches low,
  Oft made my young heart bound,
When I have stood in wonderment
  And listened to the sound.

Auld Ruglin Brig, where many **a night**
  I've stood and watched the river
Flow gently in the calm moonlight,
  When scarce a leaf did quiver;
And where I've stood when winter's blasts
  Did rend the oak asunder,
And swollen floods gushed loud **and fast**
  And filled the arches under.

And where I've watched the gloamin' close
  The long bright summer's day,
And doubted not that fairies dwelt
  On Cathkin's bonnie braes.
Auld Ruglin Brig and Cathkin braes
  And Clyde's meandering stream,
Ye shall be subject of my lays
  As ye are of my dreams.

The early home, the hawthorn tree,
  The bridge that spans the river,
And the green holms where we used to be
  Shall be forgotten never.

Mr. Ramsay's school days began in his seventh year and terminated ere he had reached the age of ten. He confesses that he made no distinguished record as a scholar. He was not a favorite with the schoolmaster, and he availed himself of every possible excuse that presented itself to prevent his attending school. Wandering about the outskirts of the city, stealing rides on canal boats and watching the glass-blowers or pottery men was more congenial to him than poring over his lessons. "And so," he says, "when I was big enough to earn half-a-crown a week, I gladly exchanged the school-room for the work-shop." He started as a boy-of-all-work in the establishment of Messrs. J. W. Robertson & Co., valentine manufacturers, and in this way became a printer.

His employment with this firm lasted about seven years, during which time many changes had come to him. Sickness and death had visited his home and carried off his father and three of his brothers, leaving him to take care of his mother and two younger brothers. His mother was of a cheerful disposition and worked hard and nobly to keep out of debt. She was truly independent, he says, and would have starved rather than ask assistance of her friends. He had how-ever become imbued with a desire for learning, and a wish to improve his condition in life. His work had brought him into contact with all sorts of books, and he had acquired an extensive knowledge of various departments of literature. There were a number of second-hand book stalls in Glasgow, and he became a regular frequenter of them. It was seldom that he had the means to purchase such books as he took a fancy for, but he sometimes picked up a cheap copy of Thomson, or Shenstone, or Prior, and in this way soon became possessed of a good collection of standard works. It was also during this period of his life that he began to court the muses. "I naturally rhymed a little now and then," he writes, "and sometimes a funny epitaph or epigram, or a song for an occasion gave me an opportunity to show a talent for rhyming. We had a weekly paper in Glasgow called the *Penny Post*, to which I frequently sent a song or short poem, and my happiest days were those in which I waited in anticipation of seeing my lines in the 'Poet's Corner.' I was afraid to have my name appear, and signed myself 'Clutha' so that my companions could not tease me, and I had all the pleasure to myself." In 1866 he went to Dublin, thence to Liverpool, working for some time in each of those cities at his trade. In 1868 he concluded to try his fortune in the new world, and so set sail for New York. But Scotland never parted with a truer or more sorrowful son than she did when he waved a final adieu to her shores. "I was indeed pained," he writes, "at leaving my native land. My dear mother's warm and last kiss was on my lips, my two brothers stood on the pier, and as we slowly sailed away the words of a song I had written some years before in a juvenile way, for a friend about to cross the Atlantic, came back to me:

> Farewell sweet river Clyde,
>   Pensive and slow
> Down thy dear stream I glide
>   Mournful I go,
> On to the ocean wide
>   O'er the broad sea,
> **O, thou sweet** winding Clyde!
>   Farewell to thee.
> Oft on thy velvet banks
>   Boyhood and man
> Thoughtful I've wandered
>   Or happy I've ran,
> Gathered the gowans bright,
>   Careless and free;
> O, thou sweet winding Clyde,
>   Farewell to thee!"

After landing in New York he proceeded to Boston, where **he has** since remained, with the exception of one year which he spent in Minnesota on account of his health. The poetical writings of Mr. Ramsay are numerous and of excellent quality. They are invariably pure and elevating, even while depicting some humorous phase of life or character. Besides showing a complete mastery over rhyme and rhythm they prove him to be possessed of a poetic imagination, a true love of nature, **a** correct taste, and **a** tender and sympathetic sense of feeling. Many of his smaller compositions are truly pathetic, both in incident and language. Take the following little piece as a specimen:

THE SHADOWS.

> Green are the fields and fair the skies,
>   And bright is the world to-day;
> But over my home a shadow lies
>   And it will not go away.
> And my heart is held with a fearful dread;
> For my love lies pale on a weary bed.
>
> **Over the lawn** my little boy,
>   Chases a butterfly,
> His laugh has a ring of careless joy
>   And happiness beams from his eye;
> Ah, **me! It is well that he** cannot see
> The **awful shadow that frightens me.**

The doctor is gone, I have closed the door,
  And what were the words he said ?
Alas! I have thought them o'er and o'er,
  And they weigh on my heart like lead.
And I sit me down in dark despair
And the awful shadow lingers there.

Our author's introduction to the writings of Robert Burns is thus amusingly referred to by himself. He says: " There was a genial old man named Gemmell that kept a small stationery shop on George street where the school children used to buy pencils, etc., and he had a circulating library composed mostly of cheap editions, sixpenny and shilling volumes. I had heard of Burns, but not much, and when I was about twelve years old, one rainy night I produced my penny (always in advance) and was handed down the wonderful volume. I ran with it out into the street, but could not wait until I reached home. I opened it under the first lamp that I came to, and in a short time became so deeply interested in the 'Twa Dogs' that the book was almost spoiled by the rain." Since that time he has become the possessor of many fine editions of Burns, and he occasionally makes a leisure hour pass pleasantly by composing a sonnet or a poem, either on or in connection with some incident in the life of the Ayrshire Bard. A short specimen of these delightful musings may be given:

THE DAISY.

Last night, while holding converse with a friend,
A man of rare intelligence and worth,
He beckoned me aside and smiling, said:
" I'll show you something which, perhaps, you know."
He then produced a volume, pocket-worn,
And opening it, displayed between the leaves
A wee red-tipped daisy culled afar,
In classic field in Scotland. What was it
That made him prize this little foreign flower ?

A hundred years ago the ploughman Burns
Laid waste a little daisy in the earth;
But there uprose from out the poet's soul,
A sympathetic prayer, showing the bigness
Of a human heart that sympathized
Even with a modest daisy crimson-tipped.

And **so** we hold the little flower up,
And look at one of God's wee instruments
That touch the cords of tenderness in man
And make us feel that we are mortal **all.**

Mr. Ramsay **is exceedingly partial towards his mother** tongue, **and** uses it, certainly to advantage, **on** every possible occasion. Indeed, the majority of his best poems are written in the Doric. Many of **them** are decidedly beautiful in conception, and form pleasant reading, even while in some cases a thread of sorrow is woven into them. The following piece will give an idea of his work in this direction:

JEANNIE BELL.

A SCOTTISH IDYL.

Fair Jeannie Bell! a sweet braw lass was she,
  As ever stept upon **the** fresh green grass,
A happy innocence sparkled in her e'e,
  An' her sweet voice nae birdie's could surpass.

At early morning on the dewy gowan lee,
  When scent o' hawthorn filled the balmy air,
An' happy warblers sang frae ilka tree,
  I aft did sit and wait for Jeannie there.

The bark **o'** Rover, tauld me o' her comin',
  An' ower the brae, like morning sun she cam',
Wi' some sweet tune she felt a joy in hummin',
  An' at her feet a snaw-white wee pet lamb.

I felt the glamour o' her witchin' glance;
  She smiled and passed, but did not speak **to me,**
For I was shy, and only looked askance,
  Happy to meet her on the golden lee.

O, Thou! *who dwellest beyond earth and air,*
  To whose great law subservient are all Powers,
*I thank Thee, that **I've seen** a form so fair!*
  So *angel like, upon this earth of ours.*

The summer passed, the flowers a' bloomed and died,
  The blast o' winter shook the leafless tree,
I wandered pensively by flowing Clyde,
  But bonnie Jeannie I could'na see.

I longed to see the sweet return o' spring,
　The pleasing sunshine an' the fresh green grass,
Frac ilka tree to hear the birds a' sing,
　But mair than a', to see my bonnie lass.

My hopes were crushed, for soon the tidings spread
　My Jeannie faded, died, and was nae mair,
I could na greet, I only bowed my head
　An' turned awa, wi' something like despair.

Wi' sad, sad hearts they laid her in the clay,
　An' lingered lang till gloamin' shadows fell,
Wi' lanesome hearts, they hameward bent their way,
　Nae mair to see their bonnie Jeannie Bell.

When a' were gane, I stood beside the mound,
　Forget that kirkyard scene, I never can,
I bowed my head in sorrow to the ground,
　A truer tear ne'er fell frae cheek o' man.

The songs of Scotland naturally contain numerous charms for our author and he loves to dwell on the grandeur and inspiring qualities of those renowned compositions. In a poem addressed to the late Mr. David Kennedy he says:

The auld Scotch sangs I lo'e them weel,
　Sae tender and sae real, man,
They touch oor heart an' mak us feel
　As only Scots can feel, man,
They waukin thocts o' ither days,
　An' scenes oor childhood saw, man,
Again we wander ower the braes
　In Scotland far awa', man,

Again by Clyde's sweet banks sae green,
　Or thro' the silent grove, man,
At gloamin', wi' some bonnie Jean,
　In memory we rove, man,
An' then their witty sparks o' fire
　Oor very souls they raise, man,
Frae life's puir diggin' in the mire,
　To sweeter, brighter days, man.

That he understands the true value and importance of a good lyric is very evident from the remarks which he makes in an epistle addressed to his warm friend and brother-poet, Mr. Duncan MacGregor Crerar, on his first reading the latter's verses entitled "My Hero True Frae Benachie:"

TO DUNCAN MacGREGOR CRERAR, POET.

I saw a sang in Scottish dress,
O' some bit lassie's sair distress,
Sic waefu'ness it did express
  It touched the vera heart o' me.
Quo' I wha wrote this bonnie sang?
Was't Stevenson or Andrew Lang?
Frae some true poet's heart it sprang,
  This plaintive Highland melody.

My interest grew an' lookin' nearer,
There stood the name *MacGregor Crerar*,
Ah then! the wee bit sang grew dearer,
  And it was quite a joy to me.
An incident sae sweetly told,
In Scottish verse o' classic mould
Does honor to our country old
  And to the lad frae Benachie.

Oh, wad that pleasant sangs an' rhymes
Had mair acceptance o' these times,
O' heartless trade and selfish crimes,
  An' social disability.
What future has the millionaire,
With a' his wark and a' his care?
The writer o' a sang has mair
  At interest with posterity.

Two short specimens of Mr. Ramsay's own lyrical productions will be appreciated here:

LOVE'S WHISPER.

Somebody whispered to me yestreen,
 Somebody whispered to me;
And my heart gaed a flutter, and flew away clean
 As somebody whispered to me,
And the rose, that I fand in my tangled hair,
Was a token o' love I ween.

An airm gaed roun' my waist yestreen,
  An airm sae strang, an' true;
An' I laid my heid on his breast yestreen,
  For, what could a puir thing do?
An' my heart is his forever mair,
An' naething will come between.

BONNIE MAY MacALISTER.

Bonnie May MacAlister!
I remember when
You were only eight years old,
And I was only ten.
And, in our childish rambles,
How much I thought of you,
While playing on the banks o' Clyde,
Whaur red-tipped gowans grew.

A misty cloud hangs 'tween our lives,
For twenty years and more.
On separate paths, diverging wide,
Along thro' life we've bore.
And you are wedded long ago;
But do you think of when
You were only eight years old,
And I was only ten.

Do smiles of happiness still lurk
Within those eyes so rare?
Or has the hard world's weary work
Strained them with anxious care?
I trust that you have seen more joys
Than he who knew you when,   *
You were only eight years old,
And I was only ten.

Our author is senior partner in the Heliotype Printing Company, and occupies the position of manager and treasurer. He is a life member of the Scot's Charitable Society, and is extensively and favorably known throughout Boston and its vicinity. His home is among the prettiest of those situated in the romantic little village of Roslindale, and his muse frequently becomes enraptured with the quiet place and its surroundings:

When shadows creep across the square,
  And slanting rays of evening sun
Light up my walls with sudden glare,
  My day's toil in the city's done.
My pen is wiped, my books are closed,
  And all the cares that they entail
Are laid aside, while I have dosed
  A half hour's ride to Roslindale.
      The quiet haunts of Roslindale,
      The green hillsides of Roslindale,
      The shady nook, the murmuring brook,
      The pleasing look of Roslindale.

Mr. Ramsay was married in 1872 to Miss Maggie Rust, daughter of William Rust, Esq., of Roxbury, Mass. In 1879, his Maggie died, leaving two boys—Willie and Allen—who still survive. It was during her sickness that the poem, " The Shadows," was written. In 1883, he was again married to Miss Lillian Whitefield, daughter of Edwin Whitefield, Esq., artist and author. She is an accomplished and delightful lady of high education and culture. They have been blessed with one child, a bright little girl, now four years of age, named Flora, who, we need hardly assure our readers, is an ever-increasing joy and delight to her estimable parents.

In concluding our sketch it may not be out of place to introduce to our readers an acrostic which Mr. Ramsay worked out of his wife's name:

          Love found me in a dreary waste,
          In which was nothing cheering,
          Love led me to a maiden chaste,
          Listless I followed fearing.
          In her I found a cheerful ray,
          And night changed to a sunny day,
          No cloud at all appearing.

DR. JOHN MASSIE.

I know thee not—I never heard thy voice;
    Yet, could I choose a friend from all mankind,
Thy spirit high should be my spirit's choice,
    Thy heart should guide my heart, thy mind my mind.

DR. JOHN MASSIE, Colborne, Ontario, has long since established an enviable reputation for himself as the author of a considerable number of poems of a superior order of merit. He is spoken of by one of his friends as a genial, generous, cultivated gentleman, learned and honorable in all his dealings with his fellow-men. His writings prove him to be a perfect master of Doric speech, and, while many of his finest and best-known poems are cast in that mould, there are also those among his English productions which display both talent and skill and entitle him to a foremost position among his brother bards. His style is vigorous, terse and attractive at all times, and his verse is generally musical and rich in true touches of nature. Many exceptionally fine thoughts are woven into his earlier poems, although, on the whole, his latter productions are the best. In connection with this it might be stated that his "Jubilee Poem," consisting of twenty-five stanzas, and published last year, was widely copied by the Canadian and British press and received the indorsement of many eminent critics as being "the finest set of verses which appeared on this illustrious occasion." Two stanzas will give a general idea of the poem:

One wish, one thought intense, one impulse strong,
    Hath governed all thy long, eventful reign;
Imbued thy days of sadness and of song
    With sweetest sympathy for all thy train;
    And strengthened thy strong heart and nerved thy brain
To do the work an empire lays on thee;
    Tis love for thine own people doth sustain
The pillars of thy throne. Love makes them free,
And guides thy ship of state o'er Time's tempestuous sea.

And as a face smile lit, wakes up a smile,
  Or bright, contagious laughter glads the eye,
Or joy gets joy, or cheerfulness, like oil,
  Lays all the troubled waters, making dry
  The cheek tear-dewed; or skylark soaring high
Lifts up man's heart, impelling him to sing;
  We watch the eagle's flight and wish to fly,
And feel within, the spirit's quivering wing;
So thy kind heart, love lit, lights every living thing.

Dr. Massie was born in Frazerburgh, Aberdeenshire, Scotland, on the eighth of April, 1833. His father's name was also John, and his mother was Isabel Falconer, a native of Strichen. The family emigrated to Canada and settled in Kingston just as our author was entering upon his fourth birthday. A few years later they went out into the wilderness of Canadian woods, settling on a " bush farm " in the then new township of Seymour, situated about twenty-five miles northwest from Belleville. But previous to this there were troublesome times in the province. The rebellion of 1837 broke out and Mr. Massie, the poet's father, who removed to Belleville in the autumn of 1837, where he remained for one year and nine months, was the first man to enlist in the militia at Belleville to help maintain law and order. When all was quiet again and peace brooded over the land he returned to Kingston and devoted much of his spare time in aiding those who were anxious to learn vocal music. Among his more prominent pupils was the Hon. Oliver Mowat, Premier of Ontario. On his leaving for his wild wood farm in the new settlement he was the recipient of many gratifying testimonials from his pupils and others. Our author at this time was about nine years of age, and soon had ample experience of the life of a Canadian pioneer in all its phases.

" The country was so wild," he writes, " and roads so few that we had to follow a ' blaze,' *i. e.*, a mark made on the trees, in order to reach the locality of our future home." Here, however, he gained that knowledge of the lives of the brave, and too often neglected, women who cheerfully accompany their husbands into the wilds of the forests in a noble effort to secure independence and a home. Such women were no doubt in his thoughts—perhaps his own mother, who was a lovable, gentle, devoted woman of quiet patient industry and remarkably strong common sense—when years afterwards in one of his poems he wrote the following truthful lines:

The record of the buried lives
Of helpful, hopeful, patient wives;
Who thoughtful still of every need
Of every creature's wants took heed,
With cheerful true self-abnegation,
Content with their laborious station,
Heroic mothers of a nation.

Dr. Massie remained with his parents until his twenty-sixth year, when he went to the village of Castleton as teacher of the public school. His own education had been acquired by what he terms odds and ends, after leaving Kingston. He had however absorbed knowledge from books, periodicals, newspapers, etc. When other lads were enjoying themselves in the usual youthful pleasures and games he was poring over Burns, Scott, Campbell, Cowley, Milton, Shakspeare, Moore, etc., and storing his mind with his native country's history and song. "Robertson's History of Scotland," "Rollins' Ancient History," other histories and different works as he could obtain them, were all carefully read and studied over, but above all he loved Scotland's Bard—her Burns—and among both his early and later productions are several very able and readable pieces on the subject of his favorite poet:

Praise to the Bard, whose mighty hand
Has placed our loved, our native land,
    On fame's celestial height,
To be through time's most distant page
For every dim succeeding age
    A blazing beacon light.

Who knits all human hearts as one
And charms all lands beneath the sun
    With music from above;
And all our minds with wisdom stored,
And bound us with a golden cord
    Of sympathy and love.

Who taught us independence true
And rung the changes through and through
    His own immortal rhymes;
And gathers as of kindred blood,
In one fraternal brotherhood
    All peoples of all climes.

Who taught the lords of lofty domes
That worth may dwell in lowly homes
    And noble patriot pride,
And points the great Creator's plan
Till man's humanity to man
    Shall stem oppression's tide.

Shall drain the springs of sorrow dry,
And wipe the tear from every eye,
    And raise the drooping soul;
And all the brotherhood of man
Shall bow to God's and nature's **plan**
    In one eternal whole.

In the autumn of 1858 **our author attended an** examination **of**
teachers at the High School of Colborne and succeeded in securing **a**
second-class county **certificate,** after which he taught school for a year
very successfully, quite **a number of** advance pupils attending his
classes.   The next year, **however,** owing **to** frequent **and severe** head-
aches, he left teaching **and returned home to** the old **farm, where he**
spent a year working, studying, **and** courting the **muses.   And this**
period we may say ended his youthful career or labors **as a poet, for**
after teaching another year he began the **study of medicine, and grad-**
uated in March, 1865, at Queen's University, Kingston, with great
credit.

His college vacations produced a few stray pieces, but his time was
now too much occupied with the actualities, trials and responsibilities
of existence to allow **even an** approach **to the** state of mind **and** feeling which finds vent in poetic thought and expression; and for a period
extending over many years thereafter he composed **not a** solitary line
of poetry.   Indeed it is only within the last few years **that** he has
strung anew his old and long neglected harp, which vibrates **now** in
mellowed and softer, yet richer tones.   A **number of** small **poems,**
odes, songs, addresses and fragmentary pieces have appeared **in rapid**
succession **from his pen of** late, and so hearty **has been the** reception
accorded to **these that he is now** seriously contemplating **the** publica-
tion of a selection from his **writings** in book **form at** an early date.
They **are** certainly all worthy of the attention which has been
bestowed upon them.   Take the following piece as a specimen of **the**
peculiar subjects on which his muse sometimes alights, and the simple
but expressive manner in which he places his thoughts before us:

ODE TO THE OWL.

Hoot awa houlet alane on the tree
Hout-awa bird! Are you hooting at me?—
Or is it a change in the weather you bring,
Or do you rejoice in the birth o' the spring,
Or wailing the past sadly mourn o'er thy lot
Till the depths o' the forest re-echo thy note?

When the music of birds and the humming of bees
Are hushed on the breast of the evening breeze;
When nature is laid on the lap of repose,
And harmony reigns in the bosom of foes;
When the world is asleep and the last ray of light
Is swept from the earth by the besom of night,
Thou art seen on the wing (though we cannot well see,
For thy daylight is darkness, ours darkness to thee),
Thou art seen on the wing, by the pale moonlight,
To flit like a ghost on the shadow of night;
Or, perched on a tree, art heard nightly to croon
Thy sorrowful tale to the wandering moon.

Oh, child of the night! cease to echo along
The mournful "to-whoo" of thy midnight song;
Or the sprites of the night will assemble to hear,
And the elves of the wood will be caught in a tear.
Dost thou mourn in sad numbers a lover's disdain,
And pour out thy passion in amorous strain?
Ah! surely thy notes are the language of care,
Commingled with tenderness, love and despair!

Mayhap the sole friend of thy bosom hath fled
And left thee to mourn o'er the bones of the dead;
Or the feathery brood that so often were prest
With a motherly tenderness close to thy breast,
Have fled thee ungrateful and left thee to mourn
O'er thy woes and thy sorrows alone and forlorn.

Hoot awa houlet—thy song on the tree,
Is woe to my soul, and is tears to my e'e,
For my lot may be dark, and like thee I may mourn,
O'er the joys of the past that can never return;
Forsaken by friends and forgotton by foes,
I may sink in the arms of unconcious repose;
May read the last lesson of life's rugged page,
With no one to soothe in the sorrow of age.

Oh, child of the night, on thy sentinel tree;
Why not take a lesson of patience from thee!
Why pine o'er the blights of ephemeral clay!
Why weep o'er the transient woes of a day!
For tho' dark be my youth yet my end may be calm,
And the evening of life bathe my sorrows in balm,
And the spirit long pent in its casket of clay,
Spread its pinions aloft, and go smiling away.

"Wedded Love," "On the Visit of the Prince of Wales to Canada in 1860" (one hundred and eighty lines), "The Old Maid's Complaint" and the epistle to Kingston's bard (Mr. Evan MacColl) are excellent poems on their several subjects, and display true poetic inspiration in their composition. Nor can we omit to refer in the very highest terms to the Doctor's numerous lyrical pieces. These include "The Willow Tree," "Aggie's Tryst," "Will ye Gang to the Highland Hills," "Jenny's Resolve," "Annie's Awa," etc. Had he written nothing else, these alone would have entitled him to a prominent place among living Scottish poets. We quote the last-named piece to show how eminently qualified he is for this style of composition:

ANNIE'S AWA.

There's wae hearts for Annie; but less that she's gane,
Than just that we never may see her again;
Frae the hame o' her childhood, kind neighbors and a',
And the leal hearts that lo'ed her, she's far, far awa':
　　Oh! Annie's awa', kind Annie's awa';
　　We'll ne'er see anither like Annie awa'.

The tentless wee lammies now toyte o'er the lea,
Wi' a waesome-like face, and a pityfu' e'e;
E'en Collie seems lost-like, " his back's to the wa',"
They've a' lost a frien' in young Annie awa';
　　Sweet Annie awa', kind Annie awa';
　　We'll ne'er see anither like Annie awa'.

The poor little birdies, sae wont to be gay,
Now sit 'mang the branches, a' sangless and wae;
Nae mair their saft warblings are heard i' the shaw,
Their wee hearts are burstin' for Annie awa':
　　Young Annie awa', kind Annie awa';
　　We'll ne'er see anither like Annie awa'.

At kirk, and at bridals, nae mair can we see
The light and the love o' her bonnie black e'e
But the tear may be seen, o' hearts broken in twa,
And the calm o' deep sorrow for Annie awa'.
    Young Annie awa', kind Annie awa';
    We'll ne'er see anither like Annie awa'.

Ah! life's blythest morning may darken ere noon,
And the sun o' it's simmer gang wearily doon;
The fairest o' flow'rets be mantled in snaw;
O! Fortune! deal kindly wi' Annie awa':
    Young Annie awa', kind Annie awa';
    We'll ne'er see anither like Annie awa',

In April, 1866, our poet Doctor was united in marriage to Miss Ada J. Marvyn, niece and adopted daughter of the Rev. James Hughes and wife, of Colborne. She is a woman of good education and fine literary ability. One daughter, now seventeen, and one son, now twelve years of age, remain to them out of a family of five. The daughter, Edith Falconer Massie, seems to inherit her parents' literary talents, as she was awarded the first prize in 1887 for an original work of fiction offered by the proprietor of the *Montreal Witness.* And so we leave our author happy in the enjoyment of a comfortable home and a large circle of friends. He is now in possession of that peace and leisure required for the exercising of his poetic gifts, and we look forward with sincere pleasure to the publication of a collection of his poems in book form. He certainly deserves to be successful in such an undertaking, and we have no hesitancy in predicting a favorable reception of his volume at the hands of the public and the press.

NOW READY, PRICE $2.50.

IN ONE LARGE 8vo. VOLUME, 400 PAGES, CLOTH, GILT TOP.

CELEBRATED

SONGS OF SCOTLAND,

FROM KING JAMES V to HENRY SCOTT RIDDELL,

EDITED WITH MEMOIRS, NOTES, GLOSSARY AND AN INDEX,

—BY—

JOHN D. ROSS,

Author of "Scottish Poets In America."

EXTRACTS FROM PRESS NOTICES, ETC.

* * It is an excellent and very complete collection, printed in large and legible type. The notes and biographical memoranda are valuable.—*New York Sun.*

* * It is a large and handsomely bound book of about 400 pages and is dedicated to General Grant, with his permission given in 1884. Every lover of Scotch songs, and this comprises every song-lover, should have a copy of this work.—*New York Sunday News.*

* * This collection includes the best songs from the time of James V to Henry Scott Riddell—about four hundred double-column pages. It is a very good and valuable selection, and if it has any faults they are not those of omission.—*Julian Hawthorne in the New York World.*

* * There are something like 700 songs in the collection and it is needless to say that such a gathering which includes some of the latest song makers of the Scots country is calculated to rouse an enthusiam equal to that inspired by the gathering of the Clans. An important and novel feature is the giving of a history of nearly every song that is included. A table of first lines and a glossary are appended.—*New York Star.*

Readers of the *Home Journal* will remember with pleasure a series of papers which were contributed not long ago by Mr. John D. Ross, on Scottish poets and poetry. These biographical sketches, with revisions and additions, have been incorporated by the author in a handsome volume entitled, "Celebrated Songs of Scotland." The memoirs are supplemented with an ample selection of poems illustrating the style of the authors and the notable wealth of this department of Scottish literature. The book presents the subject in a most attractive form for study and enjoyment.—*The Home Journal.*

In adding another to the long list of collections of Scottish songs, which range from the voluminous publications of Chambers, Cunningham, Scott, Ramsay, etc., to the little book in the Golden Treasury, Mr. Ross has apparently desired to bring together the largest possible number of pieces in a cheap form. * * His book is to be praised for its comprehensiveness, its good index, and the general adequacy of the historical and biographical notices.—*New York Tribune.*

* * It extends to about 400 large pages and embraces all, or nearly all, of the principal pieces for which Scotland is so famous. There are copious notes explanatory of the songs and descriptive of the lives of the authors. The whole forms a convenient and excellent collection of Scottish songs.—*Brooklyn Eagle.*

* ♥ * Mr. Ross' collection is a good one for popular reading, and his Memoirs and Notes, as far as we have been able to examine them, leave but little to be desired.—*Mail and Express.*